The sensation was like a drug; he needed to touch her again.

He splayed his hands on the rough bark of the Redwood, in ___ ___ her head, resisting the urge to stroke her ___ ___ ___ ___ and brush that long neck.

Why could ___ ___ ___ ___ ___ mind flashed back to the ___ ___ Skinwalker. Cesar had read *his* tho___ ___dn't he? And ___ that instant, he recogniz___ ___ ___ what he had done. His fingers mov___ ___ the fabric of her blouse as he leaned i___ ___ ___ ___ ___ the subtle, airy fragrance of ___ ___ To read her, he must touch her again and t___ ___ ___ ___ to do, despite the danger. ___ ___ ___ ___ and he stroked the column ___ ___ ___ to be overcome again by rich long___ ___ ___

The power ___ ___ ___ ___d him to draw back. What ___ ___ ___ ___ him?

Dear Reader,

I'm so pleased to introduce my third story in THE TRACKERS series, featuring Native American shapeshifters called Skinwalkers. Their world is loosely based on Lakota myth and is full of dark and dangerous creatures with ancient powers, including Nagi—the Ruler of Ghosts. In *Soul Whisperer*, Nagi will stop at nothing to find the Seer of Souls. It is up to the Skinwalkers to stop him, but now they face a new, more corporeal threat.

This story features my only female Skinwalker, Bess Suncatcher—a raven shifter with the power to fly to the Spirit World and speak to those who have crossed over. She is aptly matched with Cesar Garza, a Soul Whisperer, who can witness the last moments of a life by touching the corpse. His gift, or curse, makes him an outcast among his own. And although Bess is a Halfling, making her his enemy, she intrigues him. Too bad his other gift, reading the truth at a touch, does not work on Bess.

Be sure to visit me at my web home, www.jennakernan.com, or on Twitter at Twitter.com/jennakernan.

Fondly,

Jenna Kernan

SOUL WHISPERER

JENNA KERNAN

First published in Great Britain 2013
by Mills & Boon, an imprint of Harlequin (UK) Limited,
Eton House, 18-24 Paradise Road, Richmond, Surrey TW9 1SR

© Jeannette H. Monaco 2011

ISBN: 978 0 263 90395 9
ebook ISBN: 978 1 472 00579 3

089-0313

Harlequin (UK) policy is to use papers that are natural, renewable and recyclable products and made from wood grown in sustainable forests. The logging and manufacturing processes conform to the legal environmental regulations of the country of origin.

Printed and bound in Spain
by Blackprint CPI, Barcelona

Jenna Kernan writes fast-paced romantic adventures set in out-of-the-way places and populated by larger-than-life characters.

Happily married to her college sweetheart, Jenna shares a love of the outdoors with her husband. The couple enjoys treasure hunting all over the country, searching for natural gold nuggets and precious and semiprecious stones.

Jenna has been nominated for two RITA® Awards for her Western romances and received a Book Buyers Best Award for paranormal romance in 2010. Visit Jenna at her internet home, www.jennakernan.com, or at Twitter. com/jennakernan for up-to-the-minute news.

Mine eyes will no more see
those that are most dear to me.

In loving memory of my two feathery writing muses,
Mango & Corona

Prologue

Nagi, ruler of ghosts, arrived at the battleground too late. His army of evil spirits had been defeated and sent for judgment by the Seer of Souls.

He must kill the Seer, but how to find her now that the grizzly Skinwalker had destroyed the mark? Her meddlesome mate had healed the Spirit Wound Nagi had inflicted, the mark that allowed him to track the Seer. But they may have left other clues. Nagi hovered above the field of battle searching for some sign of his prey. He spun in a slow circle, and seeing nothing, turned away in disgust. Gone then, without trace. An instant before returning to the Circle of Ghosts he spied a fleeing raven. Hope welled in his vaporous body.

Not all the Skinwalkers had escaped.

Nagi was torn between using the raven to find the Seer and returning to his newest pursuit—fathering living Halflings of his own.

If that clod Tob Tob, the Spirit Bear, and that arrogant bastard Niyan, guardian of mankind, could father offspring, then he certainly could. Of course, they both had corporal bodies, while his was less tangible.

His experiments thus far had led to accidently suffocating his vessels while mating. But he was persistent and some had lived. He hoped one of his human incubators might yet bear fruit.

He tried to picture his children, alive with beating hearts. Would they have the power to shift form like the Skinwalkers, or be connected to the soul like the Spirit Children? He only knew that they would be mighty like their Sire.

But for now his curiosity must wait. Nagi fixed his yellow eyes on the retreating black speck on the wide blue sky and began to formulate a plan.

Chapter 1

Three months later
Redwood Forest, California

Bess Suncatcher smelled the human body from a long way off. Her senses were acute when she was in her raven form, and she tipped her wings to investigate, veering sharply to the west. It was unusual to find a human corpse in the forest, but not unheard-of. Despite the humans' high opinion of themselves, here in the wild they were outmatched. Their arrogance and smug superiority served them poorly against "nature red in tooth and claw." Bess thought it must be dreadful not to be able to fly.

She swept through the massive tree trunks, which

stood tall and sacred as the columns of a cathedral. As Bess circled the corpse her concentration slipped and her heart lurched. The body was a female, mauled by a predator. Bess's curiosity died in a vacuum of dread.

She landed high above the clearing on the limb of a pine and glanced down. She knew she should be detached, that her job was to see that animals had their proper share of the earth. With the balance between all creatures as her prime objective, what happened to one woman, here or there, should make no difference.

But still there was a definite knot in her throat as she looked at the thick black hair on the woman's head.

Who was waiting for this one to come home? Whose life would be changed forever by her passing? And who would be left behind?

Don't think about that. This isn't her.

But she was slim and dark-headed, just like Bess's human mother. Her mother's injuries had not been so obvious, yet they had been just as deadly.

After all these years, she still felt the ripping loss, sharp as talons, as it gripped her heart. First she'd lost her mother and then her father, too. Bess huddled against the wellspring of sorrow that choked her.

She took solace in the fact that, by guarding her heart, she would never again have to stand beside the grave of one she loved. That much, at least, she could control.

Bess dropped to the spongy carpet of moss and pine needles, transforming to her human form, then changed her feather cloak to resemble human clothing before stepping forward into the clearing. Her skin flashed first hot and then cold as adrenaline poured into her bloodstream, telling her that she was not alone. Was the predator still here?

She glanced about to see what was amiss, her keen eyes absorbing every detail. It took only a moment to spot him. He was closer to her than she would have liked and looked straight at her, so she could not transform without him seeing. The inside of Bess's mouth seemed rough as an emery board and she could not swallow.

Was this the murderer?

Her gaze swept the man, tall and powerful, standing with unnatural stillness and a calm that radiated confidence.

Bess's instinct told her to flee, but she did not follow the urging of her animal-self because, despite her fear, she knew she could escape in an instant where he could never follow. And she wanted to know who he was. His eyes narrowed as she made no effort to step back, but waited for him to close the distance between them.

Oh, but he was fine to look at. She ran her tongue along her bottom lip. He hesitated, lowering his chin, confused at her mixed signals.

Taking a handsome man to her bed was an easy way to connect on some physical level, while maintaining complete autonomy over her heart. She cocked her head to study him. If he hurt this woman, she'd see him pay, even if it wasn't her purpose. But if not…she allowed her mind to wander.

What was with the designer suit? She took in his tailored gray jacket and the pristine white shirt that did little to disguise the brawn beneath. His tie was drab, but his black leather belt sported a showy silver-and-turquoise buckle and those cockroach-killer cowboy boots with silver tips were definitely not standard garb for business types. Something about the way his jacket hung suggested he wore a shoulder holster. Did it make him feel safe here in the wild?

His posture radiated complete assurance. But then he didn't know what he was dealing with yet, did he?

Her eyes narrowed on his face. Was he a business type out on some strange corporate survival seminar or a murderer caught in the act?

He took a graceful step closer now. She allowed it for it brought him near enough for her to see that his eyes were not dark brown, as she had first thought, but a deep shimmering gray full of the heat only adrenaline could bring.

"Where'd you come from?"

His gravelly voice resonated through her insides, the epicenter of the tremor now quaking through her.

She pointed up into the canopy of branches far above them and he chuckled. Bess smiled in response.

He reached, as if to capture her upper arm. She nearly allowed it, but at the last instant she stepped away. His brow rose. Did her speed surprise him?

Bess let her gaze dip to glance at his strong jawline, his high cheekbones and full sensual mouth. That coupled with the healthy coppery glow of his skin made her wonder if he might also have some Native heritage. Peak sexual prowess, she thought, and then wondered where that notion came from.

"Who are you?" he asked.

What are you? would have been a more appropriate question and one that she wished to ask him, as well. Something about him raised alarm bells. So she kept a safe distance.

He frowned. Had he expected her to answer simply because he asked?

With a body like that, she surmised he didn't often face resistance of any sort from human females. What a bore that must be. Then again, that was her general experience with human males. She wondered if he was up for a little challenge.

He lifted his index finger and inched toward her hand.

He leaned closer, repeating his question as she permitted his fingers to brush hers. The brief contact sent her skin to gooseflesh as the prickle of an electric charge swept up her arm and into her chest. She gasped in surprise as her heart galloped, sending blood throbbing in her ears and pulsing in her core.

She stared into his deep, dark eyes, seeing them widen in astonishment. So, he hadn't expected that, either. He broke the tingling contact between them, but not the contact of their eyes.

His pupils dilated and she felt her breathing quicken in response. His full lips curled down and he stepped farther back.

What had just happened?

Bess was used to choosing her partners and enjoyed the rush of heat and excitement of this man, but some instinct held her in check. She coupled that with the potential involvement with the dead woman and increased her vigilance.

Bess conceded that he had a killer body. Such a form as his was designed for hunting, and she had unintentionally become his prey. Not all chases wound up with killing. Some ended with coupling. So was she his next conquest or next victim?

She stepped away to better assess the pulsing salmon-colored aura of sexual energy and only then glimpsed the constant golden glow that encircled him.

Most of her kind could not read auras, which put them at a disadvantage when they met something not quite human, like this Niyanoka standing far too close.

But she knew.

The golden aura told her he was born of the Spirit Niyan, protector of men—the other Halfling race. So, he was not responsible for the killing. More than likely he was here to investigate, for it was their mission to protect man at the expense of all else. And instead of the murderer, he had found her.

Bess's eyes narrowed as she took in the clear white vibration of spiritual energy but stilled at what she saw next. The white light spiked out past the gold and was capped with black. Her breath caught. She had never seen one like it. His body was encircled with the aura of death just like the shell of an egg encircles the albumen.

This Niyanoka dealt with the dead or perhaps just with killing. She did not know what he was, but her instinct for survival now overrode her sexual interest. He was dangerous. Far more dangerous than his significant physical presence first made her believe.

She surmised he was a warrior, but what could this blending of auras mean, clear white and inky black? They were polar opposites.

Was he one of the army who brought death to the mighty Fleetfoot, the leader of the uprising against his kind? Bess recalled the face of her father's killer. This was not that man, but he could still be one of the vigilantes.

Something inside her turned to stone and her icy calm returned.

Ah, she saw it now in his eyes, the flicker of confusion and then the narrowing as he recognized her for what she was and hated her for it. The lustful hot pink aura spiked red with anger and then he moved too close for her to see his aura, pinning her against the trunk of the tree. His hips pressed to her stomach and his arms bunched at each side of her head in a posture that was both possessive and hostile. She lifted her chin in defiance as he leaned in, her pride keeping her from transforming. Did he see the hot angry flush as blood coursed with greater power? Her neck and face burned and her hands grew slick with perspiration. Still she faced him, refusing to acknowledge her fear. She would not flee like some little rabbit. She was his equal, no matter what he and his kind thought.

"Skinwalker," he hissed. "What shape do you take?"

She was tempted to show him since she no longer needed hide who and what she was. She could leave if she wished, but her curiosity stayed her. Most of his kind never set foot off the sidewalks of major cities.

What was he doing here and how was he connected to this death?

Cesar Garza pressed the beautiful Skinwalker back against the trunk of the tree, wishing this proximity did not make him long to stroke her soft skin again. His lungs now acted as bellows, gobbling up the air that suddenly seemed too thin to satisfy him, while lower down his body responded to her proximity in the most basic way possible. She was an animal, only half human, yet the reality of this simply fueled his hunger for her. It was said that female Skinwalkers were irresistible to the males of his kind. Was she bringing this dizzy, giddy rush to him? Was she the cause of his body going haywire?

What did she know of this death?

His questions yielded nothing and that had never happened before. How was she immune to his touch…his gift? As a Truth Seeker, he had always been able to divine the answers to any spoken question simply by touching a person. But he could read nothing from her but emotion.

And he had certainly never experienced the shot of pure sexual awareness that had come when he touched her naked flesh. The sensation was like a drug; he needed to touch her again, not for answers but for the pure lustful heat. Was that why all contact with her kind was forbidden? He splayed his hands on the rough bark of the redwood, inches from her head, resisting the urge to stroke her. He could lift one finger and brush that long neck.

Why couldn't he read her? His mind flashed back to the dying male Skinwalker. Cesar had read *his* thoughts, hadn't he? And in that instant recognized with horror what he had done. His fingers moved across the fabric of her blouse as he leaned in, breathing deep of the subtle, airy fragrance of her skin. To read her, he must touch her again and that was what he wanted to do, despite the danger. His resistance crumbled and he stroked the column of her neck only to be overcome again by rich longing and hunger. The power of this connection caused him to draw back. What was she doing to him?

It must be some power she had, some defense, for when he touched her, all he read was heat. He'd never touched a she-walker before, so for all he knew his response could be normal. But he was uncertain.

Damn, he couldn't think around her. She was as arousing as hell.

He gazed down, forgetting again about his mission, forgetting everything but the deep, churning waters of her dark eyes. They shimmered with promises he would see she kept. Her high arching brows lifted like the wings of a bird as she continued to stare at him—majestic, proud.

She was tall for a woman, nearly looking him in the eye, but fine boned with the bearing of a dancer. He pressed her more firmly to the tree, feeling her curves as their hips aligned in perfect union, or it *would* be perfect if she were naked.

He forced himself to focus, trying again to pry answers from her mind.

"How do you know what I am, beauty?" He crooked one finger and used it to stroke the downy skin of her jawline, expecting to read the answer to his question. But instead he got another blast of fierce need that caused the wind to leave him in one long exhalation. Had that been his desire or hers?

The she-walker bit her bottom lip, as if also struggling with her need. Had she felt it, too, this yearning to press naked flesh to naked flesh? That thought aroused him further, causing his blood to pulse and pound.

When she spoke, her voice was breathless and halting.

"I can see your aura."

"Impossible." He didn't need to pin her hips to the tree with his own in order to read her, but he could not seem to convince his body to leave her. It was as if she had woven some spell over him.

His mind flicked back to the stories, old lore of men seduced by beautiful Skinwalkers, the white buffalo woman who turned her male lovers' bodies into snakes and bones. Was this her—the legendary temptress of old? A sheen of sweat, as fine as sea spray, now covered his chest and back. Uncertainty stilled him.

But the tales were cautionary—weren't they? A reminder that Skinwalkers made poor wives. And now, the communities were buzzing with the news of two female Niyanoka who had been banished for marrying Skinwalkers. With his body molded to her every curve and the scent of her arousal filling the air all about him, he now understood why one of his kind might commit such an unforgivable act.

He frowned, thinking of the stories of the incident in Montana. He had interviewed the parents of one Spirit Child, a Dream Walker. But they would not speak of her and he could not speak to her, because of her banishment. It was the correct thing, to disown her, but it made his investigation difficult. He was not permitted to use his touch gift on his own kind, not that they would allow him to touch them, and it did not work on her.

Now he faced a similar problem, how to get answers without using his gifts.

He arched away, keeping them connected at the hip, letting her feel his desire. Her eyes flashed a warning, which he was tempted to ignore. Instead, he straightened his arms, keeping her trapped between his hands, but breaking the contact between them. He tensed, resisting the urge to take her in his arms.

She gave an audible exhalation of breath that seemed laced with relief. Her response irritated him. Since he could not read her thoughts, he did not know for sure if she held a similar desire. He had only the looks she had given him. That had been yearning, hadn't it? Yes, she had wanted him, too, until she recognized what he was. He was certain.

Now all that had changed. Perhaps she was wiser than he or more able to rein in her passions, while his body shook with the wanting she raised. Damn her and her shifter magic.

She straightened her skirts. They fluttered about her like downy feathers. He noted she was dressed completely in black, from the crisscrossing straps of her Roman-style sandals to the low-cut, tight-fitting leather bustier. An odd choice of attire for a walk in the woods, but she could turn her hide into anything, couldn't she? So why choose black? His eye caught on the center of her throat, fixing on the only thing she wore that held color.

Her necklace.

A strand of black crystal beads hung about her slender neck. At the center lay the carving of a bird. In its open beak sat a red faceted jewel. The stone flashed bright—a ruby?

He recognized the symbolism immediately—raven stealing the sun.

The jewel exactly matched the red of her lips. He glanced from her mouth to the necklace and back to her beautiful face, putting it together. The realization jolted him as if he'd been pushed from behind. Yes, he decided, that was the perfect fit for this female, who epitomized grace and power. She'd be smart, too. Had to be.

"A raven," he said.

She made a slight throaty sound that might have been a laugh. "And I thought you were all brawn."

Their eyes met and held. She broke the contact first, glancing toward the sky. Her natural home, he realized. Why hadn't she changed and escaped him?

His instinct was to keep her here with him, against her will if necessary. So he grasped her upper arm and held fast, preparing for the change that she could summon as easily as he could draw answers from a human's mind.

"Stay," he coaxed.

Her smile was all seduction. "Why?"

He cleared his throat, changing tactics. "I'm Cesar Garza."

Her mouth quirked.

"And you are?"

"Bess."

"Do Skinwalkers have last names?"

"Suncatcher."

Appropriate, he thought, since it was the legendary raven who stole the sun from Wakan Tanka, the Great Spirit, and brought it to earth. But the sun burned her colorful feathers and afterward, her kind dressed only in black. He smiled at Bess, feeling awkward for the first time in a century. But the feeling was not mutual, judging from the menace glinting in her eyes. He felt the resistance of her as she tried to draw away from him. Her proximity made his body roar in a mad rush of blood and heat and wanting. He had been too long in the company of human females who were more than happy to give him what he wanted.

Here was the first real challenge he'd faced in decades. And he was blowing it.

"Why are you here?"

"I believe the question is, why are *you* here?" she said in a low, musical voice. "Outside the usual territory for Niyanoka, isn't it?"

Had she seen what had done this? It was definitely possible. He had to find out what they were and if they threatened mankind.

He should go, continue his hunt, but this woman… *No, she's not a woman, not completely, at least*.

Cesar lowered his chin. "Did you see what happened?"

Bess glanced in the direction of the victim, but Cesar knew the corpse was beyond her line of sight. She showed none of the horror or disgust he would have expected from a typical female.

"I need to know." It wasn't a question, exactly, but neither did it force him to stoop to asking her for help, while still allowing her to offer it.

"I didn't see." She hesitated. "But I can smell them." She met his gaze. "I've never scented anything like this before. What are they?"

"They?"

She inclined her head. "Two."

His mouth pressed into a grim line. "I'm not sure yet. I have to read the body."

She nodded, her eyes slightly wider now.

He waited, swallowing against the bitter taste in his mouth, because he knew what would happen next, what always happened after he revealed himself. But she said nothing.

"Well?" he asked, his voice full of venom.

She shrugged. "Well what?"

"I'm a Soul Whisperer."

She cocked her head as if she were part retriever, instead of a raven.

He pressed his lips together in frustration. She was going to make him spell it out for her.

"Don't you know what that means?"

She made no reply to his question, just continued her quizzical stare.

His nostrils flared as he breathed deep of the moist air and then spoke slowly, as if to a child, enunciating so there could be no mistake. "I touch the dead."

"Your aura already told me that."

He waited for the condemnation he had faced every day since he first learned of his awful gift. But still she said nothing more.

"It's unclean. I'm unclean because I touch the dead."

She screwed up her face as if tasting something sour. "But that doesn't make sense. Touching the dead is natural, isn't it? How else would we consume prey or bury a loved one?"

Cesar's jaw actually dropped.

"Are you teasing me, about the unclean thing?" she asked.

It took a moment to comprehend that she might not know, might not understand how it was with him. Was she really ignorant of the stigma endured by Soul Whisperers? Still he could not quite believe his ears.

Cesar brushed a thumb along her high cheek and still could not read her thoughts, but he did feel her emotions—curiosity and confusion, but no disgust. He'd never read emotions before.

He sensed that she knew the truth and still she did not turn away in revulsion or shy from his touch.

How remarkable.

Chapter 2

Silence stretched between them as Bess stared at the Soul Whisperer who stood glaring at her. Was his hatred for her kind so strong, or was this a very personal chip on his shoulder? If he was teasing her about the unclean thing, he didn't show it. He looked deadly serious and seemed to be trying to size her up as she engaged in the same activity.

His people were different from hers, so it was not surprising that they did not understand each other.

"Are you going to watch me?" he asked.

"Is it safe?"

He nodded. "But no one ever watched before."

She lifted one shoulder. "First time for everything."

"I'll blank out for a few moments."

She glanced about the forest, her keen eyes checking for any threat. She listened intently, but she heard only the gentle rustle of the wind in the branches and the scurry of ground squirrels about their business. Nowhere could she sense any danger. Her search concluded, she returned her attention to the son of Niyan.

"I'll watch your back, then."

His eyebrows lifted again, then fell, low and dangerous over his narrowing eyes. "Since when does a Skinwalker protect a Spirit Child?"

She motioned toward the body. "Common interest."

He made no move toward the corpse. "Is this a trick to escape me?"

She laughed. "No one holds a raven, unless she wants to be held. If I wished to escape, I'd already be gone."

There was that uncertain expression again as if he did not know what to believe. He apparently made up his mind because he gave the slightest nod of his chin, spun and then stalked to the body. Bess had witnessed many gruesome sights and tried to convince herself that this was no different. But it was, because of the body's resemblance to her mother.

Her mother's death had been sudden, accidents

usually were, and even her father's special gifts could not save her. It seemed cruel that a man who could see the future of complete strangers could not foresee the day he would kiss his wife for the last time. Bess had been there, witnessed her mother's death and been equally helpless to prevent her passing. All she could do was hold her mother as she died. Could that really be over a hundred years ago now? Still her chest filled with a hollow ache that made it difficult to draw an even breath.

She swallowed back the knot that squeezed her throat, determined to keep her face placid and remain as still as the silent giants surrounding them. The redwoods endured and so could she. When she glanced at the Niyanoka, she found him studying her again.

"You don't have to watch," he said.

"I know."

Still he did not touch the body, waiting.

"Who have you lost?"

"Is it so obvious?"

His smile never reached his slate-colored eyes. "Only to one who sees so much death."

"My mother was also slim and dark-headed."

"Ah," he said, nodding his understanding. "My situation is just the opposite. My mother is alive and just wishes I were dead."

Bess's mouth dropped open as she watched for some indication that he was making a bad joke. He gave none as he kept his attention pinned upon her.

"You shouldn't watch."

Her eyes widened with interest and she leaned forward. "Why? What will happen?"

He gave a befuddled shake of his head as if her questions made no sense. "Nothing you can see, but it's unnecessary."

Bess bristled. She shouldn't have mentioned her mother. Now he felt sorry for her. "Skinwalkers are made of sterner stuff than that, Niyanoka. I'll wager I have looked on death as often as you."

He held her gaze a moment longer and she knew from the sadness in his eyes and the long intake of breath that she had been wrong. This man had stared often into the face of death, far more often than she ever would. Still he nodded and then sank to his knees, pressing a hand to the woman's forehead. His eyes fluttered closed. The only change she could detect was in his heartbeat and the rate of his breathing. Beyond that he was the picture of tranquility.

As she watched, his expression grew strained as the color ebbed from his tanned face, until his skin exactly matched the grayish shade of the corpse. Bess stepped closer and noted his eyeballs moving erratically beneath his closed lids as if he were deep in dreaming. At last he broke the connection with the body and sank back to his heels, capturing a huge breath of air. Cesar blinked down at the woman and then seemed to remember Bess and turned toward her.

"How long?" he asked.

"Were you...?" She pointed at the woman. "Maybe five minutes. Your color isn't good."

"Temporary," he said, rising to his feet and dusting off his knees.

"Do you just see what she saw?"

He broke the contact of their gaze and stared down at the deceased. "No. I can hear their thoughts, as well."

That would be hard enough, she realized. "But not what they feel?"

He was studying her again. "Yes and no. I feel their emotions, fears, sorrows, the person they think of when they know they'll die. But I don't experience the pain of their final moments." He glanced back at the victim. "She was killed giving birth, twins again, just like the first case."

"First? Are you some kind of Dream Child cop?"

"I help humans investigate difficult cases. Work with the FBI."

"They know what you are?"

He shook his head once. "Same rules for us as for you. Human's don't know about us—ever." He rubbed his palms on his trousers. "She was also only in her first trimester."

"That's impossible."

"Apparently not. Also the newborns can walk, run actually." He pointed. "That way. That's why the self-made cesarean. They were too big to be born."

"Are you sure they were not some kind of parasite?"

"I'm sure. They are small, with ash-gray skin. Their teeth are long, pointy and sharp and they have bright yellow eyes, like a cat's."

Yellow eyes. She stilled, wondering why this tidbit made her entire scalp tingle.

"If they're Skinwalkers, they are like none I've ever seen," Cesar continued, without noticing Bess's rising concern.

"We are always born in human form and don't change until we hit puberty."

"That's what I was taught."

Taught in his little racist Niyanoka schools, where they learned to hate her kind.

Cesar seemed oblivious to her seething anger for he continued on.

"What I'm not sure about is what they'll grow into and if they are a threat to mankind."

Bess pressed her lips together in disapproval. He didn't give a fig if the little terrors killed every animal within fifty miles as long as they didn't kill men.

"Do you care nothing for The Balance—the give and take between species that is as fragile as a butterfly's wing?"

He made a face. "I don't like insects."

"Yet you protect men who are more voracious than grasshoppers in their need to devour the land."

"Spoken like a true tree-hugger."

"Better than cutting them all down to build redwood decks for your Jacuzzis."

They faced off in silence now, his jaw ticking and her fists clenched as she fought the soaring urge to fight. She had been so taken with him that she had nearly forgotten that they were born enemies.

"You're not going to help me find them?"

She couldn't quite disguise her surprise. Had he just requested her help?

"You asking?"

He shrugged.

She turned away.

"Wait. I'm asking."

"How much of a head start?"

"Two hours."

"I'll take a look. Where shall I meet you?"

"Here. But if you find them, don't get too close. They may be dangerous."

She made a face. "I can handle myself."

He gave her a serious look, then opened his mouth as if to say more, and closed it again.

"What?"

"Nothing." He glanced back at his crime scene. "I have to call this in."

"They think you're human?"

He nodded.

"Meet you here, then." She lifted her arms but he grabbed her hand. The zip of adrenaline shot through her as well as the sensation of anxiety.

"Be careful, okay?"

She pulled her hand free. "Yes, okay." Bess rubbed her wrist, but could not quite eliminate the strong feeling of worry and the nearly irresistible need to protect. Had she just read his emotions?

She did not know what was more disturbing, sensing his feelings or having him worry over her as if she were something more to him than a way to get answers.

She kept her eye on him.

He pinned her with an intense gaze. The corner of his mouth quirked and she felt an ache begin deep inside her.

"You going to watch?" she asked.

He grinned. "Oh, yeah."

"No one ever watched before."

His full smile dazzled her.

"First time for everything."

Yes, this one was dangerous in an entirely different way. Bess backed away. Once clear, she lifted her arms and pushed off the earth, feeling the electric zing of power as she changed to her raven form and burst into the sky. She glanced back to see him staring, slack-jawed, before he disappeared into the forest below. It was surprisingly exhilarating to have someone know what she was, see her other self and not turn in horror. The law prohibited her from ever showing herself to a human unless in mortal danger. But now, this man could see what she was and he had not shown anything but wonder.

She flew low through the trees, swooping and dodging around the mighty trunks, listening for a disturbance and watching with her sharp eyes. Bess flew in widening circles, seeing nothing for what she gauged to be an hour. She had almost decided to turn back when she spotted the carcass of the freshly killed moose.

She perched on a limb and stared down. What she saw next made her stomach pitch.

The animal beside the moose was gray as the ash of a campfire, but its flesh had the pocked appearance of burned charcoal. There was no fur or feathers. It hopped like a human from one leg to the other and already stood three feet tall. This thing was only two hours old?

She studied the knobby head and batlike ears. The creature's eyes were huge, wide and yellow-green with black pinprick pupils.

The dead moose shook and the other twin crawled from within the empty body cavity, dragging a section of glistening intestine between sharp white teeth.

A cry of horror escaped her. One creature looked up, staring with the fixed biopic focus of all predators.

She opened her wings as the thing leaped to the tree and climbed the forty feet that separated them with unnatural speed, reaching her just as she threw herself into the sky. Wings stretched wide, she flapped to put distance between them and then saw the second, identical thing on the ground. It snarled and snapped, then lifted into the air like smoke.

Another glance showed that the first thing was also airborne. It did not fly like any natural creature. Instead, it darted after her as if something shot from a gun, rocketing and billowing.

Fear sent a hot burst of blood and adrenaline to

her muscles as she veered this way and that, darting through the trees in an effort to evade her pursuers. Not Nagi, her mind shouted, but what then?

Something brushed her tail. She cried out, flying low to the ground, dipping, swerving. No more time to look back. She beat her wings with greater urgency as she fled the twins.

She did not turn her head until she had gone two miles and found no sign of them. They could fly! And two of them, big as bear cubs and just as dangerous.

Dangerous did not even begin to describe these creatures.

It took some time for her breathing to return to normal as she flew straight for Cesar, coming instead into the middle of a police crime scene. Just like most humans, they were so preoccupied with their own concerns they did not notice a raven winging through the middle of the proceedings. But Cesar did. She landed on the boughs of a redwood, and watched the men crawl about the scene like ants. Cesar indicated to her that she should meet him at the parking area.

While she waited for him, she dressed in a conservative black suit fashioned after a particular favorite from the fall collection of a top New York designer. She was excellent at mimicking such clothing, changing her feathers into whatever suited her, though she was just as likely to buy the real thing and wear her skin in the form of only her necklace. She brushed the crease of her trousers, admiring the fabric. She did love fashion.

Cesar appeared from the wooded trail, so she stepped into view. As she crossed the lot a young officer moved before her.

"Crime scene, ma'am. You can't—"

Cesar cut him off. "She's with me. Consultant."

The officer dropped his hand and stepped aside, allowing her to pass.

"Any luck?" he asked.

"Yes, all bad. I found them. They're about five miles northeast of here. Dangerous as hell. They killed a bull moose, just the two of them and had the innards eaten already."

Cesar folded his arms across his wide chest.

She expected him to say something, but he didn't.

"Well?"

"They're entitled to eat."

She threw her arms up in exasperation. "Would you say that if they had killed a hiker?"

He gave her a withering look. "Of course not."

"Well, they're attacking animals. That means they're my concern, even if they're not yours."

"I didn't say I'm not concerned. I'm just not going

to hunt something that is only…" He clamped his mouth shut.

"Only killing animals?"

He didn't deny that this was what he was about to say.

"What about Skinwalkers? Because they also attacked me."

His hard expression dissolved and his eyes rounded. He reached out, clasping her hand. She felt his emotions blast her like a warm wind—anxiety, then fear. His gaze swept her as she regained custody of her hand. How did he do that?

"Did they hurt you?"

"No, just took a swipe at me." She twisted her hip, and glanced back, her hand sweeping over her posterior. "Might interest you to know that they can fly."

The cloth of her trousers was sticky and wet.

"They can…what?" he said.

She lifted her hand to examine it, staring with disbelief at the crimson stain coating her palm. He captured her wrist and suddenly his horror was hers.

"You're bleeding!" Cesar turned toward the officer. "Get the EMTs over here, now!"

"No." She grasped his shoulder with her clean hand, feeling the warmth of his body even through the fabric of his blazer. She swayed and closed her eyes, sending a silent signal for help, knowing that any Skinwalker within a wide range would come immediately to her aid. When she opened her eyes it was to see a look of exasperation on his handsome face.

"Why not?"

"I prefer to work in my own HMO."

He shook his head, clearly not understanding. She sighed. For reasons she could not quite fathom, she didn't want him thinking of her animal half. Spelling it out for him would only remind him.

His brow furrowed and he glanced toward the officer behind them. "I'm getting help."

She grabbed his arm. "No. If they anesthetize me, I'll turn."

He paused, looking back at her. "To a raven?"

She nodded, meeting his wide-eyed stare. He understood now.

"Well, you need treatment."

"Not an emergency. I've sent for help already."

"When?"

"As soon as I realized I was injured. We have a kind of emergency call system. When one of us is ill, in danger or in great emotional distress, a signal goes out. Any Skinwalker within a few hundred miles will read it. They would also have perceived my danger in the forest and plus I just sent a call a moment ago that I am wounded."

Cesar glanced around, looking uncomfortable for the first time since she'd met him.

"They'll come?" he asked.

"Most definitely. Until then, could you take me home?"

He wrapped an arm about her shoulders and guided her toward his vehicle, a nondescript blue sedan. Unlike his attire, his vehicle seemed chosen to be invisible among them.

His fingers grazed her neck as they walked side by side.

Bess's head swam as apprehension swept in, followed by guilt marching through her like an army of ants. It took a moment to recognize these were not her emotions.

"Let go," she whispered.

"What?"

"You're making me dizzy."

The finger that stroked her neck dropped away, but he immediately captured her shoulder as he drew out a remote and unlocked the car doors.

"Do you need to tell your partner that you're leaving?" she asked, and then felt his grip tighten.

"I work alone."

She studied the grim line that now replaced the

sensual curve of his mouth and the glittering rage that turned his eyes cold as gray marble. She lifted a hand to his face and read betrayal.

"What happened?" she asked.

He squinted, giving her a slight shrug of incomprehension. "What?"

"With your old partner, the one you're still so pissed at?"

His eyes popped open and he removed her hand from his face, placing it on the door frame then stepping away, clamping his jaws shut as tight as an alligator grabbing a turtle.

"Oh, like that, is it? All right, not my business." She glanced at the car's interior. "I'm going to bleed all over your upholstery. You have a blanket or something?"

He released the trunk and returned with a yellow rain slicker, laying it out on the seat. "You sure I shouldn't take you to a hospital?"

She slipped in and groaned as her injured hip twinged. Blood smeared the yellow slicker. She glanced at the stain, wondering if she'd underestimated the seriousness of her injury.

"Where do you live?" he asked, starting the car and pulling out of the park lot.

"Summit of Russian Hill."

He made a sound in his throat that could have been recognition or a growl of irritation.

"What?"

"Appropriate for a raven. Bird's-eye view of the city and all." He glanced at the blood pooling rapidly beneath her. "But too damn far. We're going to a hospital."

"No."

"I'm driving. Not up to you."

"I can still fly." She met his steady gaze until he returned his attention to the road.

"My place then. I'm in SoMa, practically under the bridge."

"Hmm. I remember when that was a swamp." She was feeling woozy now and wondered if she had lost more blood than she had initially thought. She laid her head back on the seat rest. The adrenaline had abandoned her now, replaced with exhaustion and an unnerving trembling in her hands. She pressed her palms down onto her twitching thighs and let her tired eyelids fall shut.

"Don't pass out on me," he growled.

She opened one eye and noticed his white knuckles on the wheel and the fact that they were going entirely too fast.

"And don't wrap us around a tree."

She placed her hand over her wound and pressed,

feeling the blood continue to ooze between her fingers. Her eyes jerked open when they drew to the shoulder of the road. He threw the transmission into Park and removed that silly, boring tie then threaded it beneath her thigh. Next he used a crisp white handkerchief to blanket her gash.

She stared at the small square of fabric.

"Who carries one of those anymore?" It was a small thing, but it pointed to his age. Had he watched a century or two turn?

"Creature of habit." He cinched the makeshift bandage and resumed their trip.

She hadn't expected to doze, but she did, wakening as they pulled into an underground parking facility beside an elevator. He held the door and she exited, stiffly but without his assistance. Her thigh burned with each step. A check of the bandage showed that she had bled through.

They reached the elevator and waited for the car.

"You're right in the middle of a pretty touristy area."

He cast her a sidelong glance. "Lots of restaurants."

"Full of people who are transient, temporary and, perhaps, open to a little fling."

He looked suddenly imperious and, were it not

for the ticking at his left eye, she would have thought she'd guessed wrong.

"Your point?"

"You live alone?"

Now he was scowling. "Makes it easier since I don't age like they do and my own family, well, let's just say I'm not expecting an invitation to Thanksgiving dinner again this year."

She lifted her hands in surrender. "Sorry. I just, well, we have that in common, too. I lost my parents when I was young."

He didn't ask her how they died. It was the usual thing to say one was sorry and then inquire as to the cause. But Cesar remained grim and silent. His behavior made her wonder if he had already guessed what had happened.

He punched the elevator button six times in rapid succession and muttered, "Come on."

The door dinged open. Bess took a step forward and wobbled badly.

"To hell with it," he said, and scooped her effortlessly up in his arms. He stepped into the compartment. "Press nine."

How odd to be captured in the arms of a Spirit Child, trapped in this small space and not feel threatened. She was wounded, vulnerable and yet Cesar Garza showed only concern over her welfare. His reaction was beyond odd. The Niyanoka she had met to date recognized her by her aura and then avoided her as if she were carrying some fatal contagious disease. Why didn't he?

Chapter 3

The elevator was always slow, but never as lethargic as now when he held Bess in his arms. The compartment was not the only thing rising. Here she was helpless in his arms and he was ready to take her right in this tiny chamber. He kept his hands securely on the fabric of her outfit. It wouldn't do for her to feel the firestorm of lust roaring through his blood.

Maka be blessed, the fragrance of her was driving him insane. She smelled of fresh summer air and pines. He closed his eyes and inhaled the scent of her hair. Sage, he realized.

"You want to step out or take another ride?" she asked, glancing up at him.

The elevator doors stood parted and, beyond, a familiar gilded table held ornate artificial flowers before a large mirror. His floor, he realized. He jerked forward. The closing doors bumped his back and her leg, simultaneously, causing her to inhale through her teeth.

"Sorry," he muttered, and hurried down the hall, lowering her to his side as he fished for his keys. Blood dripped from her pant leg onto the carpet. "How long until your HMO shows up?"

"Hard to say. A few hours—a few days."

"Days?"

"If they sense no emergency they won't be racing here."

"But you're still bleeding."

"True. Hours then."

"Who's coming?"

"I'm not sure. A wolf or a buffalo, I imagine. The grizzly is much too far north and he has…" She didn't finish.

He stilled, key in hand, as he wondered if she was teasing and then decided she wasn't. Cesar released the lock and punched in his security code, deactivating the alarm system. Then he lifted Bess again and carried her to the guest bathroom, setting her on the marble lip of the large whirlpool tub.

"You must have been saving your pennies all these decades."

"You'd have to be a total nitwit not to have millions when you've been around as long as I have."

She smiled. "True. It's a pain moving my assets around all the time, though. I've inherited my own money three times already."

He nodded and they shared a mutual smile of understanding. His faded when he saw the blood dripping down the porcelain of his tub and pooling on the marble tile floor.

"We better get you out of those clothes."

"They're not clothes." She brushed a hand over her blouse and her stylish ensemble morphed into an inky cloak of glossy feathers that came to midthigh, exposing her wound and the bandage that now gaped around her leg. "It's just a trick, turning our coats into clothing or jewelry. This is the form I take directly from the raven."

He stroked the shimmering feather cape and she allowed it. Astonishment rippled through him, causing a pleasant heat in his stomach. When was the last time he had been surprised by anything?

Cesar fingered the edge of the cloak. "And you need this to change back."

Her eyes narrowed at him, glaring as if he'd just held a gun to her head.

"I wouldn't try it."

Bess didn't like having him know her weaknesses. He understood that and nodded his comprehension. Then he withdrew his hand and stepped away. "Let's see about that wound."

Cesar knelt beside her on the plush rug and peered beneath as she studied the gash that ran from high on her hip to midthigh. The wound tore through the skin but did not look to have gored the muscle.

"It's not very deep."

"Looks like a map of the Mississippi," said Bess, pinching and poking at her skin.

Seeing her torn flesh made his stomach flip, which was funny, since he'd seen so much worse than this over the years. How much blood had she lost?

She met his gaze. "Disinfectant?"

"I have rubbing alcohol."

"Are you crazy? Why not just pour whiskey over it?"

"If you'd prefer, but rubbing alcohol is cheaper."

"Just turn on the water. I'll wash it."

He twisted the taps and adjusted the temperature.

"Do you believe *now* that they're dangerous? Or doesn't this qualify in your code book?" She indicated her injury with a graceful sweep of her hand.

"It's a book of law and I'm not sure what to think. It's possible they were defending their kill."

She pressed her lips tight and regarded him from beneath her lowered brow. With a pang of regret, he recognized that his answer had just squashed any chance of doing anything with her that he'd fantasized about in the elevator.

"You're an idiot," she said.

"I know. But I'm not hunting a creature before it has committed a crime."

"Attacking a Skinwalker doesn't meet your criteria?"

"I only track murderers."

She snorted. "Well, then, I'll fly slower next time."

Her flippant response made his heart squeeze in some emotion he could not name. What was happening here?

"That's not funny, Bess."

She flushed and then gave a defiant toss of her head that sent her silky hair back over her shoulder.

He said nothing as she turned her back to him and began washing first her hands and then the gash. Soon blood was streaming down her long leg again and sliding down his tub drain. She motioned toward a towel and he handed it to her.

Cesar rummaged in the cabinet until he found a

medical kit he'd received from a health fair in the park. Inside, thankfully, were four large butterfly bandages, gauze, Band-Aids and an ammonia capsule. He might need that himself if he had to spend much more time with Bess.

She was his sexual ideal, but forbidden by his kind. Not that she'd have him—unless she was also feeling the tingling attraction that sparked whenever they touched. He could barely think around her. He turned and the sight of the blood brought him back from his sexual musings like a slap across the face.

She'd dried her leg, making it easy to get the butterflies to stick.

"This is going to leave a scar," he said. It hurt him to see such perfection marred by violence.

"It won't. I've had worse, but my friends took care of it."

The bear, buffalo or wolf? he wanted to ask, but kept his mouth shut.

"What will it take for you to go after those things with me?" she asked.

He pressed the gauze to her leg and accidentally brushed her skin again. The hum of sexual energy rolled from her to him and their eyes met. So he wasn't the only one whose mind was wandering.

"Not now," she said, pushing his hand away and taking charge of the gauze.

Not now? Well, to his brain that meant later. He smiled.

"So, what will it take? Would they need to kill a human or what?"

"Oh." His brain snapped back to the newborns of unknown origin. "Yes, they must commit a murder and I have to have irrefutable evidence."

"I'd like to know who fathered them," said Bess.

He nodded his agreement to that. "Me, too. But I doubt a DNA test will do anything but frighten the men I work with. I've never heard of a Supernatural successfully producing offspring. So it seems likely that they are some kind of Halfling."

"Halfling?"

Bess went as pale as the marble upon which she perched.

"Yellow eyes," she said. "Oh, no."

She swayed and he grasped her shoulders to steady her.

"Easy there." He pulled her down onto the plush mat on the floor, so she wouldn't crack her head and leaned her up against the tub. "What's wrong?"

"I think…"

Bess pressed both hands to her temples. Her skin seemed even paler than a moment ago.

She began again. "I need to know if… I have to know who fathered them."

He noticed she had twice amended her words. What was it she was unwilling to say aloud?

"I'm afraid we're too late to interview their mothers."

Her eyes widened. "That's it!"

"What? Listen, Bess. I only see their actual death. That's all. I don't get to ask questions."

"But I can, by flying to the Spirit World."

"You mean you can actually…"

Her slow nod made her seem regal as any regent. "I'll find the mothers, both of them, and I'll find out what they know."

"You'd do that?"

"I need to know what these things are just as badly as you do, and I hope with all my heart that I'm wrong."

"But your leg." He hated to point out the obvious, but she'd lost blood.

"Yeah. Bad timing on that, for sure."

There was a knock on his door. His head whipped around as if someone had discharged a weapon inside his apartment. No one ever knocked on his door. Partly because he kept to himself, but also there was an excellent security system and doorman to insure that strangers didn't just appear at his threshold. He glanced back at Bess.

"This your guy?"

"Probably." She stood and brushed a hand over her feather cape. Before his eyes the glossy wrap shifted into a short cocktail dress with a frilly skirt. Her bare feet were now trimmed in high, strappy sandals.

"Wow," was all he could think to say as he stared appreciatively.

The knock came again, but suddenly he was very sure he did not want to be disturbed. He reached for her and she ducked under his arm, clearing the door, waiting in the hall.

"Answer it."

He scowled and stalked to the foyer, jerking the door open. There before him stood a man dressed from head to toe in worn denim except for his scuffed brown cowboy boots. He had a pleasant face and long black hair plaited at each side of his head. The braids were wrapped in what appeared to be bear or buffalo hide, crisscrossed with beaded leather cords. His ethnic features, hairstyle and clothing made him look like a poster boy for Native pride.

He grinned affably. Cesar took in the frayed collar of his work shirt and the distinctive brown aura that surrounded him.

Another Skinwalker.

"Hello," said the stranger. "I'm Tuff Jackson. Is Bess here?"

Tracked her like some damn bloodhound. Cesar raised his brows. Maybe he *was* a bloodhound.

"In here," called Bess.

Cesar jerked his head in invitation and stepped aside as Tuff entered his foyer. Bess was the only woman he'd ever brought to his place and Tuff was his first guest. He knew he shouldn't be so protective of his sanctuary, but he still felt as if he were being invaded. He liked his privacy and in the course of one afternoon he suddenly had a regular party of Skinwalkers at his place.

He followed his unwelcome guest into his living room, ignoring the lovely sunset over the bay and the twinkling lights of the bridge spanning the dark water in favor of the woman standing at his bar, pouring a tumbler of Scotch.

"Do we have any pop, Cesar? Tuff doesn't drink alcohol."

What's this *we* crap? he thought as he stalked to the kitchen and retrieved a can of seltzer from his nearly empty refrigerator. He gave it to Tuff and then retrieved the tumbler Bess extended to him, Scotch on the rocks, just as he liked it. He gave the glass a puzzled look.

"You only have that and beer, so it wasn't hard to figure," she said, and then turned to their guest.

Tuff cracked the can, took a long swallow and grinned. "Bubbly." He wiped his mouth with the back of the hand that held the drink.

Hadn't he had a seltzer before?

"Thank you for coming so quickly," said Bess.

He blushed. "I've got that old truck, you know. Don't like to drive much, but it's faster than walking."

"How'd you get in?" asked Cesar, the tone of his voice making the question an accusation.

Bess frowned, displeased at either his tone or line of questioning. The Skinwalker was a guest, come at her request into his home. Cesar had so few visitors he had long ago forgotten how to be gracious and this particular guest was both male and enemy. He hardly knew how to act.

If Tuff noticed Cesar's rudeness he gave no indication for his easy smile never slipped. "Oh, I just came round the back, carrying a five-gallon bucket of compound. The guy at the loading dock let me right in."

"Where is it?" asked Cesar.

He thumbed over his shoulder. "It's right outside. You need some?"

Cesar shook his head. He'd never met anyone as

guileless and gracious as this guy. It made him suspicious. He wondered what shape he took. Was this the wolf or buffalo? Cesar glanced at the rawhide cord around his neck. Whatever was on that leather thong was hidden beneath his work shirt.

Bess stepped between them. "Tuff, this is Cesar Garza, a Niyanoka."

Tuff's eyebrows lifted, but his face remained otherwise impassive. After an awkward pause he turned back to Bess.

"So what happened, Bess? You seemed pretty rattled." He gave Cesar an appraising look.

Cesar scowled at him from over the rim of his glass, refusing to acknowledge the heat in his face.

Bess proceeded to tell him everything and showed him the bandage on her thigh. She also included her assumptions about the creatures being dangerous. He didn't point out to her that she had left the world of facts and headed into supposition.

Tuff listened and asked only a few questions. Then he set aside his drink and took a step toward Bess.

"Let's fix that up."

Cesar intercepted the guy, planting his palm on the center of Tuff's chest. Tuff did not respond to the aggressive gesture in kind, but only paused, meeting Cesar's eyes.

"I only mean to restore her to health."

That was true. Cesar read it through the connection between his index finger and the skin he touched at the gap of Tuff's button-down shirt.

"It won't hurt her."

Also true. Why could he read other Skinwalkers' thoughts but not Bess's?

Bess was tugging at Cesar's arm now. Her hand brushed his and the shock of her emotion blasted through him. She was embarrassed and aroused, but he couldn't tell if it was by him or by Tuff. Rage flooded through him. He clenched his fist around worn denim and pulled Tuff forward, or he tried. Tuff blocked his wrist and spun, leaving Cesar a choice between letting go or spinning with him. Cesar released his grip.

"Cesar, what is wrong with you?" asked Bess. She had both hands on her hips now.

Tuff kept his gaze on Cesar, placid as ever. Cesar still wanted to punch him, but the rage cooled now that Bess no longer hung on his arm. He wasn't certain what was happening himself.

"You okay with this?" asked Tuff.

"Or do I have to lock you in your room?" added Bess.

Cesar shoved his hands in his pockets. He should apologize; attacking a guest in his home was unforgivable. But for the moment it took all his slipping self-control to keep his teeth clamped together. He wanted to order Tuff out. Instead he nodded, lowering his chin and glowering at the other male.

"Honestly," said Bess, giving Cesar a scowl before returning her attention to Tuff. She smiled and shook her head. "Sorry about that. Thank you for your sacrifice."

Why was she bowing to him? What would he do to her? He took a step toward her again. She lifted one finger and pointed at him.

"Sit down, Cesar. I need this healed or I can't go."

He didn't want her to go, so he took another step. She rounded on him, putting both hands on his chest. Thankfully his shirt kept her from touching skin.

"He's an old friend."

"Yeah, I got that."

"You're being ridiculous."

His vision narrowed to Tuff as the blood beat against his eardrums like a hailstorm. "I don't want him here."

"Yeah, I got that, too. Nothing subtle about your signals. So go sit down and he'll be out of here in a few minutes. If you get up off that sofa, I'm going with him."

Suddenly he couldn't get enough air into his

lungs. He wasn't letting her just walk out of here until he understood what the blazes was happening between them and that might take all night. What was he thinking? He had no claim on her. But somehow, he did—he felt it.

He folded into the sofa. She perched at the edge of the love seat and Tuff knelt at her feet. She lifted her skirt and placed one high-heeled sandal on his coffee table. Then she peeled off the bandage, showing the red scab forming along her smooth skin.

"Not too bad." Tuff closed his eyes and placed both hands on her thigh.

Cesar left his seat but was stayed again by Bess, who aimed a warning index finger at him again as if he were her pet Pomeranian. His nostrils flared as he sank back to the edge of his seat.

Tuff began to chant, words Cesar hadn't heard in over a century. His Lakota was pure and without accent, a lilting, rolling song of power and sacrifice.

Cesar glanced at Bess and saw the strain on her face. He followed the direction of her gaze and saw, to his horror, that Tuff's left leg was now bleeding through his jeans. The blood appeared in the exact place as Bess's wound. Fingers of uncertainty wriggled down his spine as he realized what was happening. Cesar's gaze flashed to hers for confirmation and she nodded. Tuff wasn't so much healing Bess as taking her injury from her. What kind of a man would willingly do such a thing?

His prayer of gratitude ended and his eyes flickered open.

"You lost a lot of blood," he said.

"I was a ways out when I got hit."

He nodded. "I can't replace blood. So you can't fly very far until you get some nourishment and rest. I'd offer to take you with me, but you know I sleep in that truck."

Cesar knew he should offer the Skinwalker a bed. He had a guest room and this sofa, but damned if he'd have him in his house a moment longer than necessary. His selfishness seemed to stand in particularly stark contrast to this man's generosity.

"She stays here," said Cesar.

Bess made a face that said otherwise. He made a note that she didn't like being told what to do.

"Or I could drive you back to your place," said Tuff.

How did he know where Bess lived? Cesar found his rage shooting him off the sofa like a geyser blast. Drive her to her place, his ass. Damned if he let her out of his sight.

Bess looked from one to the other and smiled, seeming pleased at the turmoil she'd brought to his quiet life. He'd spent so much time with the dead that he'd forgotten how the scent of a beautiful woman could affect him.

"I'll stay here…" said Bess, and then peeled the butterfly bandages from her perfect, unblemished skin.

Cesar's smug smile died as she completed her sentence.

"…in the city. And maybe tomorrow I can start my journey to the Spirit World."

"Perhaps. If you eat and rest," he said.

She rose and Tuff followed. She walked him toward the door. "Is your leg healed already?"

"Yes. That was a small one."

"What about your pants?"

He waved a dismissive hand. "Got a real pair just like these behind the seat in the cab."

Cesar trailed behind them, battling his need to defend his territory and this woman. He couldn't understand it. He was acting much more like an animal than either of these two. Weren't Niyanoka supposed to be the ones in control of their baser sides? Yet his libido seemed to be roaring like a hungry lion. How long since he'd been so eager for sex? Too damn long and never like this.

Cesar did not like how Bess clung to the man's arm.

"Can you heal anything?" he asked.

Tuff paused and then lowered his eyes in a show of modesty. "So far."

"Can you bring someone back from the dead?" Cesar stilled, waiting for his answer, wondering if this man, this half-man could have saved his brother, had he been there.

Tuff met his eyes. "I only repair the body. Once the soul has fled, I can't call it back."

Bess looped her arm in Tuff's as she escorted him to the foyer.

Cesar moved to follow, but she rounded on him. "And you are staying here."

He wanted to make sure she came back and then he realized the choice was hers. He could not quite keep the growl of frustration from escaping his clamped jaw.

Tuff smile remained placid as he faced Cesar, who stood like a gargoyle at his front door. "Thanks for the seltzer."

Tuff turned back to Bess, but she did not release the Skinwalker's arm or show any sign that she made her farewells.

"I'm walking you out," she said to Tuff, and then turned to Cesar. "See you in a bit."

He reached for her, but Bess evaded him and stepped into the hall. It surprised him how difficult it was to let her walk away.

Bess walked Tuff to the elevator, her leg feeling perfect, while Tuff limped slightly. She had last seen the buffalo Skinwalker when they had fought Nagi's ghost army, in the spring, a little over three months ago. She knew he was fearless and selfless, for she had seen him heal the injured from both sides after the battle. He was also gentle and thoughtful. Exactly the sort of man a woman should want. Why then did she feel the sensual pull only from one surly, infuriating Soul Whisperer who was absolutely wrong for her?

"He's an enemy," Tuff said, seeming tuned in to her thoughts. "Do you know what you're doing?"

She rolled her eyes. "Not particularly, no."

"The guy has a serious thing going for you."

"I thought you couldn't read auras." Bess could see the change in color of her aura and of Cesar's. They pulsed with the salmon pink of lust and the bright blue of sexual power. But to have Tuff see that embarrassed her greatly. It wasn't as if she were some teenager with hormones raging. But something sure as hell was raging.

"I can't. But I can read a male defending his territory and fighting for the rights to a female. And I can smell the pheromones in there and his testosterone." Tuff thumbed back toward Cesar's place. "I'm dizzy from the scent."

Bess flushed.

Tuff's shoulders sagged with his long sigh. "I'd warn you to be careful, but I see it's already too late. The man's in rut."

"A Spirit Child can't go into rut."

Tuff gave her an incredulous look and hit the elevator button.

"I thought they were above all those base instincts, too."

"Apparently not," he said.

"I think he just finds me attractive."

Tuff gave her a serious look and then slowly shook his head. "He's a stallion defending a mare. He's keeping you with him and he'll kick the ass of any other stallion that comes near you. His door is open right now."

The prospect of being so coveted both annoyed and titillated.

Bess looked back, seeing only the empty corridor. "How do you know that?"

"Never heard it shut behind us."

Bess couldn't keep from smiling.

The elevator doors slid open. "I can take you with me."

She felt touched by his offer and knew the instant he spoke that she was staying here. She shook her head and he gave a long sigh.

"I'll camp in the Redwood Forest until you return from your journey. Call me if you have need of me or of a male to challenge that one and bring you safely away."

"Don't be silly. He's not keeping me. I can leave whenever I like."

Tuff glanced toward Cesar's door. "I'd kiss you goodbye, but I don't want to have to kick his ass unless it's strictly necessary."

She smiled. "Thank you for all you have done."

He stepped into the car and nodded. "Walk in beauty."

The compartment closed and the engine whirred. Bess turned back to find Cesar standing in the middle of the hall, arms akimbo with fists at his hips and his chin lowered as he fixed his stare on her. She cocked her head, wondering if Tuff was right. His expression was predatory and arousing as hell.

Bess hesitated, realizing two things simultaneously. First, she was well enough to leave and, second, she recognized exactly what would happen if she returned to his apartment. She considered escaping now, troubled by the alarming yearning he stirred in her. But, at the same time, she wanted to linger and explore this exciting, arousing male. Was it already too late?

He seemed to sense her indecision, for he stalked forward ready to claim what he already thought was his.

Chapter 4

Nagi had followed the raven to its home territory. On the journey, he realized something. If he killed it, not only would he lose his only connection to the Seer of Souls, the raven's death would send the Skinwalker to Hihankara, the immortal who guarded the Spirit Road, and alert the crone about what he was up to. Hihankara could then tell his fellow Spirits. It was one thing to fight Halflings and Supernaturals, quite another to face true immortal Spirits with powers equal or greater than his own. He still hoped to possess the earth before the others learned of his efforts. It was a dilemma.

Of course, a raven could fly to the Spirit World any time it liked and so the longer it lived the better the chance the Skinwalker might tell. Still Hihankara didn't like ravens or their intrusion into her domain. They might not even speak.

Nagi fumed. For many days and nights, the raven had done nothing and contacted no one. He'd become so bored he'd slipped away to make three more attempts at fatherhood. He did not have all century to follow this damned bird. Better to find a ghost to watch her and report. That way he would be free to continue his breeding project and still have a chance to again find the Seer.

Chapter 5

Cesar stalked toward Bess, who stood motionless beside the bank of elevators on his floor. He advanced, drawn by the power of their mutual attraction. Bess squared her body, sending her long, inky hair back over her shoulder with a toss of her head. She looked as if she were preparing to do battle. He stared at her through lowered brows, unable to keep the anticipation from licking along his insides.

"I'm not going back into your apartment."

He stopped, clenching his jaw.

"Why not?" he growled.

"Because we both know what will happen if I do, and I'm not that kind of bird." She gave him a sensual smile that made his abdomen twitch. "You're taking me out to dinner."

"A few minutes ago you were bleeding so badly I had to use a tourniquet to stop it. We should stay in. I'll order something."

She shook her head and he tried again.

"It's cold outside," he said, having no idea if it was cold, but certain it was colder than his big empty bed would be right now.

Bess let out a sigh and then brushed her hand over her shoulder. A lovely, belted black trench coat of glossy curling fur appeared over her cocktail dress. Her shapely legs were now encased in tight, knee-high boots with killer heels that made her nearly as tall as he was. She touched the fur at her throat.

"Like it? It's Persian lamb. Well, it's raven actually, but you'd never know. I do faux better than any designer in the business. Ready, or would you like your coat?" She didn't wait for an answer, just turned and pressed the elevator button. "Lovely."

Cesar growled as he stormed back to his apartment, grabbed his coat and locked the door. When he returned and stepped up beside her, he found their reflections, distorted in the shining, gold metallic finish of the elevator doors. The car behind them opened a moment later, empty of the Skinwalker. Bess moved toward the compartment and he followed. Damn, he'd follow her anywhere.

She stepped into the car and turned, lounging back against the rail. He pressed the button for the lobby and then he turned to face her, breathing in her scent. He crowded her space until his legs straddled hers. She looked up at him, raising an eyebrow in a silent question, but couldn't quite keep the ghost of a smile from lifting one corner of her mouth. She knew what he wanted, damn her. They both did.

The doors whisked shut and as he closed in she smiled up at him as if she didn't know what was coming next. She'd made a mistake, trapping herself in the car with him. He placed his hands on either side of her head and leaned in, keeping their bodies separate, wanting that first electric zing of awareness to come from her lush mouth. He took his time, angling his head to align with hers. Just before he kissed her she spoke.

"How will you explain to the front desk when they capture me on their security cameras changing into a raven?"

He straightened his arms to get a better look at her. She couldn't be serious.

"You can't. You're not allowed to show your transition to humans."

Her voice dropped, yet she managed to make it

sound like a threat. "I can if I'm in danger and I will if you don't back up."

He did and the door dinged open, admitting a wiry man whose sunburned face showed beneath his Giants baseball cap. His running shoes, navy sweatpants and a gray crew-neck sweatshirt broadcast his intention to exercise. He turned to face front, inserting white earbuds into his ears and then fiddled with the controls of his MP3 player.

Cesar growled and threw himself back against the wall with a bang that rocked the car. Bess gave a musical laugh and then looked up at him. The other occupant glanced around and then sank back into his oblivion.

"So where are you taking me?" she asked.

"Dominicos," he said without thinking. It was where he took all his dates—first dates, only dates. He didn't do second dates.

She scrunched up her delectable mouth as if thinking and then gave a barely perceptible shake of her glossy head. "No. Somewhere different."

"What's wrong with Dominicos? They've got the best Italian on the bay."

"Because it was your first choice. Take me somewhere you've never been."

How did she know he was trying to make this

no different than the others? Make *her* no different. But she was and they both knew it.

He frowned. "I've been everywhere. I've lived here for…"

He hesitated, looking at their silent companion who now drew an arm across his chest, pulling it as if he were a relief pitcher being called from the bullpen instead of a weekend warrior about to go pull a hammy. The music throbbed from the earbuds.

Cesar leaned in and whispered. "Lived here for fifty years."

"Yes, but Niyanoka are creatures of habit. You visit maybe ten places."

It was true, damn it. "What kind of food do you like?"

She gave him an impatient look and pressed a delicate hand to her chest. "Raven-ravenous. We'll eat anything."

The elevator bumped to a stop and the doors opened. They followed the jogger out and headed for the street.

"Evening Mr. Garza," said the night man as he swept open the gilded-and-glass door to allow them exit.

"Call my driver, Anthony."

"Sure thing, Mr. Garza." Anthony pulled out his phone and began pressing buttons.

"We'll walk," said Bess.

Cesar ignored her and signaled for Anthony to continue his call behind her back. An hour ago he'd feared she'd bleed to death in his bathroom, now she wanted to go for a stroll.

The breeze off the bay was cool and damp, yet she didn't seem to feel the cold.

He took a hold of her elbow and moved in close to whisper in her ear. "The Skinwalker said you're weak."

Her eyes flashed fire and he couldn't hold back the smile at the indignation he saw there. He'd said *weak* and she did not like it.

"Well?" he asked.

"The car then."

She had conceded for the second time and would be trapped in his vehicle. Was that why she wanted to walk, because she could escape him instantly?

He wrapped an arm around her, tucking her against him while using his body to block the wind. She allowed it as she watched for his car.

"What about the Figurehead on Pier Two?" she asked.

"Overrated and too far."

"You've never been."

It was more statement than question but he answered anyway. "No."

"Perfect."

His Cadillac pulled up and he motioned to his driver to get back behind the wheel as he opened the door for Bess himself.

"The Figurehead, Tommy."

"The…yes, sir."

Bess smiled as she settled into the plush backseat.

The lights from the street flashed over her face, revealing her beauty. She kept her attention fixed on the road and did not speak or look at him until they reached their destination.

Once free of the car, some of the tension disappeared from her.

"You don't like driving."

She got a wistful look in her eye. "It makes me feel trapped. I don't own a car. Never needed one."

Because she could fly.

"What's it like?"

"There is nothing that compares to it."

Cesar thought that sleeping with Bess might be a close second, but he merely nodded.

She turned toward the red-and-blue neon of the restaurant.

You would never guess from her long, effortless strides that she had suffered a recent injury. He clasped her elbow, taking charge of her and controlling their pace if not their direction. She glanced at him and laughed, as if this were a game at which she excelled. Cesar took a moment to consider how many lovers she might have taken in all her years upon the earth and found he resented each and every one.

When they arrived at the restaurant the hostess was polite but Cesar missed being greeted by name and being shown to his regular table. Bess asked for a water view and the hostess led them to a table before a huge bank of windows. The smell of garlic and cooking meat made him realize that he was starving. Bess stared out at the expansive view of the water. The lights of the Bay Bridge sparkled against the approaching twilight. He stood beside her for a moment then pulled out her chair. She graced him with a lovely smile that made his empty stomach drop several inches.

"May I take your coat?" asked their hostess.

Bess slipped out of the black lamb's wool. "I think I'll keep it with me."

The hostess nodded. "Enjoy your meal."

They exchanged a look, and he smiled. It felt good to share a secret. He'd been alone with his own for so long.

He kept his hand on the back of her chair as she nestled into her place. It was not until after she was seated that he realized the coat had vanished. On

her wrist she now wore a new bangle bracelet sparkling with hundreds of tiny black crystals.

Their waiter made his introductions, listed spe-
cials and handed over the menu and wine list. Bess
studied her menu as if there would be a test later
as the waiters circled the room, lighting small oil
lamps on each table. They were early for the dinner
crowd and momentarily had the room to themselves.

Cesar ordered wine and afterward discovered
Bess didn't drink.

"Dulls the senses," she said. "And I like my
senses sharp."

The waiter returned with his wine, opening the
bottle and offering a taste to him. He nodded and
the waiter stepped back to take their order.

She requested the calamari, mussels, lobster
bisque, house salad and entrée of Columbian
salmon. Cesar silently cautioned himself to disguise his surprise at her appetite, and then ordered
the rib eye with potatoes.

"How very pedestrian." She smiled.

She sipped her sparkling water, crossing her legs
and bouncing her foot in a way that made him draw
his chair closer to hers. Two tables behind her, the
hostess seated another couple.

He tried small talk but she shut him down.

"What do you really want to talk about?" she asked.

Sex was his first thought but he managed to censor that and instead said, "Tuff."

"Ah, yes. You were very territorial, for a man who has no claim on me."

"Does someone else have a claim?"

She made him wait for the answer, all the while his stomach squeezed as if encircled by a boa constrictor.

Her musical laugh struck him in the center of his chest. This was why it was forbidden to have a Skinwalker. They were as compelling as sirens and twice as deadly.

Forbidden.

Why should he care what his people thought? They already would have nothing to do with him, repelled as they were by his useful if repugnant gift of sight. Soul Whisperers were not permitted to have connections to anyone except the dead.

But he did care. Outcast or not, he still had his position and his work. He'd lose both if they caught him with Bess. He glanced about, searching the arriving diners to see if he spotted any other golden aura. It was dangerous to be out in public with her.

When he brought his attention back to Bess it was to find her glaring at him.

"Don't worry, Cesar. I never stay in one place for long. If I decide to have you, your little racist friends won't find out."

She'd somehow guessed his thoughts, but he knew enough not to walk down that road. Besides he didn't have friends. He kept the conversation on the Skinwalker. "How does he do it?"

"Tuff? He's a buffalo."

Cesar choked on his wine, but Bess continued without pausing.

"They have the gift of sacrifice. Terrible burden, I imagine, but that is their life's purpose. He bears the pain with the dignity of his kind and can heal anything. I've seen him take on one injury after another, more agony than any one being was ever meant to bear, but he does it and he regenerates.

"The more egregious the wound, the longer it takes to heal. And it costs him more of his strength. Buffaloes are very strong, but even he must have a limit to his endurance."

"And you can fly to the Spirit World."

She lowered her water goblet, circling the rim of the crystal with her index finger until it hummed. He imagined her running that finger down his stomach and felt his muscles twitch.

"That is my purpose. But I can only travel over the Way of Souls. I can't really cross to the Spirit

World. Well, I can, but just like everyone else, I can only do so once and there is no coming back."

"And you can talk to the ones who have departed?"

"If they have entered the Spirit World. But I can't speak to my own relations or anyone I love. My mentor said it was to keep us from lingering too long or crossing the veil and losing our way. But..." She straightened and shook her head, as if warning herself not to go there.

"But what?"

She studied him for a long moment. He felt her judging him and held his breath awaiting her decision, hoping she would trust him with the answer.

At last she said, "But it didn't stop me from thinking about it after my mother died and then again after my dad. I almost crossed. All that stopped me was knowing how angry they would be at my decision."

She scowled so deeply that Cesar grew wary.

"But for years when I flew over the Ghost Road, I would try to speak to them. I called their names and waited." She lifted her hands, palms up as if offering herself to the heavens. "No answer," she whispered.

"Then you must wait for your time, just as I must wait to speak to those who have crossed before us."

She tucked her chin to her chest.

"They died together?" He didn't want to know the answer but he asked out of respect.

She regarded him steadily now and he hoped she would tell him it was none of his business. He didn't want to have one more tragic story of loss in his head. Cesar had seen so many deaths he was weary from the burden of them all.

"My human mother's death was accidental. I was ten and got into a nest of white-faced hornets. She scooped me up and ran me to safety. Today it would have been nothing, but back then, well, who ever heard of bee-sting allergies or epinephrine? We were both stung. It hardly affected me, but the swelling closed her throat. She couldn't breathe and I couldn't do anything to save her." She swallowed but her eyes remained dry, which surprised him. "After that it was just me and my dad."

She met his gaze and it was hard for him not to flinch or look away from the pain he saw in her eyes.

"He was murdered two years later in what your kind called The Cleansing."

He'd been afraid of this. So it was her father who was the Skinwalker and he'd been killed after the bloody war between their races.

The Skinwalkers wrongly believed that keeping

the balance of nature meant killing men and their protectors, the Niyanoka. The war that followed had been bloody and long, but after the defeat of their great leader, Fleetfoot, the Skinwalkers had scattered like the animals they were. In time, his people brought the rest of Fleetfoot's followers to justice. This final blow brought the remaining Skinwalkers to the negotiation table. An uneasy truce had lasted through the century. But neither race trusted the other and his people still did not gather in large communities in order to make it harder for the Skinwalkers to find them the next time. Most were certain there would be a next time.

She was his natural enemy. How had he let a touch make him forget that?

"He fought?" asked Cesar, still staring down at the bloodred wine.

"No. But it didn't matter. None of your people cared who was guilty or innocent."

"Times have changed since then. We have rules against such things now."

She folded her arms across her chest and hunched over as if he had punched her.

"I know of your rules. They shot my father out of the sky before my eyes. So don't speak to me of Niyanoka rules, for I have seen them."

His face fell, losing any hint of superiority. "No wonder you hate us."

"I do. You and all the rest of them. Others of my people have forgotten, but not me. Because I know what lies beneath all those fancy words."

"It was war."

"It was *after* the war. The vigilantes just chose to ignore the truce."

"Because of the losses we suffered. It took some time to bring them back to their right minds and restore order."

"Stop it. You say you were too young to take part, and I believe you, Cesar. But don't you dare make excuses for the men who tracked my people down and killed them. And as for the one who shot my father, I remember his face. And I search for him still."

"Bess, you mustn't talk like that."

"Because you'll hunt me down if I kill him?"

He nodded. "I'd have to." He folded one arm over his chest and used it as a rest for his opposite elbow. He rested his chin on his fist. "Was he a raven?"

"Harrier Hawk."

"I'm sorry for your loss."

An uneasy silence followed. None of them were innocent. Not according to what he had been taught.

"Is there anything else you wish to know?"

"How did you escape them?"

"I had not yet changed and so I did not have the aura of a Skinwalker. They found me, but assumed I was human and let me go."

"That was lucky."

"Lucky." She gave a short exhalation and a half smile that seemed laced with hatred, as if she had also just recalled who and what he was. "I should go."

"No." He rested a hand on her knee and the depth of her loss rolled through him, cold as an ice storm. He drew back his hand, unable to bear it. "At least stay for supper."

Her nod was barely perceptible. He blew out the breath he'd been holding. He had her for a little while longer.

She pressed her hands together and lowered her head for a moment as if praying. But he knew better. Bess was reining in her emotions. When she lifted her chin her face was placid, but her eyes were intent as ever.

"Why do you always take your women to Dominicos?" she asked.

Now she was trying small talk. He appreciated the effort and responded with honesty that even surprised him.

"Closer to my bed, I suppose, and impressive enough to get them there."

Her eyes rounded and she pressed her hand over the smile that had returned like the sun emerging from behind a storm cloud.

"Honesty? Something I never expected from one of your kind."

"And you, Bess. What keeps you from boredom as the decades inch past?"

"My work you mean? I'm with the National Wilderness Coalition. Mostly on the coast, but I do travel domestically if there is a natural disaster that affects wildlife. It's all about The Balance, for us, as you know."

To the point of making man extinct, he thought, but said nothing. The Skinwalkers made the most militant of animal rights groups seem like a litter of kittens by comparison. Still, he did not want to say anything that would add further cracks to their fragile truce, so he held his tongue.

The waiter brought all Bess's appetizers at once, as she requested. Cesar wondered if their discussion had spoiled her appetite, but she attacked the calamari with singular attention.

"It's been so long since I've been in human form. I'd forgotten the pleasure of eating fried food."

Her comment reminded him of all the reasons

that teaming up with a raven was a bad idea. Such a liaison would have consequences for them both.

But he found himself saying, "Been a long time since I enjoyed a conversation with a fellow Halfling."

She lifted her gaze to his, her eyes searching his face for what was left unsaid. But he had years of practice and knew his expression revealed nothing.

"I thought Niyanoka lived in tight groups. You must have many opportunities to converse."

In answer he lifted his wine and took a large swallow.

She leaned forward. "They really won't talk to you?"

He lowered the wine and glared at her, heartily sorry he had brought it up.

She flopped back in her chair, indignation making her cheeks turn an appealing pink. Did she know how lovely she looked?

"That cracks it. Only Spirit Children would make an outcast of one of their own and one who holds such a valuable gift."

Valuable? Now there was a word he had never heard associated with his ability. Nor was it a gift, but rather a curse.

"I'm tainted by the dead."

Bess waved a dismissive hand, graceful as a conductor leading an orchestra. Then she used her fingers to pick up a piece of fried calamari, its brown batter-coated tentacles twisted in some representation of a dreadful second death in the fryer. She lifted it between them.

"Dead," she said, and then popped it into her mouth. "And they are hypocrites unless they are all vegans."

"It's different."

She rolled her eyes and headed back to the bisque. It was both refreshing and maddening to have someone not understand how impossibly difficult it was to be outcast by his own people. He didn't tell her that he was a double outcast, first for what he was and second for what he had done.

"So you only date human women then?"

He nodded. It was lonely passing like a shadow among them.

"That's depressing. Not that I've managed anything long-term, except for Gordon. I was with him twenty-one years. One day he didn't come home. I found his remains in the snow. An eagle got him."

"An eagle? How could an eagle kill a full-grown man?"

She met his eyes and held them, her expression unapologetic. "Gordon was exceptionally bright and terribly handsome. But not human. Raven, full raven, not a Inanoka. We met in British Columbia in the 1920s."

He couldn't quite get his mind around that. "You stayed with a raven, a bird, for twenty years?"

She cast him a look ripe with annoyance. "Twenty-one, and yes. He was very attentive and a great provider."

"Did he know what you were?"

"Of course. It didn't matter to him."

Cesar lifted the bottle and poured himself another full glass as their dinners arrived. Bess held on to the calamari but had finished everything else.

"What about you? Any Soul Whisperer ladies in your life?"

"I'm the only one of my kind," he answered.

"What? How can that be?"

"One at a time, that's the deal."

"How does that work?"

He knew only that it seemed as if the world had been structured to close him out.

He shrugged. "I'm not really sure. I was born a Truth Seeker. It wasn't until…well, no one realized for some time that I was a Soul Whisperer. I was thirteen before it was discovered." He'd nearly told her, nearly mentioned how he'd learned of his terrible curse. He wondered if she noticed his hesitation. Cesar reached for his water glass and took a swallow. His mouth still felt dry.

"Your people have too many rules."

"Designed to keep us safe while working toward the betterment of mankind."

She gave him that enigmatic stare and then she cut into her salmon.

Cesar tried to keep his attention on his steak, but he was distracted by his thoughts and the woman. How did she call to him without saying a word? He should ask for the check and leave her here. That was the proper thing to do. His people used their ability to read auras to avoid such encounters. This was exactly why. He reconsidered bringing her back to his place. After all, she might take a cleaver to him while he slept.

For all his training, he'd failed to recognize a Skinwalker when he finally met one. But she knew him on sight. Until today he never knew any of her kind could spot them the same way. It made him wonder what else the textbooks got wrong.

Bess finished first, licked her lips and eyed the remains of his steak.

He exhaled in a gesture of bewilderment. "You cannot possibly still be hungry?"

"Always," she said and smiled.

He slid his plate a little closer to himself and she

laughed outright. He liked the sound because her mirth had a rich genuine tone to it.

"So, you don't work with a partner?"

He lowered his fork. It was a touchy subject, but she couldn't know that, could she?

He was careful to keep his tone level, to prevent her seeing the depth of pain this question caused. But inside he coiled like a nest of rattlers.

"No partner," he managed.

"So what makes you so furious, not having one or what the last one did?"

"I'm not furious."

She slung one arm over the back of her chair and motioned with one finger. "Your aura says differently."

He should have thought of that. The nice dark room and candlelit tables made for perfect conditions to read auras. No wonder she seemed to know what he was thinking. She just made educated guesses from his changing auras.

"I'm not discussing my past with you."

Bess's smile turned wicked. "What about your job with the FBI?"

Cesar glanced around. A few patrons now sat within earshot but seemed absorbed in their own conversations.

He lowered his voice. "I don't talk about my work

with…" He was going to say his women but decided against it.

"Of course. Why should you have to explain anything to the likes of me? It must be so frustrating to have to deal with an inferior species."

He lowered his knife and fork to the table. "I didn't say that."

She snorted. "You do, with every breath."

"We do not have to be enemies in this. What do they say about common interest leading to strange bedfellows?"

"That's politics and why does everything lead back to bed with you?" She studied him in silence as if trying to decide if she should waste her breath on him. "Despite what you Niyanoka think, Inanoka have perfectly good minds. But if you feel you cannot speak of your work, I assume you don't need my help. You'll likely solve the case, eventually. No need for me to tell you what I discover from those young mothers."

"Bess, that's not fair."

"Really? I thought you worked alone."

He lifted his gaze from his plate and saw her leaning in, her chin lifted in a clear challenge.

"Is that what you really want to know, why I work alone?" he asked.

"I want to know how you've existed without

anyone to talk to about something other than the weather. You want my help. That entitles me to some answers and I don't give a damn if you aren't accustomed to sharing."

He pushed the remains of his meal aside and looked for the waiter. He was interested in sleeping with this Skinwalker. Conversation was not part of the deal.

The waiter caught Cesar's eye and hustled right over. "All finished?"

Cesar nodded and the plates were cleared, leaving them alone amid the other diners, who were unaware of the threat posed by the two Halflings among them.

"Sharing goes both ways," he said.

She gave a nod in concession to that point.

"So if I tell you, you'll promise to share what you find out from the two deceased women and explain to me about your powers."

She hesitated. That boded well, for a quick acceptance might mean she did not intend to keep her word. But Bess deliberated over her answer and then gave a slow, thoughtful nod.

"Done." She sat back, regarding him, as if deciding where to begin, but he asked the first question, comfortable in that role.

"So you can read auras, travel the Way of Souls, speak to the dead. Anything else?"

"I can't speak to the dead. I can only speak to those who have followed the Red Road, led a decent life and gained entrance to the Spirit World. I can't see the ghosts who remain upon the earth, nor can I speak to those who have failed to cross because of their misdeeds upon the earth. Those, as you know, have fallen into the Circle of Ghosts. Besides that, I have all the powers of a raven. I can fly, I can see exceedingly well and I am a more than passable thief, though I shouldn't say so in present company. I do love glitter and flash. Gemstones especially. What about you?"

"Besides the ability to see how a person died, you mean?"

"But you can't talk to them."

He was reluctant to tell her but decided it wasn't worth watching her walk away if he didn't, so he answered.

"That's right. I see and hear only what has already occurred but it is usually enough to discover supernatural interference with mankind and identify simple murderers."

She glanced about the busy room and then back to him. "Can you witness an animal's death?"

He was about to ask to what purpose, when he remembered the mountain lion shifter and nodded.

"That's interesting. And you said you are a Truth Seeker. I have heard of that. How does it work exactly?"

"I can tell if someone is lying by touching them." Except her, apparently. He kept that bit of information back, for it was foolish to tell an enemy your weaknesses.

"You can read minds?" she asked.

"That's not exactly how it works. I have to ask a question."

"Show me."

He really should have expected that. He pushed back the strong urge to touch her. Her silly ultimatum had now trapped him. Cesar stared out at her from the corner he had backed himself into. He'd have to use some stranger as illustration or she'd discover herself immune to his Truth Seeking gift. And so there would be no taking of her hands, no asking her everything he wanted to know and no satisfaction in learning all her secrets. He had read every woman he'd ever met for more than a century.

But not Bess.

She was the exception to his rule and that fact both annoyed and fascinated.

Chapter 6

Before he could get himself into further trouble, the waiter turned up carrying a tray laden with sweets, capturing Bess's attention. He decided the wisest way to demonstrate his Truth Seeking was to do so on a human. That way he wouldn't have to reveal that he could not read the answers to questions he posed to her.

"Have we saved room for dessert?" asked the waiter.

Cesar sat bemused as Bess leaned in to inhale.

"They all smell delicious," said Bess as if she hadn't eaten in days.

"Which do you recommend?" said Cesar, lightly brushing the back of the man's hand.

Bess went silent as she witnessed the gesture and her eyes flashed from one to the other.

"Oh, the chocolate lava cake is our bestseller."

"And you recommend it because it is the most expensive and you are out of the crème brûlée."

The waiter flushed. "The cherry cobbler is also excellent."

"I'll try the cobbler," she said without taking her attention from Cesar.

"Coffee, black," he said.

The waiter smiled weakly and retreated.

"So you just ask a question and then touch them for the answer?" she asked.

"That's it."

"Try me." She offered her hand, palm up.

He already knew he couldn't read her, because he had tried and failed on several occasions. It was one thing to know he couldn't tell if she was lying, quite another to let her know. So he stalled.

"That would be rude."

"I insist." Her eyes held a challenge.

"Bess, we both know what will happen when I touch you. It's why we're here."

She extended her hand to him.

"How do you stay so slim?" he asked, and clasped her hand in his.

"I work out two hours a day on a treadmill." Her

words trailed off and she stilled as her soft mouth parted.

But he barely heard her answer, because the brush of his palm on hers sent tendrils of excitement all the way to his heart, which began galloping as if he'd just been given a shot of adrenaline. He saw the sheen of moisture appear on her face and the lovely blossoming of pink creep up her neck and into her cheeks. She pulled back, but he tightened his grip instinctively, unwilling to let her go. His mind engaged a moment later and he opened his hand, releasing her.

"Wow," he said.

"Did you get an answer?"

"All I know is that I don't want to wait for dessert."

She made a sound in her throat and then wiped her hands on her napkin as if trying to remove all evidence of his touch. But her breathing gave her away. The woman was like heroin. Each time he touched her, he wanted more. He reached and she dropped her hands from the table to her lap, protecting herself from him.

"Does that happen when you touch anyone?"

He shook his head.

"Just me?"

He inclined his chin.

She pursed her lips as if giving a silent whistle. "What's happening between us?"

"I'm not sure. But I can't read you, Bess."

There. He'd said it.

Her expression still looked grave. "I'm glad you told me."

"That's not all. I have one more power."

She narrowed her eyes. "Three. Isn't that unusual?"

He nodded. "I was born a Truth Seeker and my parents were pleased. My father had the same gift. I developed the other two after..." He'd almost said after his brother's death. But he stopped himself just in time. "I didn't discover I was a Soul Whisperer until after I went through puberty."

Bess held his gaze in a speculative sort of way that made him think she had noticed his blunder. But she let it go.

"That's the way it is for Skinwalkers. We turn and our mentor arrives to take us from our families. If the Inanoka who sired us is a part of the family, they might choose to act as mentor and take their son or daughter away for training. I knew what I was since birth, so my change was less traumatic than some."

She scrunched up her mouth and her eyes grew glassy before she dropped her chin. Her hair fell like a dark curtain, shielding her face from his scrutiny. Her father had been killed by his people after the war. So her father could not have been her mentor.

She lifted her chin and forced a smile. "So what's giftie number three?"

"I can make people forget they ever met me."

She laughed. But when he did not join in she fell silent, studying him once more.

"How is that possible?

He shrugged. "Dunno."

"So why don't you make all of your people forget that you are a Soul Whisperer?"

"Doesn't work like that. I can only remove one memory at a time and only if I touch them."

"Does it work on Skinwalkers?"

"I'm not sure. I never tried."

She drew her chair back several inches and did not ask him to demonstrate this gift. The vibration of her aura showed apprehension.

"It's called Memory Walking."

"Have you used it on your kind?"

"It's against the law to do so without the permission of the District Council."

"That's not what I asked."

"No."

She shifted in her seat, uneasy now. "You'd make an excellent thief."

"I suppose, if I lacked a moral compass. I'm an FBI special agent, remember?"

She didn't smile. "And you'd make a fine rapist."

Cesar couldn't let that accusation slide off his back so easily. "I don't use my powers to take advantage of women. I use them to help find bad guys."

She held his gaze for a good long while and he glared back, waiting for her to call him a liar. It was a deal breaker. He didn't need her or anyone else badly enough to have them call him that.

"All right then, Soul Whisperer, Truth Seeker and the invisible man."

"Memory Walker."

"Cesar?" She stared earnestly at him and he wondered what else she could possibly want to know. "Before, when you mentioned not learning you were a Soul Whisperer until after you hit puberty?"

He knew he was sitting across from her, but he also saw ahead to what she was about to say and at the same time, back to the day he learned what he was. He didn't want her to go there, to finish what she started, but he sat there in mute silence waiting for her to ask, fearing for her to ask, knowing she would ask.

"What where you about to say, before you stopped yourself?"

He paused, feeling the familiar clamping down in his gut as he lowered his shields against such invasions.

Cesar exhaled through his nose as if trying to remove a dreadful stink from his nostrils.

Her voice was a low whisper. "I think you must have touched a dead body. Am I right?"

He lifted his water glass, all that was left to him by the overzealous waitstaff, and took another swallow, but was unable to dislodge the lump in his throat. Most days he only thought of Carlos a time or two. But some days were worse.

He read sympathy in her encouraging smile.

"Who was it, Cesar?"

He fiddled with his tie clip for a moment, trying to decide. It would be good to say it out loud to one who understood some of the issues faced by Halflings. He gave himself permission to tell her part of it.

"We were living among the humans in Illinois. Just three families, Dream Walkers, Truth Seekers and a few Peacemakers. My dad was a Truth Seeker and my mother a Dream Walker. He was elected to the state judiciary and she worked in a hospital. They supposed that we would have one of their gifts."

If she wondered who "we" included, she did not

ask, just sat still as he went on. He drew his napkin through his hands, strangling it beneath the snowy white cloth, trying to pretend she wasn't listening.

"That's usually the way. I manifested the Truth Seeker gift very early. Niyanoka are born with our gifts, but my brother, Carlos, did not seem to have one."

There, he'd said his name aloud. He glanced at her. Bess kept her steady dark eyes fixed upon him, but did not interrupt or try to fill the long silence.

"It troubled my parents greatly. My father used his ability to ask Carlos if he had any powers and my mother walked in his dreams, but his capabilities remained a mystery. I tried once, but I got such a headache I had to quit."

"Strange," she said. "Our second form comes only after we are grown."

"Spirit Children occasionally develop late. It is not unheard-of, but it caused a strain. We moved a lot. There is a ten-year maximum per locality for Niyanoka with children, twenty if you don't. Keeps folks from noticing that we don't age."

Bess nodded her understanding of this. Likely she moved around as well. "But my parents were ready to leave early. I'm not sure if it was because they were embarrassed about Carlos or because they were both ill. Our healers suggested a different climate. Carlos didn't want to leave his friends, human ones. He didn't understand yet that such friendships were temporary. We moved and Carlos was miserable. He didn't like the small town in Georgia. There was nobody his age close by. I was fourteen, was interested in girls and I didn't want him bothering us." He pressed his hand over his mouth as the wave of grief made his stomach flip. He closed his eyes at the memories.

He'd never told anyone this much, not a human or a Spirit Child. Yet here he was about to spill his guts. He pulled back, clamping his lips tight and shaking his head. He wouldn't say it aloud. Not to her. Not to anyone.

His coffee arrived and the waiter confirmed that she did not want coffee or tea, then deposited her cobbler and vanished into the crowded room.

The steaming coffee nearly burned him as he tried to swallow it. Bess did not touch her cobbler and seemed more intent on his story.

Cesar thought about what came next and the black grief rushed in like a rising tide, swallowing him whole. Then Bess laid a hand upon his and his breathing got easier. A gentle calm rippled out from the point of contact, carrying with it the recognition that her curiosity came only from concern for him.

She released him, sitting back. One look at her

and he knew she had not come away from the brief touch so well. She clamped her jaw, working the muscle there as he took in how pale she now looked.

"Finish it," she whispered, keeping her intent gaze upon him. Her eyes told him that she already knew.

He recognized that she had experienced his grief as he had absorbed her serenity. He didn't want her to know what happened next.

It occurred to him only then that he could tell her and then afterward make her forget the conversation. He could unburden himself, release the demons he carried locked in his heart and let one person know how deeply he bled. Then he could take back the memory, reabsorb the tiny bit of energy that held those recollections, so that she did not have the power to use this information against him.

"Yes," he said. "I'll finish. This was summer, 1893. My friends and I built a tree house way up in a big old oak behind the house. I wouldn't let Carlos up there. It was off-limits. He tried to talk me into letting him up, but I chased him off. Told him it was his fault we had to leave our old home."

He rubbed his temples. She reached for him again, but he lifted his hand to stop her.

"Don't. I can do this without your help. Carlos left the house that night." Cesar's voice broke. "He climbed up into that damned oak tree and shinnied out on the limb."

"Oh, Cesar. No." She reached again.

He pushed his chair back, evading, while needing to hurry to get this out before the tears choked him. "I heard him scream and I was the first one there. When I touched him I could see from his eyes. I thought I was falling." Cesar pressed his hand over his eyes at the memory, still feeling that drop. "I let go then, not understanding what was happening."

He removed the protective cover of his hand and stared at her, needing her to understand that terrible day. The day he lost his brother and discovered what he was.

"I was touching my first corpse and I was experiencing his death. I started screaming for Mom and Dad. I told them how he fell."

Cesar used his index finger to follow the crease in the center of the tablecloth but in his mind, it was over a hundred and twenty years ago and he was crying in the wet grass beneath the great oak with the fireflies blinking all about him.

He spoke just above a whisper, the shame choking him, but he forced his words past the clamping fingers of disgrace. "When I told them all that, my father thought I'd been there and I hadn't stopped Carlos. He attacked me, slapped me in the face while my mother screamed. I tried to tell him that I didn't know until after I'd touched him. If I had understood what would happen next I would have let him beat me, kill me. Anything would have been better than having them discover what I was."

"You didn't know until that day you were a Soul Whisperer."

He lowered his head. "You have to touch a body to know. My father figured it out. When he had me by the neck, he read the truth. It was as if I had suddenly become contagious. He leaped away and dragged my mother back toward the house. 'Whisperer,' he told her, and pulled her inside. I wasn't welcome under their roof after that."

"But you were only fourteen."

He shrugged. "My parent's told the cops that I had pushed my brother to his death and they arrested me."

"But you didn't."

"I learned about my memory gift in reform school. Came in handy to erase the guard's memories."

"What about your parents?"

"I haven't seen them since that night." He finally lifted his head and saw her pitying expression. That ripped a new hole in him. Thank God she wouldn't remember this conversation. He couldn't stand to see that look again.

"But you did nothing wrong. I don't understand how they could abandon you."

"It's just custom. Soul Whisperers are unclean."

"I don't believe that."

"They do. They all do. I lost my mother and my father and my little brother all in one day. I wish I could tell him…." His voice failed him and he rubbed his knuckles over his mouth while he composed himself. "I wish I had let him up in that damn tree house. It was such a pointless way to die."

"Cesar, it was an accident."

He tapped his index finger on the lip of the saucer, impatient at being told the obvious. "I know that." He hadn't meant for his voice to sound so sharp. He reined himself in. "Accidents can be prevented. I could have…" He shook his head. Carlos was gone and he couldn't do a damned thing about it, then or now.

His stomach heaved and he realized he was a breath away from humiliating himself by puking. He clamped a hand to his mouth, pinched his eyes closed and swallowed hard.

Cesar's other hand remained on the table and it was a small reach for Bess to place hers upon it. Sympathy danced over him like warm summer rain. Their eyes met.

She sat back. He watched her hand retreating to her side of the table.

"Thanks," he said.

She nodded.

He noticed his damned hands were shaking. He drew them around the coffee cup.

Bess's shoulders were uncharacteristically hunched over and she looked grim as if bone-weary from what he had told her or was it from what she had felt when she touched him? When she touched him again, he'd take back his memory.

"You're very hard on yourself. Teenagers make mistakes. It's what they do best. They are also self-absorbed. It's hardly surprising that you were not mindful of Carlos's needs. Your brother would not want you to hurt like this."

"His pain was worse."

She stared at him with those dark eyes, wide and full of compassion. "If you could speak to him, what would you say?"

"What difference does that make now?"

"Humor me."

"I'd ask his forgiveness. I'd tell him I miss him still." How he got the words past the squeezing fingers of grief that clamped around his vocal cords, he did not know.

Bess leaned forward, reaching across the white linen tablecloth to grasp his hand. He met her partway, allowing himself to experience the gentle comfort of her touch. Just a moment longer, he told himself, knowing that while he was bathed in her compassion, she suffered the burden of the visceral pain tearing through him.

He stroked his thumb over her knuckles and closed his eyes, searching for where she had hidden their conversation, finding it easily. Then he concentrated on calling the energy back to him. An instant later he pulled back, forcing a smile.

"How do you feel?" he asked. He knew the process of retrieving a memory could leave the other person feeling momentarily disoriented or even sick.

"Fine. Well, sad, of course."

Some people retained the emotion of the conversation if not the details, so her feelings were hardly a surprise.

She gave him a quizzical look. No wonder, since she likely didn't recall the past several minutes.

"How's that cobbler?"

She frowned. "I'm not sure… Cesar, are you all right?"

"Me? Why?" He held his brittle smile like a

mask before him, but the dread was already creep-ing through him like poison.

"Because I don't understand. One moment you are telling me about your little brother and the next you're asking me about cobbler."

Chapter 7

She remembered all of it. Cesar fell back in his seat so hard that the wood gave way. The crack sounded like a rifle report and the vibrations seemed to reverberate in his ears like white noise.

He couldn't take it back.

The realization slapped him in the guts. His mouth went dry as he hardened his lips into a grim, tight line and straightened.

"Cesar? You've gone pale."

He sat like a store mannequin, rigid, frozen. What had he just done? Revealed a secret to a woman who hated him. Given an enemy power over him.

Bess suddenly seemed preoccupied with her cobbler. He noted she didn't eat, but just prodded, succeeding in getting the insides to spill out.

She did not look up as she asked her next question.

"Did you try to take the memory, Cesar?"

When their eyes met he saw the accusation there. She was smart, this one. She would make a marvelous ally and a terrible enemy.

"I didn't know I could not take it back."

"So this is some game you play. Confessing your secrets and then stealing them back?"

When he first touched her he discovered that he couldn't use his Truth Seeking gift on her. Why had he assumed that his Memory Walking would work on her? Had his need to unburden himself so blinded him that he could not see the real possibility that she would recall everything?

"I've never spoken of this to anyone."

She nodded her acceptance of this. "I'm not sure that counts since you believed I wouldn't remember."

He had just wanted to connect with another like him, if only for a moment. But his attempt had backfired, exploding in his face like a mortar.

Bess lifted a scoop of cobbler onto her fork. "Seems you'll have to deal with the fallout."

She slipped the bite of red cobbler into her mouth.

It appeared she had trouble swallowing. It made him pause to study her reaction, instead of dwelling on his own. Upset, he decided, judging from the erratic pulse of her aura. But was she upset by what he had just tried to pull or by what he had revealed? He didn't know but was quite certain she wouldn't let him touch her right now.

Bess set her fork upon the plate and gave the dish a little nudge away from her. Then she lifted her dark eyes to him.

"I've spoiled your appetite."

She didn't deny it.

"Do you pray for him?"

They both knew that to enter the Spirit World a man or woman must walk the Red Road and live a life of balance and responsibility to oneself, one's community and to the earth. Otherwise a soul was condemned to the Circle of Ghosts. Once there, only time and the earnest prayers of the living might bring release. Was she implying that Carlos needed his prayers?

"He was ten. What sins could he have had?"

"Just a question."

She could find Carlos, he realized. Sweat popped out on Cesar's face, drenched his back and armpits. She could actually speak to him. Cesar's ears buzzed again. He was unsure if he wanted to ask her to do that. He did not want to be in her debt, nor was he certain he could bear to hear from his brother. His heart seemed to shrink into a hard lump, like a clod of cold mud.

"I pray for him every day." He lifted the cup and drained the contents. It was dark and bitter, like his thoughts.

Cesar bobbled the cup and it clattered to the saucer. Bess said nothing.

The waiter presented the bill and he offered his card. He was helping Bess on with her coat, which had reappeared, when the card was returned and they headed out.

Cesar offered Bess his elbow, uneasy now, as if the ground beneath him was no longer level. He tried to suppress his surprise when she took it.

It was so unexpected to have someone know what he was and still not flinch when he touched her. He let his fingers brush her neck, experiencing again the electric sizzle that passed between them. What was that, anyway?

He lifted his cell phone but she shook her head.

"Let's walk a bit."

"The air is damp and you need to take it easy." She didn't argue but simply withdrew her arm and turned away from the road, walking down the pier.

The woman was obviously used to doing as she liked.

He walked at her side, breathing in the salty mist that made the lights hazy. When they reached the end, they stood side by side. The waves slapped against the pylons with a rhythmic thrum he could feel through the soles of his shoes. The motion reminded him of the pounding rhythm of sex. He checked to see if Bess was shivering, but she seemed warmer than he was. She stood with her nose lifted to the wind, which blew her thick hair out behind her in an undulating black curtain of silk.

"So when do you use this Memory Walking, exactly?" she asked.

He hesitated, preparing to lie out of habit and then deciding to tell her. "Mostly after examining witnesses for investigations I don't want humans to remember. You have the same law. Humans can't find out about us."

She stared at him, her head cocked in a way that did remind him of a bird. Her face glowed pale in the high florescent lights of the pier, making her aura invisible to him. An inky lock of hair blew beneath her nose for a moment before she tucked it behind her ear.

"What about on Skinwalkers?"

"Before tonight, I never tried Memory Walking on one."

"You've never apprehended one?"

He wondered if she noticed his hesitation before he shook his head. It was true. He'd never apprehended one. But it was only part of the truth.

"And if you did?"

"If apprehended, I'd turn them over to your people by arrangement in the treaty. Human criminals are delivered to their judicial system. Niyanoka are remanded to our legal system—"

She interrupted. "I'll bet that doesn't happen a lot."

Did she mean that Skinwalkers weren't turned over or that Niyanoka were not prosecuted? Either way, she was right. He hoped his aura wasn't showing his discomfort and inched farther into the circle of artificial light. Bess knew too much about him already. He didn't want her to know about the only time he'd taken a Skinwalker alive and then failed to deliver the suspect.

"Not often," he admitted.

Her smile was knowing and still it caused a tiny jolt in his heart, like an electrical charge.

"I expected you to lie."

But he hadn't. How did she know?

He tried for a smile, hoping she wouldn't notice

it didn't reach his eyes or his heart. He didn't enjoy being interrogated and was not accustomed to answering questions. So he tried for a distraction, an amusing anecdote after which he'd steer them back to his car or leave her here.

"I nearly caught a Supernatural once."

"You've faced Supernaturals?"

Did that impress her? He realized he wanted to. "Once."

Bess's eyes widened. "Which one?"

"Ksa, Goddess of Water. She brought a terrible storm and I had to confront her."

"She could have killed you."

He shrugged. "Worse things than that."

Bess knew this all too well.

"Trouble was half a dozen people on the waterfront saw her, right out in the bay, riding an orca."

Bess winced.

"Took some doing to erase all that."

There, he'd taken control again and ceased her endless questions.

"Do you use your memory gift with your lovers?"

The smile died upon his lips, but there was no hesitation in his answer. "No."

"But you could?"

"It's unethical."

"What about when you tire of them and they

won't go away like good little girls, and instead they get attached, leave their cosmetics in your medicine cabinet and start shopping for engagement rings?"

"I do what every other man does."

"What's that?"

"Make sure they find me with another woman."

Bess laughed and nodded. "I've done that, too, but only with the stubborn ones. You can't let them stay too long. They notice we don't age and start asking questions we can't answer."

Cesar could feel his own pain as he considered parting from Bess and he hadn't even managed to slip around with her between his satin sheets.

She stuck her hands in her pockets and continued to the end of the pier. He kept pace with her. "Did you ever stay with one too long?"

"No. My affairs are very brief. You?" he asked.

"Yes, usually. Ours will be, as well."

That did not disappoint him very much as it meant she was planning to have an affair with him. He'd begun to doubt she would. Cesar cautioned himself not to do a fist pump as she faced him, looking him dead in the eye.

"Don't even think about falling in love with me, Cesar, because I'm not going there. I don't do attachments, especially with a Spirit Child."

He scowled, lowering his chin like a bull preparing to charge. She had quite an ego on her. "I don't even like you."

"That's not a requirement."

"Maybe *you'll* fall in love with *me*."

"Don't count on it."

He leaned in, his nose almost touching hers. "So how's about we just stick to what interests us both and sleep together. I don't know if it's because you're a Skinwalker or what, but I've never wanted anyone more. Have you?"

"Flattering, but…"

He grasped her arm and turned her to face him, demanding an answer. "Have you?"

She broke the contact of their eyes. "No. Never. It scares me."

"Thrill is how I would describe it."

"But what is it? I don't know and neither do you. It could be dangerous."

"Or extremely arousing."

She gave her head a little sideward nod as if conceding his point. Then she placed her hand on his arm, silently demanding that he release her. He didn't want to and hesitated a moment too long, for her expression went black as her aura turned from brown to red. He let her go, dropping his hands to his sides.

She stared out over the dark water. When he remembered that she could throw herself from the pier and into the air, he inched closer, cautioning himself not to say anything else to upset her. He wanted, no, that wasn't right, he needed to get her back to his place.

He tried persuasion. "You're as aroused as I am. I can see that pulsing bright pink aura from a block away."

She smiled. "Yes, but unlike a man, I can resist temptation. And unlike a human, I follow my instincts. Ravens are not known for being reckless, and sleeping with you feels reckless to me. I'll pass for now."

He needed her now and would not let her just slip away from him.

"You can't resist this," he insisted, reaching for her.

Bess took a step backward, off the pier, falling down toward the icy water of San Francisco Bay.

He dropped to his knees and watched her descent. There was a flash of brilliant white light, as if St. Elmo's fire burned beneath the pier and then a raven glided below him, dark wings against dark water.

It seemed that Bess could resist temptation after all.

Bess dipped low over the churning water. She'd slept with men for many reasons, loneliness mostly, and grief and the need to be touched. But the raw passion that Cesar Garza roused in her was angry red and pulsing like a thumb struck with a hammer. She knew she couldn't ignore it for long. No matter which way she turned it was there in the promise in dark eyes, the half smile of his sensual mouth and the aura that reached out to hers before he did.

Perilous. That was what this was. What if she slept with him and it didn't go away? What if it got worse?

She veered right, away from the city and toward the cool, soothing darkness of the Redwood Forest. She didn't need him. Surely this would pass in time.

It had to. Dark clouds streaked across the moon, casting their edges in silver as she swept from the bay to the hills beyond. She flew deep into the old-growth forest, briefly considering staying in her lodge, which was only a few miles from this spot. Her retreat was large, secluded and fully stocked. But finally she rejected the idea because she needed to stay in her animal form. Here she had more control of her impulses for Cesar. If she changed back, she'd turn right around and take him up on his offer.

She perched in the top branches of the tallest tree, gazing out over the canopy stretched out before her. She could hear the campers in the state forest, their voices low as they sat in circles, huddled

about their little fires. They didn't know what was
out there tonight.

Bess thought about the strange gray newborns
that had nearly outflown a raven. She ruffled her
feathers, allowing them to settle back in place. She
did not like the new, vulnerable feeling wriggling
in her belly. This was her forest and she would not
tremble like a rabbit in the grass, or look over her
shoulder when she landed to drink at a stream. They
did not belong here. So she must drive them out.
And that meant finding out what they were. If it
would help her be free of the intruders, she would
even work with Garza, but only in order to be rid
of those things. Yes, that was the reason she must
see him again.

But she could not go on her journey to the Way
of Souls tonight. The short flight across the bay
had confirmed her fears. She was still weak from
the blood loss. She would have to be patient as her
body replaced the vital fluids. In a day or two she
would be strong enough.

So in the meantime, should she stay here with
those gray demons or occupy herself with Cesar
Garza?

Bess listened to the unfamiliar sounds below her,
a sort of scratching combined with a low growl.
Never before was there a sound here that she could

not instantly identify. She craned her neck to look behind her as she remembered how fast the one climbed the tree. The starlight glinted off dark branches. This place, cradled high in the redwood pines, always brought her the peace of knowing her predators could not reach her. But now they could. The damn things could fly.

Right now they prowled the night in her forest. The growling grew closer. Bess stood, her talons gripping the rough bark as she cocked her head and lifted the feathers over her ear holes to listen. They were below her on the floor of the forest, scratching in the pine. She was certain. In an instant they could be up the tree and, weak as she was, she was doubtful she could outfly them again.

Bess pushed off and flew toward the bright glowing lights that man had invented to protect himself from the darkness. It hurt her that she needed to seek the refuge of humans. But her pride would survive and so would she.

Those things had stolen her peace. She meant to have it back, even if she had to work with a Soul Whisperer to do it.

Chapter 8

Cesar waited on the pier until the moist salty air coated him with a fine sheen of brine. Hoping she'd come back, waiting for her to come back. She didn't come back.

"To hell with this," he said to the churning water below his feet. Bess had gone where he could not pursue her and he didn't like it.

Cesar reached for his phone and summoned his driver, who met him at the curb a few minutes later and then dropped Cesar at his front door. It was the last place he wanted to be. He hesitated before the glass door, held open by Anthony. If she came back, it might be to his place. Did he want her to find him waiting like some lovelorn puppy?

He briefly considered trolling the tourist bars as he had done for ten years, just to show her she wasn't missed. But the prospect of another such encounter left him empty inside. Bess's sudden intrusion and departure from his life only served to draw attention to the meaninglessness of his relationships. If you could even call them that.

"Going out again, Mr. Garza? Shall I call back your car?"

He shook his head. "No, Anthony. You have a good night."

Cesar swept by him and headed for the elevators.

He waited, hands balled in his pockets as he thought of her beside him and how she looked by candlelight there at his table in the restaurant, her lovely aura circling her like a halo.

Maybe she didn't understand the loneliness that surrounded him. But if anyone in the world could, it was Bess. She'd lived among humans and among animals while always being separate from them. She understood loss, for she would have also had to watch them all die as she lived on.

But she had the other shifters. If she needed them, they were there for her, as the appearance of Tuff proved. While he had no one. He could not even join the communities as a voting member. Cesar was permitted, albeit grudgingly, to speak to the committee when necessary. Though he knew not one of his kind would come to his aid if he were wounded. In fact, when he had been wounded in the shooting, they had left him to human surgeons.

Cesar lowered his chin to his chest, trying to ignore the burn of shame filling his chest.

He still had his work and that was what he lived for. It was enough to know what he did was valuable. He didn't need their acceptance.

The elevator arrived and he stepped aboard, hitting the floor button and dropping back against the wall. As the car rose, he tried not to think of Bess here, her lips a whisper from his.

He punched the wall with the side of his fist and then knocked the back of his head once against the same wall.

Was she with that buffalo-man right now?

A few moments later he'd reached the empty sanctuary of his condo and was headed for his bar, pausing as he recalled the whiskey he had before dinner and the bottle of wine he'd finished unassisted. He lifted the empty tumbler she'd given him, the ice now melted to water, and threw it with all his might. It exploded against the wall, sending a shower of shards raining down on his black leather sofa.

"Go to bed," he muttered. He hoped he could

sleep. Sleep was one of the few refuges left to him. There he might again be part of a family, loved by his parents and adored by his younger brother.

But sometimes he faced the opposite, his brother as he had last seen him, broken, bleeding from his mouth and ears.

Cesar pinched his eyes closed and shook his head to vanquish the image. Then he stalked down the hall to the bathroom. He paused at the wadded white towel stained bright red with Bess's blood. He used it to mop up the floor and tub and then threw the thing in the hamper. But his efforts to remove all signs of her failed, because his brain kept flashing him images of Bess.

Cesar stripped out of his clothes and into a hot shower. Water droplets jetted against his skin like tiny stinging needles of heat. The room billowed with steam as he soaped and rinsed. It wasn't until he switched off the taps and reached for the fluffy white towel that he heard the rhythmic rapping. He looked around, trying to identify the unfamiliar noise. It reminded him of the sound of a slack jib of a sailboat thumping against the mast.

The tapping changed to a different sequence. *Tap tap tap-tap tap.* Pause. *Tap tap.* It came again, in the direction of his bedroom. And then he understood.

Bess.

He wrapped the towel about his hips and headed for the bedroom. He unlocked the window and drew up the sash. There she stood, a large, glossy black raven staring at him with those bead-black eyes.

He stepped back. She walked across the threshold and onto the inner sill.

"Bess, can you understand me?"

She cocked her head. Then she opened her beak and spoke. Her voice crackled, but it was perfectly clear. "Not in the least."

The flash of white light nearly blinded him and when he opened his eyes, she stood before him, dressed in a black silk robe, which revealed an enticing glimpse of formfitting lace on her bosom.

"Leave it to a Spirit Child to assume that we can't think when in animal form."

Her choice of attire and arrival in his bedroom certainly boded well, but her prickliness did not.

"Why did you disappear on me?"

"Because you were looking at me as if I were dessert."

He gave her that same look. "Then why come back?"

Her brow knitted, giving her an uncharacteristic troubled look that lasted only a heartbeat before she recovered. The smooth mask of confidence slid back into place as she gave him a seductive smile. What was she afraid of? She didn't trust him. That was understandable. But he could be trusted. If she'd stay, he'd prove it to her.

"Just a public service, really. Trying to protect the other women in the area."

"That's *my* job."

She laughed and slid off the sill. "Yes, but I meant from you."

Had she been back there, to the forest? Had she seen them again? It would explain her return.

If they had driven her to him, he should be grateful. Instead he felt hurt.

Still he offered her what he believed she sought. "I could protect *you,* tonight."

There was that forlorn look again. Had he guessed correctly? The need to shelter her pounded within him with each heartbeat.

Again he saw that look of vulnerability, but she masked it with a slow smoldering scan of his body. Her leisurely assessment concluded when she glanced toward his bed. Cesar's muscles tightened, all coiled potential waiting for her to decide. That was the way with her kind. The females chose their mate and the males did all that they could to be worthy. He glanced at his bed, as well. Did she find his nest suitable? Would she see him as a good provider, attentive? He hoped she would let him stroke her fine long legs and more secret places. It was hard to remain still when his body screamed for him to take her in his arms, fling her to his bed and devour her. He hadn't even kissed her, yet here he was, wanting her more than any other woman he had ever met in his long, lonely life.

Say yes, Bess.

She didn't move. He stepped toward her and she slid away, so he paused, waiting for her to come to him.

Bess motioned to his chest and he felt a foreshadowing.

"Is that a gunshot wound?" She motioned to the puckering scar below his collarbone.

"In the line of duty."

"Who shot you?"

He hesitated, not wanting to go there. "Long story for another time."

Was she going to be stubborn? She regarded him a long moment. "You'll tell me sometime?"

He nodded, trying not to sigh in relief at the reprieve.

"It looks like it's over your heart."

He rubbed the tiny puckering scar under his collarbone with his index finger.

"It missed."

"Good news for you and for me."

"Come here," he ordered.

She didn't.

"I've got concerns," she said. "The same thing that makes this coupling unique is also what disturbs me."

Coupling. Yes, that was what he wanted, to couple, to quench the hot, thrumming need to mate and claim her as no one else had ever done. His body rang like a bell with his need.

"I don't want attachments. So you understand. I'm not here for that."

"Except the obvious one," he said.

She smiled. "Yes. There's that."

"I'm not going to fall in love with you, Bess. I'm only going to make love to you, all night if you let me."

"And then let me go."

"If that's what you want."

"That's the way it must be. At the end of the day, you are still my enemy."

Some of his desire died in the knowledge that she didn't want him any more than any of the women of his race. She came to him at night, under cover of darkness as if he was some dirty secret she didn't want anyone to know about.

Why did he let that hurt him? He was getting what he wanted, wasn't he? And he didn't need a

Skinwalker in his life any more than she wanted a Spirit Child in hers. Still he couldn't keep his jaw from locking as all of the tenderness left him. She wanted what he gave the others, a night of ecstasy followed by a quick goodbye.

"One night. No strings," he promised.

She cocked her head at him again, as if uncertain. "We need to get this out of our systems, whatever it is. Don't you agree?"

He nodded, knowing it was a lie. He'd never get Bess out of his system. She continued on.

"It's distracting. Better to face it head-on than ignore it. We'll satisfy the need in the normal way, find release and then we can get back to our lives."

"You said you'd fly to the Spirit World, speak to the mothers."

"I will."

He wondered if she kept her promises.

"We'll find out who sired those things. Then when we part, it will be for good."

When. Not if, *when* we part.

His lip twitched in that uncontrollable tell of his rage and shame.

"Sure, baby, anything you say."

Her eyes narrowed on him. Oh, she didn't like being called baby? Well, he didn't like her showing him the door before he even knocked.

"Maybe this is a bad idea," she hedged.

"Maybe. So you going to fly away or you want to screw?"

Her neck increased in length as she stared haughtily at him. He lowered his chin and glared, his lust cementing into wrath.

"I think I deserved that."

Now she had him off balance again. What did she deserve?

"When I left you, I went back to the forest."

A cold chill went through him, as he imagined her there in the darkness with those things, out where he couldn't protect her.

"That was stupid."

"I live there, remember?"

He hadn't. "I thought you lived on Russian Hill."

"Rarely. I live in the forest, sometimes in human form. I also have a lodge just outside the state park with a king-size bed, but most nights I sleep near the top of a redwood with other ravens. On a clear night I can see the moon reflecting on the waves of the ocean."

"But now it's not safe. So you came here."

She nodded.

He hated the idea of being her last hope when he wanted to be her first thought and only desire.

"You can stay here without sleeping with me."

"Cesar, I could have gone to my lodge or back to my apartment or anywhere else in the wide world. I have enough money to buy this building and I have friends who would protect me with their lives. But I didn't go to them. I came here."

The desire was back, simmering like hot sugar, thickening with each bubbling beat of blood.

"I'm sorry about my earlier comment."

She nodded. "You excite me, Cesar. Intrigue me. This connection makes me curious. It's my nature to be curious." She stepped toward him.

"Thank God for that, then." He met her halfway. "I'm curious, too."

She opened her robe, holding the lapels out so he could see her body. The satin fabric billowed like wings. Beneath, she wore a sheer concoction of molded lace that clung to every perfect curve and hollow, while revealing her cinnamon-colored nipples through the sheer fabric. Her form was slim and lithe as a dancer, her waist narrow, her hips barely flared. The high-cut panties made her legs look impossibly long.

"This your style?" she asked. "Or this?"

The soft lace and satin ribbons grew solid, transforming before his eyes into a shiny leather bustier and formfitting pants. She stood on heels so high that he thought he'd need a stepladder just to reach her mouth. Bess made the ideal dominatrix. But he didn't swing that way.

"Take it off."

"What?"

"You asked about my style. I want to see you naked in my bed. That's my style. So your feather cape, take it off."

Bess pressed a hand to her throat and felt her own pulse pounding there. No one had ever said that to her.

Cesar did not cower. He was not driven away by fear of her power, for he had powers equal to her own. And that made this a first all around.

She smiled, knowing already it would be so good between them. Superficial, of course, but good. He had everything he needed to keep her content and she already itched to run her hands over all that exposed, damp male flesh.

Bess touched her shoulder and the shiny leather facade slipped away, leaving her in her human form, shielded by her feather mantle all the way to midthigh. The glossy cloak shone iridescent, flashing deep green, blue and purple as she moved to release the cord about her neck. She used her index finger and thumb to draw the leather tie, releasing the bow.

Cesar seemed to be holding his breath. His jaw clenched and his expression reminded her of a man in pain. Yes, the wanting was like that with her, too, so strong it hurt.

"Dim the lights, so we can see our auras."

Cesar moved to the window, needing to close it to bar her escape.

"Leave it," she commanded. "I like the cool air and the scent of the salt water."

He didn't want to, but feared reversing her decision to stay. Bess had released the cape that now draped her shoulders, leaving an enticing band of bare skin down her middle. Her two collarbones stood out. She was right about being slim. His eyes descended. But not so slim as to interfere with the tempting swell of her breasts, free now from her restrictive clothing. Her belly had only the slightest swell and her navel lay, small and puckered, at the center of her stomach.

Her dark thatch of hair was manicured as the rest of her into a narrow swatch that seemed especially thick and glossy, the color of the hair on her head, but also like her feathers. Would it be just as soft, or coarse and curly?

"Have you ever done this before with one of my kind?"

He shook his head. "It's forbidden. You?"

"Never."

She lifted a slim hand to the cape, sweeping it from her shoulders with the flourish of a matador. Then she set her precious hide on the chair beside the window, leaving her bare to his gaze and his touch. She had removed it for him, making herself vulnerable, unable to shift without it. Should he capture that cloak, she would be trapped in her human form.

Cesar was many things and he had made many mistakes, but he vowed in that moment to be worthy of the trust she showed him.

He took a step to close the distance separating them.

"The light," she whispered.

Cesar reached back flicked the switch off. The room came alive with colored light, bouncing off the ceiling and walls as if he had a disco ball installed as a chandelier. But this light came from them. The turquoise of wanting swirled like smoke to mix with the virile blue of strong sexual energy. Bess's aura surrounded her, flaring high and casting her in silhouette, while all about him the light shimmered and danced from deep within him.

He grew cautious and his voice dropped. "You ever seen anything like this?"

"No," she whispered.

Chapter 9

Bess stood separated from him by the distance of his bedroom. Behind her, the damp night air fanned her flanks. Her fingers twitched with the urge to touch his moist skin while her tongue licked away the droplets of water clinging to his naked flesh.

But she resisted.

She had spent too many years avoiding his kind and nursing her grievances. She feared she could not set her hostility aside for even one night. Despite the seemingly peaceful unions of her two dearest friends and their Niyanoka wives, she did not trust his race, never would trust them. Not after witnessing the hunts following Fleetfoot's defeat. She retreated a step and then looked again at their auras.

Hers surrounded her, illuminating her skin as if by candlelight. She had seen a weaker version of this glow before, when she was highly aroused, but never had her energy field reached for another's as it did now. The two bands of light met in the center of the room, like the aurora borealis, swirling and merging, the mixture of blues becoming a bright, shimmering amber hue, which she had not seen before.

Her curiosity brought her a step closer. The light glowed brighter, iridescent now, as if filled with tiny bits of mica. They swirled like dust motes in a beam of sunlight, spinning faster as she closed the distance between them.

Cesar showed only certainty as he reached for her, taking possession of her shoulders and drawing her forward until their bodies connected. And then she no longer cared about their auras, because Cesar was kissing her. She gave herself over to his touch, relishing the contrast of his soft lips and the roughness of his stubbled jaw. He pressed her tight to his hard muscular frame, letting her feel the power of his body and his willingness to use his strength to delight her senses. He rubbed his chest back and forth, his skin arousing hers until her breasts ached and her nipples beaded, turning to hard knots of sensation with each gentle stroke of his flesh on hers. She could feel her desire rising, but something more, something new, a kind of expansion of pleasure as if she felt more than her own delight.

She slid her hands up and down his broad back, from the taut curve of his ass to the wide wings of his shoulders. At his head, her fingers turned to talons, fisting his short hair and tugging him closer. The effect was like spurring a wild horse. Her need raged and her mind filled with raw, sensual images that were not her own.

He growled as he flanked each side of her torso with his splayed hands, lifting her until her feet no longer touched the thick pile of the Berber carpet beside his bed. She held his head between her hands, refusing to relinquish control, needing him to kiss her neck, her shoulders, every square inch of her.

He surprised her by bringing her near and then lowering her slowly inch by delicious inch, letting her body slide along his. Her thighs touched his arousal first as it jutted from him, hard and ready. He opened his mouth and stared at her breasts and she knew what he would do. Anticipation quickened her breathing and she slid down until her nipple drew parallel to his open mouth. He latched onto her like a starving man. She threw her head back at the torturous joy of his sucking and arched to let him take her as he would. Sharp shards of pleasure darted inside her. He released one breast and shifted her to enjoy the other as she tugged him closer and called out his name.

The images flooded her mind again, visions of her entangled in his sheets, lying with her legs spread as he kissed her between her thighs. She gasped, as understanding dawned.

"Your thoughts," she whispered.

"What?"

Before she could answer he tossed her to his bed. Had she been wearing her cloak she would have turned, in that instant she found herself airborne. Instead she had time only to perform a half turn as she landed with a bounce on the soft pile of his comforter. She glanced back at him and knew that tonight she would not be bored or lonely or full of the pain that not even the touch of a man would allay. Tonight would be magic. Cesar would make her forget that she was alone, that she would always be alone. In his arms she found a hunger to match her own.

Let the feasting begin.

His mouth quirked as he stalked toward her. She lifted to one elbow to enjoy the sight of him in motion. Cesar rested one knee upon the bedding, the muscles of his thigh bunched as he loomed over her, closing the gap, claiming what she offered. He tried to kiss her but she rolled away, in a mock attempt to escape him. He wrapped one strong arm about her middle and pulled, bringing her bottom tight against his middle. Ah, yes. This was exactly where she wanted to be, locked against him, his male to her female, his hard arousal against her wet, yielding flesh.

He pressed his lips to her ear, his voice a half growl. "Is this how you want me?"

In answer she reached between her legs, wetting her hand on the juices of her own body and then encircled him with that hand. The slickness and the friction made him gasp. Then his teeth scored her neck and his hand came up to toy with her breasts.

He moved his hand lower to touch her wet, needy flesh. She rocked against him, but he did not enter her. His fingers teased her most sensitive places as he stroked her to madness.

He lifted one leg to flank her hip, positioning himself for entry. Then he rocked back. She braced to accept his thrust, which came with a hot rush of pleasure. They moved in opposition but both toward the same goal. He gripped her hips, increasing the speed and depth of his penetration. Bess bit her lip, but did not succeed in stifling the long sigh of pleasure at the perfect friction of their joining.

She threw herself back against him as the first orgasm burst from within her like dawn. All about her the light vibrated outward, emanating in dancing iridescent pink light. Still he took her again and again, as her body trembled in the cascading pleasure coming in a second cresting wave. She knew he was reaching his release now from the new tension building in him and gave herself over to the rising need within. His long deep thrusts brought her to the most spectacular orgasm in her very long life. She cried out again and heard his answering call, deep, animalistic and raw as their lovemaking.

He carried her forward to the bedding, pressing her flat with his body half on and half off her own. They gasped from their exertions as their muscles twitched and shuddered, finally spent.

After her breathing had slowed and the warm flush left her skin, she opened her eyes. Her aura glowed a soft pale brown as always and his, a sedate pale blue, capped with gold. What had happened to the white and black she had first seen?

As she stared the blue dissolved, replaced by the golden aura of all Niyanoka and then the now familiar white, pulsing out from him in jagged spears, the pale wave capped with the black of death. The unique aura of this Soul Whisperer had returned.

She closed her eyes, letting the lethargy take her,

drifting in her mind as her body lay half beneath his. Exhausted, yet she was not. Bess opened one eye as she recognized that was not her feelings, but his. She lifted a hand and rested it upon his naked back, drawing his emotions more easily now. He was sated and something he rarely felt…at peace. She smiled in satisfaction for she had brought that to him. Could he read her mood, as well?

He rolled onto his back, capturing her hand as he laced hers with his while breaking all other connections between them. The flesh of her palm tingled pleasantly from the point of contact. Her body continued to hum, like the vibration of a string after it is plucked, but now her thoughts grew confused, a jumble.

She had taken him just like an animal. Rough and raw. Had he expected otherwise? Humans make love face-to-face. She was not human. Was it her animal side that made the joining so intense?

Bess drew her hand free as she recognized these were not her thoughts, but his. Her animal side? Then she remembered him asking if this was how she wanted him. Was that what he meant? Did his humans and his Niyanoka lovers always lie placid upon their backs as he worked above them?

Shame filled her. He rolled onto his side and

reached to stroke her, but she escaped from the other side of the bed.

"Is that why you slept with me?"

"Bess?" He tried for a look of bewilderment and failed. "Can you read my emotions, too?"

She glowered at him.

"And your thoughts."

Why had she opened herself up to this? She knew what his kind thought of hers. These were the mind hunters who tricked her people into stepping off cliffs or sleeping naked in the snow. They were diabolical. And he was one of them.

Why had she let herself pretend he would ever see her as anything but beneath him?

He reached for her and she stepped back.

"Bess, listen."

"I've heard enough." She snatched up her feather cape and threw it onto her back. She could not believe she had been stupid enough to completely remove it. Temporary insanity. It was the only explanation for such a complete lapse in judgment.

The cape molded to her skin as she called on the deep inner power to shift. Energy surged through her frame as the world seemed to change with her transforming vision.

He called to her as she reached the window ledge.

"Bess. Wait."

She opened her wings and jumped, soaring out into the night, away from this latest humiliation. Away from the Soul Whisperer who had managed to make her feel precious one moment and like a beast the next. Well, she didn't need him. She didn't need anyone.

Cesar watched until Bess vanished into the night, her dark feathers aiding in her disappearance. Usually he was the one to walk away and he always felt worse afterward, but never this bad. It hurt to know that he was equally unsuitable to her when by all rights it should be the other way around.

Most of his people viewed Skinwalkers as the inferior species and he had accepted those teachings without much thought. The Inanoka had attacked his people in the most cowardly fashion imaginable. Now it was forbidden to even speak to one. He was holding on to his citizenship by his fingernails and he'd risked it all to have Bess. For what?

Cesar sat on the bed. What the devil had he been thinking before she'd leaped up? That she was lovely, sensual. That he'd never been laid like that and thought that, even if he reached his four hundredth year, he never would be again. Nothing insulting there.

He'd been remembering the strange way their

auras had spiked and glittered as they merged, wondering why he enjoyed her so much. He'd speculated that it was because…

And then he knew. He'd wondered if her animal self had made their joining so thrilling.

"Shit," he muttered, realizing too late that he'd ruined any chance of ever having her again.

He didn't know Bess well, but he understood a prideful woman.

She wasn't coming back.

When he was cast out by his people, he had told himself that the universe had seen fit to make him what he was for a reason. He didn't need anyone because his work was what mattered most.

Until tonight, he'd nearly believed it.

Tonight he had touched a woman who was not past feeling, past caring. Bess positively pulsed with life, her heartbeat as strong as the stroke of her wide, beautiful wings. He had touched magic and she had left him, too. It was ironic that the same thing that had brought her to him, her complete ignorance of how unacceptable it was to touch him, was also what had driven her away.

He wondered briefly if women of his kind could also read his thoughts and then recognized, glumly that he would never find out. Soul Whisperers did not have friends, confidants or lovers. What they had was solitude and work.

He hated his power. If he had the choice to set it aside and become a human, he would do it, anything to avoid the curse of this half life.

Cesar stepped to the window. He leaned far out, staring at the place where she had disappeared.

He shouted his fury to the night. "Do you think I want this? Well, I don't! I don't want any of it. Why couldn't I be a Dream Walker, like mother, or just a Truth Seeker, like father? Why this curse and why me?"

As always he received no answer. He slammed the window closed and spun around to reach for his clothing.

He tugged on his shirt, flipped on the bathroom light and then paused as the scent of pine and sage tickled his nostrils.

He dragged off his shirt and threw it as far as he could.

Cesar refused to be reminded of her, of her rejection. He dressed carefully in clean clothing and then headed for the lobby. She might have abandoned him, but he still had his work. There were at least two sets of twins out there with a likelihood of supernatural parentage. It was his job to assess the threat and determine how to proceed.

Bess was gone and the sooner he forgot her, the better off he'd be. He would do what he always did when faced with the emptiness. Move. Move forward, move up, move beyond. As long as he kept moving, the deadness inside him could not overtake him.

When Nagi had finished with the human female, he summoned the ghost that he had set to follow the raven. The loathsome specter appeared a moment later, groveling before him in a brownish fog, his immortal soul dull beneath a gray film of evil.

"My lord and master, how can I serve you?"

"Has the Skinwalker raven contacted any others of her kind?"

"No, Lord." The edges of his soul curled up, billowing back into his central core.

"What has she been doing?"

"Only meeting with a Spirit Child, Lord, a Soul Whisperer."

"What?"

Chapter 10

Bess did not return to the forest. Instead she landed on the balcony of her high-rise penthouse on Russian Hill. Most days she loved the view here, but tonight she barely noticed the sparkling lights of the city spread beneath her feet. Cesar's assessment of her as some hot, lusty animal cut her just as assuredly as the talons of those gray menaces in the forest.

Niyanoka were never to be trusted. She knew it and could not conceive how she had forgotten even for a moment. She was honest enough to know that her body had needs and that when the mind and body were at odds, her body usually got its way. So what if she had given in? She had done nothing more than scratch an itch. Now it was over and done with.

She would not have to see him again. Except she did have to, said a small voice in her mind.

You promised to fly to the Spirit World, speak to the mothers of those monsters and share with Cesar what you learn.

Damn. Bess stroked her feather cape, transforming the skin into a thick terry-cloth robe almost instantly. Then she punched in the code to deactivate the alarm and slipped through one of the large glass-paneled doors, that retracted, accordion-style, to allow her to bring the outside in. There she paused, listening to the buzz of the human world. The air conditioner purred, the refrigerator hummed and even the cable box emitted a low whine. There was no silence here, no peace. She found that only in the air.

Bess checked the refrigerator, fully stocked thanks to her housekeeper, Judy. The older woman would have to be replaced soon. She had been with her long enough to begin to notice something was not quite right with her employer. Bess could safely stay here another five or six years, but no longer.

She pulled out the sparkling cider, sliced ham and the loaf of bread. Judy would be surprised to see she had been here. How long ago was it now, two months, three?

She wasn't sure. Bess returned to the way she had come to prefer eating—alfresco. On the outdoor bar she screwed off the gold-tone cap and then drank from the bottle.

Bess finished much of the ham and half the loaf, then washed her mouth with one more swallow of cider. How long until her blood regenerated and she could take the road that no other living thing had ever traveled? Tuff had said she needed food and rest. That meant she might have to sit in this dreadful little concrete-and-steel box for a night or two before departing. Perhaps she would go to her lodge in the forest. It was peaceful there and closer to the mighty trees she loved.

Bess glanced toward SoMa, where Cesar lived. She'd not go back there no matter how good the sex had been. They shared a common interest, but that was as much of a connection as they would ever share. Now that she knew what he really thought of her, she would not share his bed again. He'd been oh, so polite and sophisticated at dinner. A facade, like the clothing humans wore to make them appear other than what they were—naked, afraid, vulnerable.

She shifted on the cushioned chaise longue,

knowing that it would be a fight not to do as she liked and what she liked was feeling Cesar move inside her as their auras danced a tango all about them.

Two days later, Cesar stood at another crime scene in the Redwood Forest, the State Park, this time, just off the Avenue of Giants and just inside the Whispering Springs Camp sight. They'd cordoned off the area. The papers were calling the recent deaths the work of a pattern killer, but Cesar knew the births of the little gray newborns had caused the deaths and hoped not to find another dead mother in the forest.

His connections to the Niyanoka law enforcement had turned up nothing. No other district had seen evidence of the births of some new supernatural creature. But they were now on alert.

Cesar ducked under the tape, nodding at the men posted on the perimeter. The human sheriffs and park service had cleared out all the tourists from the area, sending them and their pop-up/pop-out RVs to Gilbert Flats so they couldn't see the nice new camper that something had turned into a recycling project. The metal skin and particleboard had been shredded and the foam-and-fabric interior scattered, leaving debris a good fifteen feet back.

Now the RV looked more like a spent piñata than a former residence.

Two of the uniforms eyed him as if *he* were the curiosity. That was the trouble with humans; they were more interested in covering their asses than making sure something didn't bite theirs off.

Although the family had been away at the time of the attack, Cesar had already seen the bloody remains of the family's German shepherd.

He followed the tracks the hunter had made, now half the size of a man, into the forest, but paused when he got the feeling he was being watched. He scanned among the trunks, looking beyond the rough, folded bark to the salmonberry bushes and waxy rhododendrons that covered the forest floor. If they were moving on the ground, he'd see it first there.

Did they sense him? Did they know he was not human, either?

He pushed back his jacket and released the strap holding his service revolver.

"Don't do it, boys. I don't want to kill you," he whispered.

Sunlight poured between the branches in columns of light, turning the ground cover beneath it a soft, spring green. Something moved to his left. His gun was drawn and aimed the instant the creature darted from cover, making its way obliquely toward a closer tree. If he didn't know better he would have sworn it was a shadow. But there was nothing to cast such an outline.

Bess had been right, of course. It was ash-gray, with batlike ears. He couldn't see the eyes.

"Come out!" he called.

It didn't. Instead a second creature scurried with unnatural speed after its fellow, staying low in the cover of the ferns. There followed a cacophony of screeches and yowls that sounded as if two cats were mating. Cesar inched closer, bringing the distance to a hundred yards.

"Come out!" he called again.

This time one of the creatures jutted its head around the tree to look at him with a fixed biopic stare. Its large yellow eyes reminded Cesar of a great horned owl. He tried and failed to see the creature's aura before a hand reached out from behind the cover and clenched the thing's ear, dragging it back. More yowling ensued.

The two creatures bounded out together, but in the opposite direction. Cesar gave chase. They sprang along on two legs like monkeys, jumping five to six feet at a bound. Cesar increased his speed. One of his targets glanced back, howled and transformed into a black cloud that resembled the emission from a diesel engine of a city bus. Cesar broke stride as the other followed, launching itself into the air and flying up into the treetops to disappear into the branches.

"Damned if I can follow you there," he muttered.

His next thought was to go to Bess, confirm that what she had told him was right. The excitement of having someone he could share this with momentarily eclipsed the fact that she would have nothing more to do with him. He stood staring at the giant pines and the canopy that was her home. Should he track her down and apologize or give her space?

All depends on if you want to see her again. See her, don't see her, the relationship had been DOA. No chance that two of their races would ever survive as a couple. But there were rumors of a Niyanoka far north who had taken up with a great grizzly Skinwalker and he had met the mother of the Dream Walker who was banished for consorting with a wolf shifter. He faced the same if he continued with Bess. He almost thought she'd be worth it, though, if she didn't hate him.

He and Bess still shared an interest in these Halflings, for he was now certain that was what they were. He was positive they were not of his race and Bess seemed certain they were not of hers. He was less convinced and still believed they were a new sort of Skinwalker, perhaps half bat or owl. The ears and yellow eyes seemed animalistic to him and they had the ability to transform, something none of his kind could do.

He needed to talk to her, exchange theories. It gave him as good an excuse as he was likely to find and he seized it with both hands.

Now how long would it take for him to uncover her address? Well, he loved a challenge.

He headed back to his car to begin his search of Russian Hill for a very elusive raven. With the help of his smartphone Cesar had discovered a likely penthouse apartment at the Infinity Tower on Folsom. The 2.5-million-dollar unit was owned by a group called, Covrid Enterprises. Had Bess used the scientific name for her animal species as a corporate cover?

He drove back to the city, his eagerness to see Bess filling him up like rainwater. He reached the Infinity Towers and used his badge to gain access to the apartment, and then his gift to make the manager forget he'd ever been there. The building security couldn't keep him out, but he had no way to keep Bess from taking off the moment she saw him.

But as it happened, things didn't go as he'd pictured for when he reached her place, he found it empty. Had Bess gone to the Spirit Road or just disappeared?

Bess returned to the world of light and time to discover she had been gone only six hours. The journey that, to her had taken the better part of two days, had bent back upon itself and she had returned barely after she had left. The opposite could also happen. More than once she had returned after a day or two, flying fast and hard, to discover she had been gone the better part of a month.

She landed on the rail of her apartment in a steady gentle rain and then hopped down to her favorite chair, protected from the weather by the awning above her. There she transformed into her human self and stretched out upon the thick cushions in her feather cape, which was now covered with pearly drops of rain. She loved this sheltered balcony for the privacy and the view. Today the misty rain had gobbled up her usual vista of the bay lapping around Alcatraz and sweeping beneath the Golden Gate Bridge.

She closed her eyes to better enjoy the cool moist air, giving a groan in pleasure to finally be at rest. Her joints ached and her muscles trembled from the exertion, but she had done it. She raked her fingers through her damp hair and let her head fall back to the cushions, letting the weariness ebb from her body.

Her journey had confirmed her suspicions. She knew what had sired those newborns in her forest. And soon even that stubborn Soul Whisperer could not refute that they were as dangerous as flying rattlesnakes.

She needed to tell her friends and she had promised to tell Cesar. He wouldn't expect her to keep her word and that was why she was going to.

That *was* the only reason, wasn't it?

Bess lifted from her seat with a groan and slipped in through the glass doors. Her eyes went to the only unfamiliar thing in the room the instant she entered her condo and she knew someone other than her housekeeper had been here.

The white hydrangeas, roses and lilies were in full bloom, but not one had yet begun to droop. Her heart hammered at the possibility that Cesar had found her, excitement racing through her vessels with the rushing blood.

Stop it. He'll make a fool of you again.

But she couldn't keep from admiring the bouquet. Instead of the usual baby's breath, the blossoms were punctuated with sprigs of evergreen and soft gray-green foliage she could not at first identify, until she inhaled. Mixed with the scent of roses and fresh pine came the distinctive aroma of sage. What an odd choice. It almost seemed her admirer had picked the arrangement by scent.

She smiled, pleased with the gift. They could not compare with their wild counterparts, but she did love flowers.

Bess lifted the card, slipped it from the tiny white envelope and read:

Call me. We need to talk.

He had not signed the note, but he had included his cell number. Was that to prevent others from seeing his name or to keep him from having to choose a closing to the card? Bess's smile faded as her satisfaction died.

Cesar had found her so easily. She glanced at the locked door of her high-security apartment. He had invaded her space. She briefly considered moving, but discarded the notion as too extreme.

Cops could find people and gain entry. It was what they did.

Bess tapped the card against her thumbnail as she headed down the hall toward her bedroom.

She was curious again and that was bad. Her curiosity often brought her trouble. Usually she liked trouble, other people's especially. But just now, she felt that this trouble would come back to roost.

Should she fly to him or make him wait? If he came here, she'd have what humans called home field advantage. But her animal side called for her to keep him away from her nest. This was her territory and she did not want him here. His place then.

She stood in the doorway to her bedroom. How did he know for certain that this was her place? Had he been in here, as well?

The room looked undisturbed, everything as she had left it, but he was an FBI officer. Surely they taught them how to maneuver without being obvious. If she had the chance to be in his apartment without him knowing she would have given his dwelling a thorough going-over. She felt certain he had done the same. What had he seen when looking at her personal possessions?

She tried to picture her bedroom as he might, as if seeing it for the first time instead of the thousandth. The eighteenth century Ottoman tapestry displayed a magnificent black tree growing on a white background, centered just behind the wall of pillows on her bed. The pillows and bed skirt were both created from a custom embroidered silk, black and white again, and if one did not look too closely they might not notice the pattern resembled feathers. Flanking the bed sat two vintage black champagne cabinets, repurposed to act as end tables. A

Japanese lacquered screen was mainly black, but did have a bronze-colored tree branch, growing from one panel and across the following two. The cherry blossoms upon the screen were slightly more pink than white. Had he stepped beyond the screen?

She did, moving into her master bath, with the huge tub, separate shower and fluffy towels. Beyond lay her walk-in closet, the deepest sanctuary of her home. She stepped along the white marble floor, the stone cold beneath her bare feet.

Inside the closet, the plush lavender carpet embraced her feet. Beyond, the upholstered hot pink and royal purple bench squatted before a magenta wall, which was mounted with rows of custom-built cubbies from floor to ceiling. They held her footwear, boots at the bottom, flats on the top and in between every variety of black shoe imaginable. Her purses, clutches, satchels and bags were displayed to the right, each in its own lavender cubby. To the left lay the wall of clothing. She needed the colored walls here, because her wardrobe had none. Nor did she want anything on her person other than black.

Had Cesar stood in this spot, trying to understand her? She studied the carpet, noting the indentation that was too long and deep to be anyone's other than a man. She stepped into the place he had vacated, looking at her clothing. Had he touched them?

She let the thrill of excitement pass through her at the thought of him here. It seemed she was not the only curious one. He might dismiss her as only partly human, but he'd been snooping like a frat boy in a sorority house. She'd a good mind to count her underwear.

Bess stroked her thumb over the words he had written, blue ink on the white card, his handwriting small and neat. Then she set the card on the dressing table and pulled open the appropriate drawer, staring down at her most intimate apparel.

"Did you go on a panty raid, Cesar?"

Bess touched her cape, transforming it into the necklace Cesar had first noticed her wearing. Tonight she would wear clothing, human clothing, and keep her cloak with her at all times. He'd already shown what he thought of her and she'd not be caught defenseless again.

She selected a black lace push-up bra and matching panties, embellished with small clear crystal beads. Next she considered her footwear, choosing high boots. Bess pushed the hangers, flicking from one skirt to the next until she came to a scrap of satin that would hug her hips but had some flounce in it. She chose a V-necked cashmere sweater with princess sleeves. Accessories. Designer clutch, wide leather belt, beaded rope necklace tied in a knot.

Men didn't notice designers. They noticed textures, soft, satiny, silken, and she had created an outfit that had all three. Beneath the sweater, her feather cape now sat transformed into just her choker and it would remain there about her neck no matter how the evening evolved.

Bess glanced at herself in the full-length mirror, deciding she needed lipstick. After applying bright ruby-red, she dropped the cylinder back in place before glancing at the card once more.

Call me.

Oh, she'd do better than that.

She lifted the card and noticed something she had missed before. The line beneath his cell phone number was, in fact, an arrow.

She flipped the card and read:

I've seen them.

Seen them? Her heart pounded and everything about her faded until she could see only his words, blue against the white paper. Was he all right?

Bess was halfway to the windows when the logical part of her mind kicked in. If he had been injured would he have come here, left flowers and a note?

She paused, her heart still hammering painfully in her chest. He was all right and she'd be damned if she'd let him know how much his note had frightened her.

Bess pressed her free hand to her forehead trying to think. What exactly had he seen? She needed to find out.

Chapter 11

The intercom phone in Cesar's apartment gave a sedate purring ring. His senses went on instant alert. None of his kind would come to his home. Was it her?

Cesar closed the electronic document of the most recent attacks on his secure computer and closed the laptop, annoyed at the way his heart galloped at the possibility that Bess might be there. Then he hesitated, realizing that if she chose to visit him, she would more likely arrive unannounced upon his balcony. It gave him a flush of shame that since their parting, he had kept his outdoor entrance unlocked just in case she wished to visit. She hadn't.

He hit the button. "Yeah?"

"Visitor, Mr. Garza. A Ms. Suncatcher to see you. Shall I send her up?"

At the name Suncatcher his insides squeezed as if bracing for a blow. He was in such a mad rush to see her again, he punched the button with unnecessary force, causing the Sheetrock, upon which it perched, to collapse like the shell of an egg.

He cursed.

"What's that, Mr. Garza?"

"Send her up." He hadn't intended for his tone to be so harsh.

"Oh, yes, sir."

He tucked in his shirt and then glanced around the place, which he began hurriedly straightening.

The doorbell chimed as he brushed his teeth. So that was what the doorbell sounded like, he thought as he retraced his steps to the front door, frowning as he took in the buzzer's now skewed position in the bowing Sheetrock.

He was still frowning when he opened the door.

Bess had run down the corridor to his apartment and pressed the bell. Now she stood, breathless from fear before his closed door, waiting for some sight of him. She knew in her mind he was all right, had waited while the attendant downstairs spoke to him. Yet, still she could scarcely breathe past the hard knot of worry in her throat. She needed to see him with her own eyes.

She tapped her fingers on her thighs as she waited, the dread creeping through her as she recalled how fast and deadly they were. They'd almost caught her. Cesar had amazing powers, but speed was not one of them. He was all right, wasn't he?

When the door swung open, the air filled her lungs in a sweet rush. There he stood, tall and whole. Thank the Great Spirit!

She forgot her cool demeanor, her affectation of sophistication and her past grievances in the rush of relief that washed over her like seawater.

Bess reached, cradling his strong stubbly jaw between her two hands as she searched for injuries. The zing of first contact tingled up her arm. He grinned at her and she read the satisfaction he derived from her worry.

She didn't care. He was safe.

He took hold of her hips and drew her in, his desire sparking inside her like a signal flare against the night sky. She responded with a hot rush of longing. He spun her inside and kicked the door closed.

"You saw them."

"Yes." His whisper was a caress.

He bent forward to kiss her.

"But you're all right?"

Cesar was pressing her backward, kissing her neck as he pushed her from the foyer to the living room. She bumped against the couch. His hands moved from her waist, sliding up her ribs until he held each of her breasts in his hands. At the sweet pressure of his touch, she threw her head back, giving him her throat.

She dropped her purse on the entryway rug.

"I visited the Ghost Road."

He lifted his lips a millimeter from her throat to whisper his reply, his hot breath fanning her wet skin. "Later."

"It's important."

"So is this."

They tumbled over the back of the couch, Bess landing first and Cesar on top of her.

"But…"

He lifted up to stare at her, his dark eyes glittering with passion. Her breath caught.

"Are you in danger?"

She shook her head. An instant later she felt his reaction—sweet relief.

"Am I?"

"No," she whispered.

His smile was wicked. "Then it can wait an hour."

Yes. It could wait, everything could wait for them

to burn this passion to ash. An hour. A perfect hour in his arms.

"All right."

Cesar tugged at her sweater. "Make it disappear."

She met his longing gaze with a satisfied smile.

"Can't. It's real. If you want it off, you'll have to do it the conventional way."

"Love to." He rolled from her and sat on the metal corner of the glass coffee table. "Stand up."

She did, rising like a phoenix, her skin aflame. He lifted her foot and she allowed it, using his shoulders to steady herself, when in fact her balance was perfect. She kneaded the thick muscles of his shoulders as he removed her shoe and cast it aside. She flinched at seeing her expensive footwear so misused. She stepped down and offered her other foot, placing it in his crotch so that the heel was poised to do serious damage.

He removed this one as well, but set it gently beside him on the coffee table and she realized he had read her distress at the treatment of its mate. She met his knowing look and nodded her approval.

She stood before him between the couch and the coffee table, where he sat.

In her bare feet, she was several inches shorter, so now her breasts were just even with his mouth. He lifted her long beaded necklace, careful to rub his knuckles over her breasts as he removed it. Bess gasped at the sheer pleasure of his touch.

How delicious.

She released her belt, held it out to her side at arm's length and dropped it on his rug. Then she reached behind herself and unhooked her skirt, lowering the zipper so the waistband slid to her hips. He reached beneath it, his hands brushing her thighs as he drew it off, letting the scrap of satin drop around her ankles. He took the time to admire the sheer thong before stroking the downy thatch of dark hair through the lace. The tingle of anticipation burrowed deep. He slipped a finger under the elastic that sat high on her hip and gave it a little snap. The pleasing sting made her twitch with anticipation.

Cesar now held the hem of her cashmere sweater. He stood to lift it, leaning in to kiss her bare stomach, taking advantage of the exposed skin revealed by her receding garment, his mouth eager and hot. For a moment soft, fluffy cashmere brushed her cheek and then his mouth was on hers again. Their tongues danced a fiery tango as he reached between her breasts and expertly released the clip that held her bra in place.

She giggled.

He drew back enough to look at her, but did not let her go. His look asked the question.

"How did you know where the clasp was?" she asked.

His shrug said he didn't kiss and tell. The man had skills and she didn't begrudge all the hours of practice, for it would now be to her benefit.

She set to work releasing the small white buttons of his shirt, pleased to see that he was not so old-fashioned that he wore an undershirt. When she finished, he unfastened his cuffs and shrugged out of his shirt as she caressed his chest and licked his nipples. He liked that, judging from his rapid breathing and the hum of pleasure. His rising excitement flowed from him to her, doubling her need.

Bess took her time returning to his mouth. Too much time, for she could feel his impatience building like a shaken bottle of champagne. He threaded his fingers in her long, loose hair and used this handhold to drag her up to receive his kiss.

Commanding. She liked that.

His fingers tightened, sending an exciting tingle through her scalp. Had he read her thrill? He pulled her back so that she could see his face.

"I want to take you right here on the carpet."

"Yes."

Cesar kicked the coffee table aside, exposing more of the plush white carpet that felt thick as sheepskin beneath her feet.

He didn't release her as he guided her down to the ground. She let him carry her to her back. He unhitched his trousers and she pushed them down over his taut backside, using her nails to score his skin. The electric pop of exhilaration from her action reached her an instant later. It was so easy to tell what he liked and for him to learn what made her senses soar.

He ducked away from her, using his teeth to grasp one side of her thong. He used his hand on the other, dragging the lace away, exposing her most sensitive skin.

Cesar held up the thong like a battle trophy, his smile triumphant. Then he wrapped the thong about his hand and used the lace to brush across her nipples, arousing her even more. She wiggled impatiently and reached for him. He didn't make her wait. Instead he used his knee like a wedge to push her legs apart, settling between them.

She locked her heels behind his lean flanks and pulled. He fell forward, catching himself on his forearms, with one hand planted at each side of her head.

"I want to kiss you," he said.

She lifted her chin and offered her lips.

"Not on the mouth."

She smiled and inclined her head. He dropped,

smothering her with the weight of his body, before moving his attention to her ear, her neck, her breasts. His hands preceded him, like an advance team, making her skin tingle with his feathery touch before his mouth even reached her naked flesh.

"You smell so good. I could eat you up."

She hoped he would.

He stroked and kissed down her ribs and over the gentle mound of her stomach as she braced in anticipation, splaying her legs wide. Was this how his human's behaved? Uncertainty niggled as she second-guessed her actions.

When his tongue reached her cleft, her head fell back at the thrill and her thoughts broke apart. That electric buzz of energy that came from each touch between them was now centered entirely on her most sensitive skin. She arched to meet his eager mouth and muscular tongue. Her breathing became erratic as her climax approached. Her hands first dug into the thick pile of the carpet and then into the thick hair at his scalp.

The cry began in her throat and ended in his as the stellar orgasm burst inside her and careened out, curling her fingers and toes. She panted and writhed, taken up in the pleasure until nothing existed but her bliss. Then she fell back, her lungs starving for oxygen, her body replete. Cesar laid his head on her belly and continued to stroke her wet cleft. He seemed to be breathing as heavily as she was, as if he'd just come as well.

That thought brought her up to her elbows. Had he?

But what if he also... She'd been anticipating feeling him inside her again and felt a jolt of disappointment.

He gave a growl that turned into a laugh as he rose to his hands and knees, giving her a perfect view of his magnificent erection.

She glanced to his face and saw his half smile.

"I did feel it. But I didn't come. Yet. That was amazing."

Cesar stalked up her body, taking his time. Bess used her foot to stroke him from hip to calf as she waited impatiently for him to enter her.

He kissed her deeply as he slid inside. The sensation was exquisite as the rush of pleasure, his and hers, merged and intensified like a cloud giving forth both thunder and lightning. Bess trembled from the pure delight as her body quickened again.

She lifted her hips to more fully enjoy the sliding friction of his thrusts and then wrapped her strong legs about him, like a python, drawing him deep. He drove as she bucked, each stroke bringing him closer. She felt it begin, crying out even before he did as the hot rush of his orgasm erupted inside his body then through hers. He arched against her, plunging deep, threw back his head and cried out his satisfaction in one guttural shout.

At last, his eyes opened and he met her gaze. The look of wonderment struck her with his feeling of awe. This joining had been more powerful than the last.

The niggling fear woke within her. She had slept with him twice and would do it again if he let her. Why had she believed she could have him and move on?

She pushed back her rising panic, hoping to disguise her emotional turbulence by breaking contact before he sensed her emotions.

In a move she hoped would appear playful, she tugged at his wrist. Bess pulled, throwing him off balance and rolling him onto his back as she splayed across his chest, belly and thighs. He was warm and lethargic and their bodies were both slick from perspiration and sex.

"Delicious," she cooed.

He slapped one palm to his forehead and closed his eyes. "Wow."

Without opening them, he cradled her head to his chest and used the other hand to grope around on the couch until he located the afghan, then made a halfhearted attempt to cover them, succeeding only in blanketing their torsos, but leaving her behind and their legs uncovered.

Had he noticed anything amiss?

She felt his body powering down, like a race car gliding after crossing the finish line. The muscles of his thighs twitched, his arm jerked once.

He hadn't.

"I thought you said an hour," she whispered.

He opened one eye and peeked at her. "That includes napping."

He pressed her head back to his chest and patted it as if she were a fretful child that he wanted to be good. She gave a laugh and closed her eyes.

"Bess?" he whispered. "You're amazing."

"No. We're amazing."

She felt her legs twitch, as well. Bess hadn't meant to sleep, but she must have, because she woke when Cesar pulled her off his chest and nestled her along his side. When she opened her eyes, he stroked her hair from her face.

She smiled up at him. He was a wonderful lover. Bess was so damned glad that nothing had happened to him out there.

He returned her smile with a tender one of his own.

"Been a long time since someone cared whether I came home or not."

"Don't read too much into it." She tried to keep her tone light, knowing he wasn't fooled. His expression told her that he'd felt her concern as surely as if it had been his own.

His smile broadened. "I'm fine, thanks."

She scowled, trying not to think about why it so irritated her that he was experiencing her concern for him right now. She shouldn't care what happened to him, really? To be worried over his welfare was nearly the same as worrying about the safety of a great white shark trapped in a swimming pool full of bathers. Yet she had rushed over here like some damned fool.

Cesar stretched. Bess stared at the rippling muscles of his chest and arms and felt a stab of desire pierce her insides.

He grinned. "Why am I thinking of a shark?"

Bess moved away, bringing the blanket with her. That was her thought and he had read it. The same thing that made sex so great also opened some kind of portal between them. She didn't like it.

"Not sure," she said, sitting up and recovering her bra, which lay on the coffee table. She located her sweater next and drew the cashmere over her head, then stood to slip into her thong and skirt.

Cesar made a sound of surprise. "They sold me this place on the view, but it's never been as good as right now." Cesar still lay on his back, but was now looking straight up her skirt.

"What are you, twelve?"

"Closer to a hundred and twenty."

"Me, too. Not quite a hundred."

Cesar sat up, using the afghan like a toga.

Bess buckled her belt and then glanced to the foyer, spotting her purse.

Cesar stood, dropping the afghan. Bess sat back on the sofa to watch him get dressed, thoroughly enjoying herself. "It's like Chippendales only in reverse."

"Don't feel obligated to stick a twenty in my G-string."

"Thanks."

He sat next to her. She turned sideways, curling her bare foot beneath her thigh and folding her hands in her lap to keep herself from brushing his thick hair from his forehead. She preferred his disheveled look. It made him seem more approachable, less fierce.

"I'm glad you came back," he said, his voice low and intimate. He could still smell the perfume of her skin, but now it was on his clothing and skin.

Cesar wondered if Bess realized how lovely she

was, with her lips swollen from his kisses and her usually perfectly arranged hair in a tangle all about her lovely heart-shaped face. Her high cheekbones, narrow nose and pointed chin all served as the perfect canvas for her wide, sloping dark eyes. Her lovely full red lips no longer shined, but still held the stain of red from the lipstick she'd applied.

He fingered the fuzzy sweater at her waist then slid along the satin of her short skirt until he touched her toned thighs. She allowed it, but did not move to take his hand.

She wasn't aroused right now, but feeling anxious and self-conscious, worried about what he thought of her because of the last time.

"Damn," he whispered, drawing back and breaking the connection. This was because she'd read his thoughts the first time, when he'd wondered about her animal urges.

"Bess? I'm sorry for upsetting you last time."

She glanced away, looking toward the windows. The rain still pattered against the glass as it had all day.

Her voice was so low he had to lean forward to hear her.

"You mean for wondering if sex was good because I'm part animal?"

"Was it?" he asked.

"Was it what?"

"Was it because you are Inanoka and I'm Ni-yanoka that our sex was so off-the-charts spectacular?"

Chapter 12

Bess blinked at him in a look of open astonishment. He'd been trying to apologize for the last time they'd been together.

Now he waited, wondering if she'd fly away again.

She sat before him, perched at the edge of the couch cushion, her posture stiff and her knees pressed tightly together.

Cesar crossed one arm over his chest and used his wrist to brace the opposite elbow, balling his fist over his mouth to keep himself from saying anything else.

"I'm not sure," she said.

He sat on the coffee table, his legs splayed on either side of hers. It would be a simple thing to touch her, but he resisted, not wanting to reveal the tumult of this thoughts.

"What do you think?" she asked.

Humor, you idiot. Say something funny and pray she lets you off the hook.

"Me? I think I should send flowers more often."

Her smile seemed forced as she studied him with her sharp, black eyes. He knew the instant he was in the clear, because she gave a slight nod. Then she tucked her hair behind her ears as if getting down to business.

"So tell me, what exactly did you see?"

He nodded his resignation. Their danger was past, but also their intimacy. Their coupling had been so damned good, he felt an ache that she could set it aside so easily.

"Well, we had a call. Something tore up a trailer."

She leaned in. "Something?"

"It was them. The more recently born twins."

"Tell me everything."

He did, beginning with the trailer that the creatures had opened like a can of tuna fish to reach the dog and the curious behavior of the one, trying, it seemed to Cesar, to get a better look at him, while the other twin urged it away.

"Why didn't they attack you?"

"Not sure."

"But you did see them?"

He nodded.

"And they saw you?"

"Yes, most definitely."

"I don't understand." Bess recalled that they had turned on her the instant she was spotted and with an unsettling ruthlessness. Yet they had let him entirely alone. It puzzled her.

"Do you think they recognized you as something other than human and other than animal, something like them?"

"Again, not sure. They were howling and barking back and forth. A disagreement, I think."

Bess rubbed her sculpted thumbnail along her lower lip as she thought. "They were speaking to one another?"

"That was my take. But I couldn't distinguish any words. Just yowling and screeching."

"Did you use your gun?"

"No, though it was out of the holster. I'm not sure they recognized the weapon as a threat."

"And you don't know if it *is* a threat. They can turn their bodies to smoke, remember?"

"True. I really don't know what they know. In any case, they were already bigger than you described. Nearly four feet now and they did a kind of jumping, leaping gallop that reminded me of the way ring-tailed lemurs move on the ground."

She gave him an incredulous look.

"Discovery Channel."

"So they saw you, watched you and then took off?"

"Then sort of exploded into a black cloud of smoke and rose up into the tree canopy."

Bess sat back. "You're lucky they didn't kill you."

"I'm not sure it was luck."

She waited, giving him time to formulate his thoughts instead of disagreeing outright.

"So far these two have killed a moose and a dog that we know of. But the campground was full of tourists in tents and RVs. It they had wanted to attack people, they surely had the opportunity."

"They killed their mother, who was human."

"All creatures have a right to be born."

"By gnawing their way out of their mother's body?"

He didn't answer, choosing retreat instead. "You want a drink?"

She nodded and followed him to the kitchen, waiting as he retrieved two glasses. She chose one of the four chairs that lined the granite counter, and then tucked in facing him.

"Water, juice, cocktail?"

She asked for juice and he mixed seltzer with the pomegranate blend he had on hand, recalling Persephone's mistake, half hoping that the concoction would have the same effect on Bess. He'd like to have her around for half the year.

He offered the glass and she accepted it. The ice cubes tinkled as their hands brushed. In that instant he felt her true emotions rushing at him like a windstorm of agitation. He righted himself, looking at her. The calm demeanor was merely a facade, then. Had he not touched her, he might never have guessed.

He retrieved a dark beer and lifted the amber bottle, clinking it against her glass in a silent salute.

Bess lifted hers to him before drinking.

"So, in summary, unless they attack a camper, your people won't do a thing, because they are only killing animals."

"Yes."

"You're giving those things a lot more credit than they deserve."

"Perhaps. But until we know what they are—"

"I know now."

He held the bottle frozen in place for an instant before setting it aside. His voice turned grave as his expression.

"Niyanoka?"

She shook her head. "Before I tell you what the mothers said, I need to explain something."

"Bess, you promised you'd tell me what you discovered."

"And I will. Just listen."

Bess's voice was breathless now and he had a hard time not staring at her lush mouth.

"I was in Montana three months ago helping a friend who was attacked by ghosts."

"Montana? This have anything to do with the daughter of a Peacemaker and his wife, a Dream Walker?"

She nodded. "How did you know?"

"The Council of Elders sent me to Montana in May to interview them. They told me their daughter had broken our..." He hesitated, sensing another battle, but instead of turning back, he charged ahead. "Our laws against fraternization with Skinwalkers." She did not take visible offense, but he knew now that her expression was not a good method of gauging her mood. He wondered if he should risk a touch and decided against it. "They said a Skinwalker had been discovered by a group of humans on a dude ranch. They reported that the Skinwalker wolf had caused injuries. But the Peacemaker reformulated their memories."

"What! That's a lie. That's not what happened."

"I sensed the Peacemaker was lying, but I can't use my Truth Seeking on other Niyanoka without permission and he was very thorough with the humans. I did see their daughter in the company of a Skinwalker, confirming that part of his story. So I reported to the Council what little I found. Jessie Healy was banished as a result."

"His name is Nicholas and he saved their daughter's life. Did you at least speak to them?"

"Was there some reason I should?"

They stared at each other from opposite sides of the stone counter, but Cesar felt the distance separating them was suddenly much greater. He reached for her hands, needing to bring her back to him, but she slid them from the granite surface and onto her lap.

She stared at him earnestly. "I was there, Cesar. Are you willing to listen to what really happened?"

He nodded.

Bess blew out a breath and launched into her story.

"It was a battle in Montana against four Skinwalkers and three Niyanoka, the two you spoke to and their daughter. We fought against Nagi's ghosts."

"Ghosts can't attack humans."

"Unless they have taken possession of humans."

Cesar's unease grew at this revelation.

"Nagi captured the one you helped banish and used her in an attempt to get Nicholas—he's the wolf—to reveal the location of his real target. Nagi sent his ghosts to possess the men and women at the ranch. When we tried to rescue Jessie, they attacked us."

She did not need to touch him to see the disbelief painted on his features.

"Tuff was there. He'll tell you the same."

His expression told her that the word of another Skinwalker was no proof at all.

Cesar's voice held a note of the type one uses to explain something to a child. "Nagi doesn't allow ghosts to attack humans. He collects evil souls and sends them for judgment."

Bess's frustration bubbled into her words. "He wasn't attacking humans! He was using them to attack us to try to find a Niyanoka."

"Who?"

"The last Seer of Souls."

Cesar stepped back. He bumped into the oven, then folded his arms protectively across his chest, avoiding her eye and Bess knew that he had heard of the Seer.

"Chatter on the internet is all. Some say there is still a Seer in the world."

"I know her."

"You've met the Seer?"

Bess nodded and Cesar's eyes grew wide. He covered his mouth with his hand, regarding her as if trying to decide how to proceed.

"I thought it was a rumor." He spoke as much to himself as to her. "I didn't believe, that is, we thought the Ghost Clan had died with Michael Proud."

"Michaela's father. He was also a Seer. He hid his daughter when he realized Nagi was stalking him and suppressed her gifts. Until recently, she thought she was human."

"How is that possible?"

"I do not know."

"And you say Nagi killed her father? Why does the Council know nothing of this?"

"I'm not certain they don't. Tuff told me that Jessie tried to tell them but they disregarded her words because she is living with one of my people."

"And called me to investigate instead?"

Bess nodded. "To be certain she no longer has the right to speak to them."

"Why didn't her parents back her up? Why turn her in?" he asked.

"They chose to protect their position instead of

their daughter. And perhaps the Council does not want others to hear of this."

She noticed he had no trouble accepting that the Council was intentionally suppressing information from his people.

"Why doesn't that surprise you?"

Cesar lowered his chin. "I have some experience with them. They have their own agenda." He tapped his first two fingers on his lower lip, staring past her to the empty room, but seeming to be looking back into his own thoughts.

Bess resisted the urge to touch him.

At last he dropped his hand. "So what really happened in Montana?"

She released a breath. At least, he was willing to listen.

"It began when her father ventured onto the Spirit Road while still alive. The journey tore his soul."

"Making it easy for Nagi to find him," Cesar finished for her.

"Exactly. Nagi had reasons to want him dead before he produced more Seers, but when he tracked the Seer, he discovered his wife was already with child."

"The current Seer?"

"No, her younger brother. Nagi killed the Seer and his wife, but was unaware that they had hidden Michaela. Nagi did not know of her until her powers manifested."

"Seers are invisible to all Spirits."

"Yes, unless they walk the Ghost Road."

"She nearly died?"

"Auto accident. Coma. She survived."

"But Nagi saw her on the Ghost Road."

Bess nodded. "Exactly."

"But why would Nagi hunt Seers?"

"Because the Seer of Souls is the only living person who can see ghosts. So she is the only person who would see him amassing those ghosts into his own private army."

His voice emerged as a tight growl. "Why?"

"To take over the living world."

Cesar gave Bess a dubious look, but she gave no indication that she was playing some elaborate joke. This didn't make any sense. "Nagi rules the Circle of Ghosts."

. She waved an impatient hand in the air. "I know. But he attacked the Seer. She suffered a Spirit Wound. He also attacked Jessie Healy, a Dream Walker. Same deal."

Cesar couldn't keep himself from flinching. Spirit Wounds worked from within through madness or by killing the soul.

"Why aren't they both dead?"

"My friend Sebastian took the Seer to Kanka for help."

"A Supernatural cannot heal a Spirit Wound." He spoke automatically, pointing at the gaping hole in her story.

Again he received the impatient look. "I know. But she did heal her body. Michaela had to learn to repair the other one herself."

"I did not know that was possible."

"Her recovery means Nagi can no longer find her, but he still wants her dead, so he attacked her husband's best friend in hopes that the injured Skinwalker would come to them to be healed."

"This Skinwalker, is a healer?"

She nodded. "A grizzly bear."

Cesar understood now. Bears were the greatest of healers, respected even among his people.

Bess continued. "But Nicholas realized what Nagi was up to and sought another healer."

"The Dream Walker in Montana," finished Cesar.

"Yes. She healed him and he saved her from Nagi, with my help."

Cesar couldn't suppress the half smile. Bess was not modest, but neither was she a braggart.

"How did you stop the ghosts?"

"We didn't. Couldn't. We only won because of

the Seer. She figured out how to send them back to the Circle. Do you understand what that means?"

"It means she can defeat his ghosts but if he finds her, she'll die."

"He can't use his ghosts. He can't win that way unless he finds and kills the Seers."

"There are more than one?"

"She's recently delivered twins. Nagi is more desperate to find her than before. But I think he figured out another way to take over the living world."

The look in her eyes told him that he sure as hell wasn't going to like what came next.

"Why didn't you tell me all this before now?"

Bess made a face. "Niyanoka are not known for listening to Inanoka. As soon as you see us, you scurry the other way."

"That's not fair."

She flapped her arms in annoyance. "I didn't know you then. I didn't trust you."

Did she trust him now?

"Fair enough. So what does this have to do with the twins we found?"

"I'm getting to that." She wet her dry lips before beginning. "First, the mothers are there, in the Spirit World. Both lived proper lives and neither knows exactly who the father is."

"How is that possible?"

"They never saw him, for one thing. He came to them in complete darkness. Both of them said they were in some kind of ecstatic trance. One said she was aroused, but it felt as if she were aroused from the inside, as if there was no lover. The other said she thought it was the Lord. Both were surprised to find themselves with child and to have the children grow so fast. They were sick from the pregnancy, very sick. Their labor was so painful that it was a relief to die. They were happy to end the pain, but sad to have left loved ones behind."

"So they *don't* know who the father is."

"No. But I think I do. You do, as well."

Cesar broke the contact of their gaze. He rubbed his hand over his mouth and stepped to the windows to stare out at the raindrops streaming down the glass in rivulets.

Something about his stillness told Bess that he had put it together.

The nail was set, so she gave it one last good, hard whack.

"They are flesh of one who has no flesh. Living, breathing, children of the ruler of the Circle of Ghosts."

He turned to meet her gaze. She held it, not letting go.

His voice was barely a whisper. "Not possible."

His denial was halfhearted at best.

"You wouldn't think so. He's a ghost himself after all with no body or not one like you and me. But he is also a true Spirit with powers equal to those who sired our races."

"If you are right, that means there is a third Halfling race in the world. And that is something the Council must know."

She shrugged. "If you think they will listen. Then you might want to also tell them *why* he's sired children. Now that the Seer can expel his ghosts, he can't use them. But living creatures would make a fine army. Tell them we must track them down and kill them before they grow, multiply and murder us all."

He was shaking his head again.

"They're infants. They've done nothing wrong. You can't just kill them because of who sired them. Plus this is just your theory. You have no evidence. Even the mothers don't know who the father is. You admitted that."

Bess spun her stool and slipped from it, pushing off the counter as she stalked toward him, standing toe to toe.

"They're ghost-children, born of Nagi. And you still don't think they pose a threat?"

"A great threat. But my job is to capture those

who *have* committed a crime. I do not hunt creatures for what they *might* do."

She tried again. "They're here because their father wants real, living, breathing soldiers. When they are mature, they will be unstoppable. And the way they're growing, that could be about next week. We have to take them before then."

"I will speak to my people."

She stood in silence broken only by the pattering rain. He did not want to fight with her. He even wished he could side with her against Nagi's children. But he would not take down a suspect without evidence again. Not even to please Bess.

"Why won't you fight them?" she whispered.

"It's not what I do," Cesar said. "I'm not an assassin. I read the dead, gather evidence and make arrests. I'm always too late to stop a crime and that sucks. But it is not my place to act as judge, jury and executioner, because that's how mistakes are made—mistakes that cannot be put right. Do you understand, Bess?"

He leaned in, breathing the fragrance of intoxication that was her skin.

She turned toward the glass as she spoke, giving him her back. "They are not human."

"They've done nothing wrong."

She stepped back, bumping into the glass as she lifted a finger at him.

"They will."

"Bess." His voice was intended to pacify, but he failed to fully purge the irritation from his tone. "You have to believe me. Hunting them is a mistake. I know it's a mistake."

"How?"

He locked his jaw, willing to give her only a slow shake of his head.

"There has to be some reason you are so adamant."

"There is."

"But you're not going to tell me. Right?"

"Right."

She gave an audible sigh, seeming to shrink several inches as she exhaled. At last she nodded, as if coming to some decision.

"I promised I would reveal what I found. I have done so."

Cesar sensed impending doom. She was leaving him because he refused to take up her cause and go hunt the little Halflings with pitchforks and scythes. Or was it because he refused to tell her why he knew better than to prevent a crime by committing one?

His mind scrambled for some reason to keep her—something, anything.

Instead, he watched her posture stiffen to defensiveness as she stalked away. He pursued.

"Bess, I can't go on a witch hunt."

She stared at him, her expression a poignant mix of sorrow and regret. "Yes. I know. You must go to your people and me to mine. I knew this would come. I just, I hoped it could be otherwise."

Chapter 13

Cesar could have stopped Bess. Instead he watched her go. He knew she'd leave him eventually. He just hadn't thought it would be so damned soon.

Well, better to have her gone than revealing to her why he couldn't do as she asked, for that secret he kept locked in his heart with his other mistakes.

The Book of Reasoning said that past errors could become a source of wisdom. It was a section of text that he has studied at length after his trial, trying to come to terms with his part in the murder. In his mind, they had tried him for the wrong crime.

If he could go back… But he couldn't.

Cesar rubbed his thumb and index finger over his closed eyelids.

Had his experience made him wiser? He didn't know.

Thinking back always ripped his guts out. That's why he stayed away from his kind, away from everyone and everything that reminded him.

"Hell."

Cesar stepped onto the balcony, letting the needles of rain sting his upturned face as he gripped the cold steel rail.

He refused to go there. Instead, he thought of Bess.

Had he really just let her go? Bess was difficult, but he knew she was the best thing that had happened to him in decades.

Would he ever see her again?

The icy rain soaked him, numbed him and finally drove him back inside. When he could no longer ignore his shivering, he retreated to his bedroom, stripped and toweled off, then dressed without much thought.

He retrieved his laptop from his briefcase and booted up, determining to work for as long as it took for his mind to stop mugging him with memories. It was going to be a long night.

Cesar reviewed everything he knew about the creatures and added what Bess had learned. Though the mothers did not directly say their offspring were born of Nagi, he had to admit that Bess's theory, though alarming, was plausible.

Despite his resolve, more than once he found himself losing focus, thinking about Bess. How exactly did she locate the Ghost Road? As it stood now, he'd probably never get the chance to ask her.

He opened a new file and entered his notes on the creatures that he now agreed were a new Half-ling race. The prospect excited him. As soon as he'd finished, he made the call to the head of his District Council, an elderly Peacemaker, named Holly Black Hawk. She was less than pleased to hear from him and resistant to having to meet with him, but he insisted, exerting his rights as a member of the community. Eventually she agreed to gather the District Council in the morning. If the seven members found merit in his concerns they would be the ones to proceed to the Council of Elders.

His rights in the community continued, even if his people would generally cross the street rather than speak to him. His ability as a Soul Whisperer was only half the reason for his infamy. The rest came from what had happened after he and his partner had captured the puma Skinwalker. Many thought his old partner had done nothing wrong and blamed Cesar for the entire incident.

After the phone call, Cesar rattled around his

apartment like a ghost before finally turning in. He had a fitful night and rose early, after giving up on the hope of sleep. He arrived at the District offices and was shown into the Council chamber. Things went badly from there.

The moment they learned that he had received some information from a Skinwalker they closed the session. Instead of the help and wisdom he had sought, he received an official reprimand and a warning that should he be seen in the company of Skinwalkers, he would lose all rights as a member of the Niyanoka community and be banished for life.

He'd brought them the truth and in return they had threatened to take the only thing left to him— his work. He'd be damned if he'd lose that, too.

After leaving the Council, his first thought was that he had to tell Bess what had happened. But he couldn't. He couldn't see her again, ever, if he wanted to remain one of his people.

He weighed the shame of banishment against his desire for Bess and didn't know what to do. All he knew was that his heart felt heavy and cold as a lump of melted lead.

His gut told him that the Council knew more than they were saying. Was Bess right? Did they already know about the Seer, Nagi and the new Halflings?

Cesar spent the rest of the day rereading all his open case files and adding to his notes on the new Halfling breed. Finally, Cesar shut down his laptop, spent forty minutes flipping from one station to the next and then gave up. He got dressed to go out to his favorite bar-restaurant and was at the door to his apartment when he felt the great yawning emptiness that his life had become.

He forced himself out and ate a tasteless meal at the bar, ignoring the attempts of several women to engage him in conversation. His physical relationships with human females now seemed repugnant. Just the thought of taking another one to his bed filled him with despair.

What the devil was wrong with him?

Cesar felt weary to the very center of his spirit. Weary and lonely and sad.

Where was Bess right now?

He went home early, disheartened and alone. But sleep eluded him again and so, when his phone buzzed like an electric razor on his bedside table at four in the morning, he opened it on the first ring.

"Garza."

He listened to the details of the crime scene, feeling a chill that had nothing to do with the breeze off the bay. He'd left his bedroom window open, just for air, he'd told himself, knowing that he wanted her back.

"Be there in twenty." He snapped the phone closed and dropped it back on the table as he headed for the bathroom. Maka, he hoped that this was not the work of the Halflings, because if they were murdering people, as Bess had predicted they would, he'd have to hunt them down.

He didn't bother to shave, just dressed, forgoing coffee in his haste to reach the scene. He arrived a little after five and flashed his badge to the young officer then double-parked behind the squad cars. He stepped out onto the wet street. At least the rain had stopped.

Cesar ducked under the yellow tape. The victim lay on her back in the alley on the wet concrete in a pool of congealed blood. Cesar saw at a glance that she had not died giving birth. Someone had set up a portable light. The bright illumination and the stillness of the corpse gave the scene the surreal look of an image captured in a momentary flash of a camera. Matted hair lay across her face and neck. She'd been killed after the storm had stopped.

Cesar squatted beside her, seeing no evidence of predation. The killer had not been after food. He sighed in relief and then looked at the detective who stood across from him. The man's face held the gray tinge of blocked arteries and the deep lines of a guy who'd seen this kind of thing a few times too often. His watery, red-rimmed eyes said the coffee he held in the disposable cup was not doing the job.

"Where's the blood coming from?"

The detective drew a slim gold pen from his front pocket and used it to lift the hair from the victim's neck, revealing a laceration that had opened the jugular.

"This like the ones you're investigating?" asked the detective.

Cesar shook his head. "Nope. You got any leads?"

"She's a business girl, so, you know, wrong place, wrong guy. She's also got three pops for meth. Could be that or a john."

Cesar stood. A shadow swept just over him and he glanced up, shading his eyes against the spotlight in time to see a raven perch on a fire escape. Suddenly his heart was doing an aerobic workout without him moving a muscle.

The detective followed the line of his sight. "Huh. You don't see them in the city very often."

Cesar waved at Bess, who gave a regal nod of her glossy head. Just the sight of her lightened his spirit.

"Anyways, no weapon," said the detective.

Cesar recalled why he was there. He squatted and touched the victim's wrist. The last moment of the woman's life played out in his mind in gruesome living color.

"Hey, Garza. Put on some gloves."

The admonishment brought him back to this time and place. Cesar stood. "Do you know her old boyfriend's name?"

"Not yet, why?"

"Because the killer's name is Harold Marin. He tried to make it look like a robbery. Nice to meet you, Detective…" He let his words trail off waiting for the man to shake his offered hand.

When he did, Cesar put the move on him, using his Memory Walking gift to draw back their conversation. As far as the detective knew, Cesar had never been there, but Cesar left one thing behind. The detective now had a real bad feeling about Marin and that would make Marin his prime suspect.

Cesar ducked under the tape and headed back to his car where he held open the passenger side door. He looked up at Bess, now perched on a streetlamp. She made a chortling sound in her throat, but did not accept his invitation. So he shut the door and returned to the driver's side.

As he pulled out, the raven swept down the middle of the street. Should he follow her?

"Hell, yes."

* * *

Bess had to stop on the top girder of the Golden Gate to wait for Cesar's car to weave through traffic. Pity Cesar could not fly.

Once his car finally appeared, she headed to a picnic area in the forest. There she waited at a table in her human form, dressed in black hiking boots, jeans and a fleece. He finally pulled into the parking lot.

He exited his sedan, looking aggravated. Driving did that to all of them, she noticed.

"You couldn't use the cell phone number I gave you?" He finger combed his hair with both hands in a gesture that looked painful.

Bess patted her empty pockets. "Must have left it in my other outfit."

They shared a look and after a long moment, his smile returned.

"Yeah, right." He laughed.

"Did you talk to your people?"

His smile dropped away. And she already knew what he would say.

"Didn't believe you?"

"Nope."

"Not surprised."

"They also told me if I ever see you again, I'm banished for life."

Now that did piss her off. Then she realized he was defying them right now, for her. The realization sent a ray of sunshine that seemed to travel through the top of her head and straight to her heart.

"Yet you followed me," she said.

"Can't seem to help myself."

"That's the sweetest thing anyone ever said to me."

He took her hand, letting his joy flow to her and feeling her pleasure vibrate back to him.

"I missed you."

"Me, too," she admitted, and then pulled back.

He let her go, pressing down his disappointment at not getting to hold her.

"Did you speak to your Council?" he asked.

"We don't have a Council. I found Tuff and told him what's what. He'll pass the news when he runs into someone else."

"Pretty low tech."

"But good for those who live off the grid, as many of us do."

Cesar rubbed his neck. "Did you bring me here for a romp, I hope?"

She laughed. "Afraid not. Though I do have a place nearby if you like a bed."

"Not necessarily." He craned his neck as if looking for a likely place for some privacy, the fatigue and annoyance now completely gone from him.

Bess pulled them back on track. "I need you to meet someone." She pointed. "The guy in camp site number twenty-two should be back from the emergency room by now."

Cesar looked cautious but took her up on the challenge. "You coming?"

"Of course. I'm your new partner, remember?" She gave a mock salute. "Detective Suncatcher, here."

"Bess? Have you been impersonating an FBI officer?"

Her smile was devilish. She looped her arm in his and set them in motion. After several moments he stopped. She glanced up at him, the question on her face.

"Partners don't walk like this," he said, glancing at her arm looped through his crooked elbow. "At least, police partners don't. Not that I'm not enjoying it."

She felt her face heat as she released him. "Oh, right."

Why was it so difficult to keep her hands off him?

Cesar approached the small detached camper, walking past the white dually that was parked at an odd angle. Bess waited in the gravel driveway as Cesar knocked on the flimsy aluminum screen door.

It opened and an athletic-looking woman filled the small door frame. Thirtyish, blonde, ruddy complexion, wearing twin braids, a T-shirt covered with images of a large variety of sea turtles all identified by type, khaki shorts and wool hiking socks without shoes.

Cesar glanced back at Bess in confusion.

"Ask to speak to her husband."

Cesar flashed his badge, introduced himself and was admitted. Bess remained outside. Cesar found himself standing in the kitchen, living-dining-sleeping room before the woman's husband. Mr. Donald Ortega sat on the little sofa, a brown, lumpy looking pull-out, with his right leg propped up on pillows. A bag of frozen peas rested under his meaty calf, which was swathed in an expert wrapping of white gauze. He seemed the perfect male counterpart to his wife in athleticism and attire, except he was smaller and darker and his T-shirt identified various kinds of animal tracks.

"I told the rangers it was no bear. Did they send you?"

Cesar explained he was investigating another matter and wondered if this incident might be connected. Ortega gave him his story. He and the wife were hiking and had come upon a dead deer. They knew this was a bad place to be and feared the predator might be the mountain lion that had been sighted on Bull Creek Flats trail, which was ironic since they picked another trail specifically to avoid encountering the big cat.

"But what ran out of the huckleberry was no cat and it sure the hell was no bear." Ortega held his hand up to approximate the size of the creature he had seen. "Grayish skin and a white mane. It had pointy ears like a German shepherd's and eyes as yellow as those taxidermy ones they use for owls. Thing came at me with claws bared and I pushed Karen to get her running. I took off after her and thought I was in the clear when it gave me this."

He lifted his leg off the peas.

"Thirty-seven stitches. What the hell was that thing?"

Cesar sat on the arm of the sofa and helped Mr. Ortega adjust the peas, being careful to touch his ankle long enough to steal the actual sighting from his mind. The hiker now remembered everything but the little Halfling coming at him. Then he turned to Mrs. Ortega.

Cesar shook her hand on the way out.

"Did you see it?"

"No. When Donny screamed, I turned back, but there was nothing there."

She'd told the truth. She hadn't seen it and so he didn't have to alter her memories.

Bess waited on the picnic table, her expression eager. "They attacked a human hiker. Happy now?"

"Of course I'm not happy."

"But you'll go after them."

"He's fine."

Bess was on her feet. "If a bear attacks a man, it's a death sentence for the bear. No exceptions."

"Not the same."

"No, it's not because these creatures are ten times as deadly as a bear. There are at least four now. How long before there are a thousand?"

"I see no crime. If they are what you say, they have operated within our laws."

"By slicing open a hiker?"

"They have a right to protect their kill from other predators."

"That's all they do—kill and eat." She stepped off the pavement and onto the 1.2 mile hiking trail. "I'm going to look for them."

He didn't understand the Halflings, but it seemed they did not kill or eat men. If they did, Mr. Ortega would have been lunch, for he knew the man could not outrun them. That meant they had retreated and left him to escape.

They had given Bess a similar injury. A warning or an attack? He didn't know.

"You coming?"

Cesar feared if he didn't join her, Bess would go off alone and that could put her in danger.

"Can I talk you out of this?"

Her look held vexation and disbelief. "Not a chance."

"Then I'm coming."

Bess took the lead up the trail that cut away from the river and climbed steadily along the hill, under the dappled light streaming through the canopy high above them. She gave Cesar credit. For an urbanite, he certainly had an easy, tireless stride. The remains of the deer were easy to spot from the buzzing clouds of flies feasting on the carcass and the odor of decay. But Cesar did not see the deer, and so she called it to his attention. The infant killers had dragged the carcass half under the trunk of a fallen redwood with scars that showed it had survived a fire. As long as the blaze did not burn the tree's thick bark completely off, they endured. She admired them that and their ability to remain seemingly unchanged by the centuries.

"This is the area of the attack."

They spent the next half hour studying the

ground, but Cesar was no tracker and she always re-lied on her vision to find food. Cesar leaned against the toppled trunk that was so huge she would have needed a twelve-foot ladder to even consider sit-ting on it.

Cesar drew out his handkerchief and offered it to her. She shook her head and he shrugged, then used the cotton cloth to swab the sweat from his brow.

He rested a hand on the tree, absently finger-ing the ridged bark. "What does it look like—the Spirit Road?"

Bess smiled, allowing him the temporary depar-ture. He'd not keep her from saying what she must this time. "The way is a shimmering silvery path, a little like this one." She indicated the hiking trail. "Only paved in sparkling pinpricks of light that re-semble sunlight on dark water. Like water, I can see through to the space beneath. If I stray from the path, I am only in the sky again. I must keep the Ghost Road under me at all times, or lose my way."

"Can you see it now?

"No. Night is best. It takes longer to find in the daylight."

She glanced to the sky and saw something large and tawny stalking Cesar from above. She acted on instinct, stepping between the crouching mountain lion and the cat's intended prey.

* * *

Bess recognized the lioness for what she was, a Skinwalker and an old one. There was no doubt the cat recognized Bess, as well. She knew this for two reasons. She had made herself visible before the attack and she had not yet pounced. But she kept her intent green eyes fixed on Cesar. The menace in that look turned Bess's skin to gooseflesh and she raised both hands to the big cat, knowing full well she was outmatched.

"Hold, sister. This is a friend."

Behind her she heard Cesar draw and cock his pistol.

"Don't move, Bess. I have a shot."

The situation was rapidly spinning out of control. Bess whirled on Cesar. "She's a Skinwalker. Put down your weapon."

He hesitated, his eyes registering surprise, then something else. If she did not know better she'd say it was dread. The hairs on Bess's neck rose up as a feeling of premonition brought her to complete stillness. Cesar lowered his pistol and released the slide, but he did not return the weapon to his shoulder holster.

Behind her there was a flash of white light. She turned to see a woman, who appeared to be middle-age, meaning she was likely over three hundred, with platinum-blond hair, a jowly face and eyes as green as an alfalfa field. Her choice of clothing was ironic, as she wore a leopard-print scarf knotted about her throat and an orange silk blouse on top. Her crouched legs were sheathed in tawny faux suede slacks and her footwear consisted of slipperlike flats that echoed the leopard print of her scarf. Now she looked like the other sort of cougar. The cat remained on the higher ground, poised above them, with one hand resting between her bent knees. She still stood prepared to strike. Bess knew that the Skinwalker could pounce and transform into her cat form before her claws ripped into Cesar's flesh.

"Step aside, sister, I have hunted this one for fifty years. Today I kill him."

"Get back, Bess," Cesar ordered.

She didn't. Instead she lowered her hands, still facing the puma. "Why him?"

"He killed my husband for a crime he never committed. Shot him before my eyes."

Bess's insides were bathed in icy cold, freezing her to the spot. She could not seem to draw any air and spots rapidly began a threatening dance in her vision. She glanced back at Cesar, expecting—no, hoping for—a denial.

Oh, Great Spirit, it was the worst of her fears

come true. He was a vigilante, just like the one who had killed her father, and she had worked with him, aided him, slept with him.

Chapter 14

"They each shot him. This one brought him down and his partner finished him. I told their Council, but who did this one believe?" The cougar slowly leaned forward as if she were falling gently into her pounce as she whispered her words in a chant.

The low feral growl vibrated through Bess's ribs and sternum.

"Stand aside, sister, for I will taste his blood."

The world seemed to press down upon her, making Bess feel heavy, barely able to move. She could hardly think and when she found herself so bewildered, she turned to instinct.

"No."

The cat never took her eyes off her prey as she

spoke. "I have no quarrel with you, raven. You may go. Walk in beauty."

Bess could not explain why she did not do as she was told. The cougar was clearly stronger and if it came to a fight, Bess would certainly lose. Still she could not leave Cesar to the cat. One of them would die, by bullet or claw.

"I can't do that. This Soul Whisperer is helping me find the children of Nagi."

The cat hesitated. She used the back of her hand to wipe her cheek as if smoothing whiskers that were no longer there, as her attention flicked to Bess.

"I have seen these creatures in the forest, but I did not know what they were. It explains the smell of death that clings to them."

"Did they see you?"

She smiled. "Of course not."

"Do not let them. They can fly."

She nodded. "I will be cautious."

"One attacked me."

"I heard your distress, but could not get to you before you left the forest."

"This Niyanoka saved me and is helping us fight Nagi."

The cat's pencil-thin eyebrows rose. "I have no fight with Nagi. But if these creatures are hunting in my territory, I have a fight with them."

"They are deadly," Bess warned. "Vicious. Extremely fast."

The cat lowered her voice to a near purr. "Then we are well matched. If I kill one, do you want me to call you, little raven?"

"Yes."

"I would still kill this one."

Bess moved before Cesar and prepared to fight a losing battle.

The cat smiled and fixed her green eyes upon Bess. "But not at the expense of your life, little sister. I respect the old ways and would not kill a raven. You may go and the killer may go." Her smile vanished as she glared her hatred at Cesar. "But if our paths cross again, I will kill you. My mate was a good husband and I will yet have my revenge. And you, little one, should be wiser than to protect our enemies."

The brilliant flash made Bess cover her eyes. When she looked again the cat was gone.

Bess felt Cesar's betrayal like a knife thrust in her sternum. The ache filled her lungs, making it hard to draw breath. She turned back to face him, waiting as he holstered his weapon. When he was done, he did not look at her, but instead rubbed the back of his neck with his shooting hand and stared at the ground.

It was true then.

"You killed a Skinwalker?"

"Yes."

"So that talk of turning my people over to our justice was a lie."

"There's more to it than that."

"Vigilante." Bess pressed her hand to her mouth as if the sight of him made her physically sick. "I would leave you here, but I'm afraid if I do, she'll kill you. Let's go."

Bess marched back the way she had come, hoping he was wise enough to follow. How could she have believed him? Lies upon lies upon lies. Bess pressed her eyes closed against the burning, wishing she could find relief in tears as she had done before the change. But this was something ravens could not do.

What difference was there between him and the men who killed her father?

None, she realized. She had let the unnatural attraction between them cloud her judgment and make her vulnerable to his deceit. Shame heated her face.

It was a long, angry, silent walk back to his vehicle. Bess could barely see past her fury, but she did not stop until they reached the parking area.

Once there Bess waited, with folded arms, praying he would have the sense to get in his damned car and drive away. She didn't want him to see how much this betrayal crushed her and she scrubbed her hands over her burning cheeks.

All the while she thought they were working together, he was using her.

"Bess, please let me explain."

"You are no better than the killers who took my father."

"It was a mistake. My mistake."

"And mine."

He reached for her, but she was too fast. He let his arm drop back to his side.

He hesitated. "I don't want to leave you here unprotected."

Her laugh held no humor. "I'd be safer with Nagi's children than with you. At least they have not yet killed one of my kind."

"Come with me."

She shook her head. "This is my home. I mean to take it back, but this time, I'll do it without you."

"Bess, please…"

"Get in your car, Cesar, and drive back to your world. I never want to see you again."

"No." He held his hands out before him as if offering himself. "Bess, I don't want to lose you."

"You already have."

Bess pressed her hand to her chest, summoning

the power which roared through her. A moment later she was high in the tree branches, looking down on the tiny man beside the blue car. He stood with his hand across his eyes like a visor, staring up at her. Then he was gone.

Such an easy matter to leave him behind, but she feared forgetting him would be harder. She could not trust this Spirit Child. Now she would turn to her own kind.

Bess headed for Nicholas's place in Montana. If she were to have help fighting Nagi's children, that was the place to start. Hopefully his new Niyanoka bride had not settled him too much, for if anyone liked a hunt, it was a wolf.

Nagi, ruler of the Circle of Ghosts, stood in the center of the revolving whirlwind of souls unworthy to enter the Spirit World. Now and then a white wisp of a soul leaped upward, like smoke caught in the draft of a fireplace flume. These were the ones redeemed by the prayers of the living.

But no matter, enrollment always exceeded attrition and his Circle only increased in size. He watched the arriving souls drop from the Spirit Road, like comets, their light extinguished upon reaching the slow treadmill of his world. They called to him for mercy, of course, but he had none to give. If he had to be here, they had to be here. He cared nothing for their suffering.

But one soul was persistent; she called that she knew him, that she had done as he asked and carried his children at the cost of her life. Nagi summoned her from the Circle, permitting her a moment of rest as the others swept endlessly on. He recalled her now, a strong soul, very dark and past redemption when he had found her in the living world.

"What is it you say?" he hissed.

He could have sworn that she thought, *They live*.

Nagi had planned to check back on the three dozen or so females whom he had chosen to carry his seed. But it had only been a few months. That was not long enough for such plantings to bear fruit. Was it? Time was so different here than on the earthly plane, but was it possible he had lost track?

He looked at the soul, a woman who he had found in prison for arson. She was strong and willing and so he had taken a small part of himself and planted it in her womb.

He read her next thought clearly. *Twins*.

The elation lifted him from the center of his Circle. The soul cried out for mercy, but he swept her back with the others. She would serve her sentence like the rest, while he would see his children. How many where there? Would they know him on sight?

Nagi swept past Hihankara, the old crone who judged each soul that crossed on the Spirit Road and who threw the unworthy ones down into his perpetual Circle.

She noted his passing as she always did. How a creature as old as she was could see so perfectly in the dark was beyond him. But she was immortal, just like him. He did not like her and she did not trust him.

He soared past her, making her duck. She threw her shock wave after him, the one that cast even the most tenacious souls from her path, but it did no more thangive him a pleasant sensation of cool. Not even the old crone could spoil his mood.

They lived.

Nagi was elated at at his success. His seeds had born fruit, growing into a living creatures, with physical bodies. They would grow and be his army and he might yet rule two worlds, that of the condemned souls and that of the living world. Nagi needed to see his offspring, now. So he swept through the veil dividing the Spirit realm from the living world.

Bess flew low over the tree line and out across open fields beneath cloudy skies in the late afternoon. This part of Montana had not received notice

that spring had arrived, judging from the frost forming on the blades of grass along the fence where five
horses grazed in bucolic bliss.

Bess tilted her wings and glanced at the ranch be-
longing to Nick Chien and a Dream Walker named
Jessie Healy. It so resembled Jessie's old home it
took a moment to recall that after the battle, Nicholas and Jessie could not return to her home for fear
Nagi would find them again and that this was a new
location. The grass remained yellowish with no sign
of new growth, looking much the same as it had in
the fall when last she visited. Despite appearances,
much had changed since then.

Her old friend and once lover had finally found
his alpha female. Funny, really, because after he'd
looked among all the Skinwalkers, he'd decided he
was destined to be a lone wolf. And then he'd fallen,
mortally wounded, into the hands of an enemy. And
instead of killing him, she had healed him.

Bess was happy for him. Admittedly, what she
and Nick had shared had been more of a cry against
the loneliness than a love affair. He sought her out
twice and she had come to him once. The mating had been physically satisfying and emotion-
ally upsetting. It had strained their friendship and
that tension remained. The momentary comfort was
not worth losing a friend like Nick. She was most

sorry for that and for telling Jessie about their past. It wouldn't make for a warm welcome.

Bess landed on the roof of the barn and looked down on the horses foraging in the pasture at the already scoured grass. With the winter still frosting their breath, the mares retained their thick, shaggy coats.

Across the road lay Nick's new home. Evening stole the colors, making the cheery yellow planking seem more ghostly white. The windows glowed golden and from time to time Nick or Jessie crossed before the kitchen window. Jessie paused at the sink and Nick stepped behind her, pinning her to the counter as he enfolded her in his arms.

Bess felt a stabbing surge of jealousy squeezing her heart, but not over losing Nick. What then?

The realization crept slowly over her as lightly as the tread of a mouse. Not jealousy, envy. She coveted what they shared, the easy camaraderie, the tender affection, the hope of many days and nights of true and lasting love. Did they know how blessed they were?

She folded her wings and nestled in to wait as the twilight crept toward evening. At last, Jessie left the house to see to her horses. They followed her eagerly along the fence, heads bobbing, hungry for grain. Bess flitted to the house. She found Nick in the garage, the door open and the lights on as he fiddled beneath the hood of a battered blue pickup. She shook her head in disgust that he would waste his time on this. It was as if she didn't even know him now.

She landed behind his truck, just outside of the circle of artificial light cast by the overhead bulb.

Before she even transformed, his head popped up as he scented the air. He had the ability to track anything that moved and so she was not surprised that his acute senses alerted him instantly to her arrival.

"Bess?" he called softly.

She stepped into the light of the garage.

"Please tell me that your silver Ferrari is in the shop."

"Sold it."

He rounded the fender, wiping his hands, that big, charming smile on his handsome face and his crystal blue eyes dancing with joy. Why couldn't she love him the way Jessie did? He, at least, was of her own kind.

He hugged her tight, like a brother, and set her aside to look down at her face. "This is a wonderful surprise."

"Not so wonderful," she said, unable to muster a

smile. She felt sad suddenly to realize that not only was he over her, but she was also over him.

He grew worried. "Sebastian and Michaela?"

"Safe. I do not contact them as I never know if the ghosts of Nagi are about. I will not make that mistake again."

"You could fly to the Spirit Road and then to Sebastian as you once did."

"If necessary. But I did not want to disturb them. They have young to raise."

Nick gave her a funny sort of grin, filled with a giddy pleasure she did not understand. It made him look different.

"Come into the house. Let me tell Jessie you're here."

He started toward the door which led inside, but she placed a hand on his forearm, staying him. "I would speak to you alone."

Nick's smile vanished. His somber expression was familiar now. This was the Nick she remembered—cautious, driven and solitary.

He shook his head. "No."

"But—"

"Whatever it is, you'll have to tell me and Jessie together."

Bess didn't like it. There was no love lost between her and the Dream Walker. But she knew that

Nick would not relent. He never did. It was one of many reasons they didn't suit—they were both too damn stubborn, like two old donkeys.

She sighed, not liking her options. "All right, then."

Nick brightened again, like the sun passing out from behind a cloud. "Jessie will be so happy to see you."

Bess knew otherwise but fixed a smile on her face. "Surprised, you mean."

"That, too."

He led the way. Bess felt overdressed in her long-sleeved suit with the knife-slit skirt, so she added a jacket with banded peak lapels and matching cuff details as they crossed the road to the barn. She refused to give up her sequined platform ankle boots despite the uneven ground.

She let Nick draw ahead of her, giving him a moment to announce her arrival before she disrupted their domestic bliss. Nothing like an old flame to put the kibosh on new love. If it came to that, she'd leave, because she cared for Nick too much to cause him such trouble.

She heard Jessie's voice, louder than Nick's murmur.

"What? Here? What's happened?"

Nick's murmur again and then Bess stepped into

the barn. Jessie exited one of the stalls, dressed in her perpetual attire of faded denim and polar fleece, now dotted with bits of hay. Her lovely long hair was pulled back severely into a ponytail, but instead of being unflattering, the style only accentuated the perfect oval of her face and made her honey-colored eyes look even larger.

Bess had been barely civil to Jessie when the Dream Walker had sheltered Nick after the grievous injuries he suffered at the hands of three humans possessed by Nagi's ghosts. The Thunderbirds had carried him to Jessie. Nick first feared the Thunderbirds had brought him to his enemy for a quick death. But the immortals must have known that he and Jessie shared the fabled soul-mate connection.

In any case, Bess had received Nicholas's distress call and found him here. When Jessie refused to let Bess take him, she had taunted that the Dream Walker would never keep him. Damn if the little Spirit Child hadn't done just that, but at the cost of being banished by her kind. Bess admired Jessie's inner strength, but she still thought she could kick the Dream Walker's ass in a fight.

Bess was certain she would be as welcome in Jessie's home as a falling hornet's nest. She waited as Jessie removed her worn leather gloves and set them aside. Then she opened her arms to Bess.

"Welcome back."

Bess glanced at Nicholas for some confirmation that his girlfriend was not planning to stick a shiv in her ribs. But he only smiled and waited as Jessie embraced her, pressing her soft cheek briefly to Bess's. This was only the second Spirit Child she had ever touched. The other was Cesar and the connection with Jessie held none of the zip of energy. In addition, she could not read Jessie's mood through the brief contact. With Cesar, one touch and she knew exactly what he was feeling, for she felt it herself.

Bess gave Jessie an awkward pat on both shoulders and then Jessie drew back.

"Nick didn't tell me you were coming."

"Because he didn't know."

It had been nearly four months since they had faced Nagi's ghost at the ranch outside of Bozeman, a fight they would have lost if Bess had not delivered her message bringing the Seer of Souls to their aid.

"Come inside. The temperature drops at night like a stone tossed down a well. I swear it feels more like December than April."

She and Nicholas exchanged a look over Jessie's head for they did not feel the cold the way humans and Niyanoka did. Bess had her feathers and he his fine wolf skin that protected them no matter their form.

Nicholas linked arms with Jessie. Bess trailed the couple, noting the way Nick needed to touch the Dream Walker, briefly as they left the barn, taking her hand to assist her through the dark. Nicholas's night vision surpassed Bess's and far surpassed the Dream Walker's, but the night was not so black as to blind the woman. Still, Nicholas did not release Jessie until they entered the house. He'd never done that with her. But Cesar did.

Stop thinking about him. He's a killer, like all Niyanoka.

Bess looked at Jessie, staring up at Nick, her aura glowing a soft, pale pink. She loved him. There was no question that these two enemies had somehow overcome their differences. But Jessie had never killed one of his pack and Nick had never fought against her people.

Did Jessie know who Nick's father was? Bess was sure that would be a deal breaker. She determined not to say a word, for she was happy for what Nick had found.

"Have you eaten? I have some stew in the Crock-Pot and a batch of corn bread."

Bess thought this was a joke and smiled. The Nick she knew ate in the finest restaurants in New

York, L.A. and London. He was the CEO of a land reclamation foundation and ran one of the largest "green" stock funds on the S&P. He didn't eat corn bread or anything that came out of a Crock-Pot.

But Nick gave her a look over Jessie's head that warned her to silence. Bess's smile faltered. Who was this guy and what had he done with Nicholas?

"Ah, that sounds…lovely."

Nicholas flashed her a grin and Bess was mildly surprised that his approval did nothing for her.

Damn Cesar.

"Great."

Plates clattered and silverware was slid into place. She accepted a drink of red grapefruit juice as Nick poured himself two fingers of bourbon. Thank the Great Spirit some things hadn't changed completely.

Jessie sat beside Nick and folded her hands on the table. The emerald-cut diamond on her left hand caught the light and flashed.

"Oh," said Bess, motioning to the ring. "Congratulations."

Jesse admired the ring briefly and then grinned at Nick.

"Thanks. We're very excited."

Then Jessie proceeded to chatter about the farm, the horses, the hay, the raccoons that had been steal-

ing the grain but had now all inexplicably disappeared. Bess looked to Nicholas, quite certain she
knew what the wolf had done with those pests, but
he didn't look up from his meal. When Bess had
finished her supper, Nicholas looked at Jessie, who
nodded her approval.

"So, what's up?" he asked.

Bess faced Nick and filled him in on the killings.

"Nicholas, I went to the Spirit World to speak to
the mothers," Bess continued. "There are two sets
of twins that I know of, but perhaps more. I'm not
certain how many more."

"What did you find out?" Nicholas sat stiffly,
with his fists bunched at each side of his bowl, bracing as if he already suspected the answer.

"Nagi is the father."

Chapter 15

"But how?" cried Jessie.

"Not possible," said Nicholas, his denial sounding not nearly as positive as Bess would have liked. He and Jessie exchanged looks.

"What do we do?" Jessie asked.

Nicholas's eyes flashed, reflecting the power and strength of his wolf self. Bess would not want to face him in battle, for he was a skilled fighter, like his father had been.

"Tell me what they look like."

She did. And then she told him about Cesar's unwillingness to hunt and kill them when they were still vulnerable.

Jessie touched Nicholas's arm and he stared at

her. She did not speak, but Nicholas nodded and then turned to Bess.

The silent exchange sent a chill down Bess's back. What was happening between these two?

It was Nicholas who spoke. "What kind of Niyanoka found the body?"

"His name is Cesar and—"

"Cesar? Cesar Garza?" Jessie interrupted, her face reflected alarm.

Nick's hand brushed Jessie's and a moment later he did a double take. Finally he shifted his ice-blue eyes back to Bess. She shivered, realizing she was witnessing the connection they had, the communication that required no words at all for perfect understanding.

"What is his gift?" he asked.

"He is a Soul Whisperer," said Bess.

Jessie cringed and instantly broke eye contact. So this was the reaction of one of his own people, the response that Cesar endured at each meeting. No wonder he was alone.

The Dream Walker fell back in her chair. "I know of him. All my people know him. He's…I'm not sure what to call him, legendary. No, that's wrong, infamous would be more accurate."

The uneasiness was back, causing Bess's stomach

to clench and her muscles to twitch. Was it worse than she'd imagined? "Why?"

"Because he worked with a famous Mind Walker, a clairvoyant named Robert Winter Elk. Winter Elk was the best known lawman my people ever had, and we were shocked when he chose a Soul Whisperer for a partner."

"What's so shocking?" asked Bess.

"They're unclean," said Jessie, as if this were the most obvious thing in the world.

Bess leaned forward, palms flat on the polished oak table. "Like Skinwalkers?"

Jessie shifted in her seat. "It's different. They speak to the dead."

Bess lifted both her brows. "While I...oh, wait, I speak to the dead, as well."

Jessie glanced to Nick for rescue and one look told Bess he'd side with her.

"Calm down, Bess," said Nicholas. His words were innocent, but his tone held a definite threat.

How dare he side with a Niyanoka over his own kind? But Jessie was his mate now. Of course he would defend her to the death, if necessary.

Bess stood and Nicholas followed. Bess considered her options—leave or keep a civil tongue. She didn't like either choice.

"Do you want to hear this or not?" he asked.

She glowered at him, her pride warring with her need to know. "I want to hear."

He pointed at the chair she had vacated. She sat, but he did not, choosing instead to flank his little Dream Walker like a bodyguard.

Jessie glanced to Nicholas, who nodded. She drew a breath and then continued.

"At the time, my people thought Winter Elk's choice was mad, but he insisted that only a man with such a power could be certain justice was done. After all, he told the communities, he could only read the minds of the living, but Cesar could read the minds of the dead. With him at Winter Elk's side, no murder would go unsolved. After Garza became Winter Elk's partner, Cesar was not accepted, but he was permitted at public gatherings, something previously unheard-of. Before that, a Soul Whisperer could not work in law enforcement. Generally there is only one born per century and it is a great misfortune to their family."

Bess felt outraged on Cesar's behalf and opened her mouth, glanced at Nicholas's scowling face and closed it again.

"By tradition, a Whisperer is called to discover how a loved one died. It is their lot to bring grieving families their loved ones' last thoughts. But some do not want a Soul Whisperer to touch their departed. Some say they bring bad luck." She glanced to Nick. "No one in my family has ever called upon a Whisperer. Their gift is very bad, dangerous and thought to bring ghosts, so only desperate people ever call one. It is equivalent to inviting a devil into your home."

"A devil?" said Bess.

Jessie nodded gravely. Bess did not know whether to laugh or scream. She held her body rigid and clamped her jaw, squeezing the muscles that locked her teeth together. It prevented her from verbally attacking Jessie. She had never heard such rubbish and the outrage on Cesar's behalf burned her stomach. These Niyanoka, with their grand academies and written laws, were as superstitious as humans.

After a moment, Bess trusted herself to speak, though her voice still shook.

"So why is Cesar infamous?"

The Dream Walker rubbed a hand across her forehead and then blew out a breath before continuing.

"I'm not sure where to start. Winter Elk used his gifts to look into the thoughts of the accused. It is impossible to lie to a Mind Walker, for they know the truth. So he could tell instantly who was guilty and who was innocent. His invulnerability was the reason it was so difficult to believe what happened next. It is my opinion and that of a few others that Garza might have felt obligated to Winter Elk for raising him above his station. And they had the permission of the Council of Elders."

Bess could not restrain the low rumble in her throat, frustrated at this babble.

"Together, they identified the killers, Winter Elk by speaking to possible suspects and Garza by touching the dead." She shivered. "Winter Elk was lead investigator after the war. Many of the other Peacekeepers, their superiors, disapproved of his choice of partners, but he would not take another Mind Walker, defending Garza when no one else would. Only his position and the years of dedicated service enabled him to do something so unconventional. It was only afterward that the true reason for his choice came to light. Winter Elk was put in charge of pursuing the war criminals among the Skinwalkers, their leaders and the ones who committed the worst atrocities. He was very effective."

Bess felt her face growing hot as she listened to this little Dream Walker speak of atrocities, while recalling the men who came for her father. Her stomach shriveled to a hard angry knot.

Nicholas placed a hand on Jessie's shoulder. She turned to him, the question on her face. Then her jaw dropped open and her ears turned pink.

Nicholas's expression was grim and he seemed to speak largely for Bess's benefit.

"Bess lost her father after the war. He was killed by a Niyanoka."

Jessie squirmed in her seat. "I'm so sorry."

The silence grew deafening. At last Nicholas squeezed Jessie's shoulder.

"Tell her the rest."

Jessie wet her lips. When she spoke again she hurried as if racing to get it all out. "Winter Elk told Garza which Skinwalkers were guilty and which were innocent. No Skinwalkers were taken alive."

Nicholas spoke. "It is not our way to be taken captive. We fight to the death."

"Cesar killed them?" Bess asked.

"Winter Elk did the killing after supposedly confirming their guilt. But Cesar helped track them." Jessie rubbed her hand over her forearm as if suddenly cold.

Jessie placed a hand over Nicholas's, which still lay on her shoulder and the hard lines about his mouth softened. Somehow, with just a touch, she soothed him.

"They were a very successful team. Garza followed Winter Elk's orders without question. But when Garza shot a mountain lion-Skinwalker on his partner's orders, things changed. The lion wasn't dead and Garza wanted to bring it in. But Winter Elk finished it. Something about the, uh, unfortunate event made Garza suspicious and he read the lion. He later testified to the Council that he had never touched a Skinwalker's corpse before, but he was able to read it, despite, uh, despite it being of a different race."

Bess held back a snort of disapproval.

"He reported at the trial that he knew at first contact that Winter Elk had lied. They had killed an innocent creature who had taken no part in the war."

"Did they lock Winter Elk up or give him a medal?" asked Bess.

Jessie flushed, making Bess wonder if there was hope for her yet.

"Garza confronted Winter Elk. He testified that he tried to convince his partner to turn himself in to the Council, but Winter Elk drew his weapon and shot Garza. All the evidence confirmed the Whisperer's story that he discharged his weapon only after Winter Elk shot him, firing in self-defense. Garza lived. Winter Elk died."

"Garza killed his partner," Bess said.

Jessie nodded, solemn as a priest giving last rites.

Bess tried to imagine Cesar, betrayed by his partner, bleeding and still trying to do the right thing. She recalled the scar under his collarbone, close to the sternum, the one he wouldn't speak of. It was the bullet shot from his partner's gun.

Cesar had been tricked by his own kind into hunting Skinwalkers. His fault was believing the word of a man he trusted. How did he feel knowing that the only man who ever treated him as an equal had really only used him?

Bess suddenly felt numb from all she had heard.

"He shot in self-defense," Bess muttered. "And he didn't know about the lion because his partner lied to him."

"Yes. He was exonerated but…"

Bess's eyes flashed fire as she vowed retribution for what had been done to Cesar.

Nicholas bared his teeth. "You are in my home territory, Bess."

She lifted a hand in surrender as she realized Nicholas had seen a threat and acted. Still Bess ached for someone to blame and then she found the culprit, the one who had flown to conclusions and refused to listen.

She had judged Cesar without giving him a chance to explain.

Jessie continued on, her voice low as if ashamed of what she must say next. "Garza lost his position with the law enforcement. I understand he works with humans now, solving their murders and the like. I have to tell you this, Bess, even though it's hard. There were many in our community who did not approve of Cesar's actions. They called him a turncoat and a traitor. They did not blame Winter Elk, in fact, many applauded him for killing Skinwalkers, regardless of their guilt or innocence. It was after the war and many thought…" She glanced at Nicholas, her eyes begging for forgiveness. "Many thought that he only did what most wished to do, kill a creature they considered to be a dangerous animal."

"This does not surprise me," said Bess.

Jessie's head hung. "Well, it shames me. As does the fact that there were some who called for Garza's banishment. He was not banished, not officially, at least."

"But he's an outcast?" asked Nicholas.

"Yes, worse than before."

Bess said, "He spoke to some Council about the new Halflings."

"His District Council?" asked Jessie.

"He mentioned me and that put an end to all discussion."

Jessie's eyebrows lifted.

Bess wondered about the Spirit Child that Cesar had killed. Shooting a fellow was a grave matter among Niyanoka, but Winter Elk had earned his death many times over and she hoped he walked in the Circle of Ghosts for eternity. A moment later she had an unsettling thought.

"Do you have an image of his partner?" Bess asked.

Jessie furrowed her brow. "I can get one, yes."

The Dream Walker retrieved her laptop as Nicholas cleared away Jessie's place setting. She set the computer in the empty space and booted up, then entered a secure site.

"This is our news source, though I've come to discover that it is highly censored. Our fight with Nagi's ghosts wasn't even mentioned. I hope it is only that they do not wish to cause panic among our kind or perhaps—"

Nick interrupted. "Maybe now isn't the time."

Jessie gave herself a little shake. "Oh, of course. Well." She clicked some keys, then waited. A moment later she spun the laptop toward Bess. "That's him."

Bess stared at the image in silence. All the blood seemed to sink to her feet. Her skin felt cold and tingly. The room disappeared until she could see nothing but the image of the face she had vowed never to forget.

Someone was shaking her. She blinked up to see

Nicholas's face before her. He released her shoulder and she could hear him now, his voice sharp.

"Bess, what?"

She pointed at the photo of the man who had haunted her dreams for nearly a century. "He's the one who came for my father."

Nicholas's expression grew deadly. He knew how her father met his end and Bess thought he felt partly responsible, since it was Nicholas's father who began the war that triggered the hunts following the Inanoka defeat.

"That means," said Nicholas, "this Soul Whisperer has avenged your father's death."

Bess tried to take it all in. She rested an elbow on the table and a hand on her forehead as her vision swam. Dizzy. Nauseous. Bewildered. The search she had made her life's mission was over. What should she do now? It felt as if she was flying through the darkest night, blind, exhausted and could find no place to land.

Winter Elk had killed her father and Cesar had shot Winter Elk. Bess waited for the rush of satisfaction from the knowledge that justice had been done. Instead she felt hollow as a pumpkin after Halloween. She had searched her entire lifetime for a dead man.

Her insides burned with an arctic cold, the kind

that bites the bones and freezes the blood. She began to shake. Her trembling brought Jessie to her feet. A moment later she draped a crocheted blanket about Bess's shoulders and offered a quick hug.

Bess lifted her face to look at them, standing side by side.

"He can't hurt anyone else," said Nicholas.

"That's right," said Jessie.

Bess opened her mouth but could not find her voice.

Jessie clicked her laptop closed, removing the image from Bess's sight. "To my knowledge, Cesar Garza only assists in difficult investigations, cases that would be unsolvable without his gifts. Because of Garza, the hunting of Skinwalkers ceased."

Bess needed to find some reason to reject him, for if she did not, then what would happen to her? She had always been the Niyanoka's strongest detractor. She was the one who would never let bygones be bygones. If she let go of her hatred for Cesar's kind, what would she have left?

She stared at Nicholas, standing beside his mate. Could Bess be like him? No. She could not, for she was not like him. It did not matter that Winter Elk was dead when there were so many, just like him, to take his place.

"Garza is hunting the children of Nagi."

Bess saw the shock register on Jessie's face as her mouth dropped open in surprise. Beside her, Nicholas's complexion grew dangerous and dark.

"Hunting?" asked Jessie.

It was on Bess's tongue to say that Cesar meant to kill them when she paused at the recognition that, like Jessie, Cesar had urged caution.

Bess was the one who called for the extermination of a race.

The floor dropped out from under her. Had she not been sitting she would have fallen. Instead she tilted as the world seemed to stop on its axis.

She was just like Winter Elk.

Bess rose in horror and staggered, before Nicholas caught her, setting her right, dragging the chair behind her and pushing her back into it.

"Bess? What's wrong?"

She judged without evidence. Was prepared to track and kill these creatures, solely because they were born of Nagi. She was no different than the vigilantes. And she would not listen when Cesar tried to explain. Why hadn't she given him the chance to explain?

But she knew and it shamed her. She needed Cesar to be guilty. If he was just like the rest of them, she wouldn't have to face the fact that she had fallen in love with him.

Bess pressed her hands to her burning cheeks. "I've made a terrible mistake."

Chapter 16

Jessie told Nick to give them some privacy as she led Bess to the living room, seating them side by side on the big, comfortable, broken-down sofa.

"I don't think he'll forgive me," she whispered.

Jessie wrapped an arm about Bess, drawing her in. Bess had not been kind to Jessie and still the Dream Child showed graciousness and love. It broke Bess's defenses. A sob bubbled up in her throat, choking off her air until she released it in a long, low cry of agony. She had fallen in love with an enemy. Bess wept.

For a time Jessie rocked her slowly as Bess sobbed. Since the change Bess could no longer produce tears, so her weeping was a dry, hoarse heaving that shamed and embarrassed her. Without tears, her pain burned like dry ice in her throat and it took some time to recover her voice.

"I'm so afraid," she whispered. "I've never felt like this with anyone and when he touches me, I swear I can feel what he is feeling."

Jessie drew back, her expression incredulous. "Do you mean you know what he is feeling?"

Bess shook her head, the prickling unease creeping up the skin of her arms and reaching the hairs of her neck. "I experience it as if it was my own emotion."

Jessie's face grew pale. "Can you hear his thoughts?"

Bess stilled, recalling when she knew that Cesar thought she made love like an animal. "Why?"

"Sebastian could read Michaela's thoughts from the beginning, but she couldn't read his until after her powers came. But for both Nick and I, it was just feeling the emotions at first, his pain when he was injured and our pleasure." Jessie flushed, her face and neck turning pink.

"What are you saying?" asked Bess, drawing back and pinning her gaze on Jessie, who now shifted uncomfortably and glanced toward the door as if wishing Nicholas had not left them as she had requested.

"Nick?" she called toward the kitchen.

Jessie gave one more anxious glance toward the empty doorway and then gave up, turning back to her guest. All her dithering made Bess more anxious.

"Tell me," she insisted.

"Bess, I think, that is, I believe the connection you two are experiencing is called the soul-mate bond."

She sucked in her breath as if Jessie had slapped her and was on her feet a moment later, searching for an open window or door. This could not be.

"No. Impossible."

"Then how do you explain it?"

"I can't but it is not possible that I should be linked to a Niyanoka." She turned to Jessie. "Don't you understand? The Niyanoka killed my father. Cesar's *partner* killed him."

"And Nick's father killed my grandparents and uncle. Perhaps that is exactly why we are connected, to make up for what happened to our families in the past."

Bess stared in shock. Nicholas had told Jessie, revealed the part of himself that shamed him most deeply and still she loved him.

Bess covered her eyes. "No. It can't be. I can't."

Nicholas's voice came from the other side of the room. "Jessie?"

His Dream Walker tried to make her movements relaxed, but Bess noted the haste with which she went to him and the relief in her face at his appearance.

"What?" he asked Bess.

"Your woman thinks that Cesar is my soul mate."

Nicholas's eyes widened and he looked to Jessie for confirmation, as if not trusting Bess to tell him the truth. Jessie's nod was barely perceptible.

"My woman is also my fiancée and you will not use this tone of voice here."

Bess fumed.

"Why do you choose to believe her over one of your own race?"

"Because she is calm and thoughtful and you are acting crazy." He drew Jessie to his side, holding her as if she were an extension of his own body. "This is my mate and I love her."

She looked at Nicholas, her eyes beseeching. "Nicholas, what if it's true?"

"You'll accept it."

"Can I do something to break it? Anything?"

He shook his head. "Bess, when I discovered our bond I was just as torn. So I know you think this is the worst thing that could happen, but you have to trust me. It's not."

"Oh, please don't tell me that this will all work out."

"But it can," said Jessie. "With him you have a chance for true love and happiness."

Not if he won't take me back, she thought.

Nagi swept through the old-growth forest, searching for his children. As he billowed along, he glowed with both pride and anticipation. He had done it, created living children, the first of a new Halfling race, combining his power with human flesh. The prospect was so new and so full of promise he tingled with hope as his mind raced with possibilities. Would they recognize him instantly and rush to him or would they fall in awe at his feet? He would teach them how to be mighty, but what exactly should he say?

He knew Niyan, the prissy guardian of man, had composed a wordy book for his people, while Tob Tob, always lazy and more informal, had gathered his first children and told them the law, which was passed from one generation to the next. But some of Tob Tob's instructions must have been lost, because he seriously doubted that he had ever told his children to exterminate the human race to protect The

Balance. Yet that was how Fleetfoot had interpreted Tob Tob's teaching in the edict beginning the war.

Nagi caught the scent of fresh blood and headed in that direction, spotting the carcass of a mule deer. He had only paused an instant when he heard the snarling and snapping. He looked in the direction of the disturbance and saw them.

There was no mistaking the pair—twins. They had his lovely eyes and their coloring matched his. But there the resemblance ended.

His smile faded as he noticed the strange pointed ears that resembled a wolf's. Their bodies were mostly hairless except for the strange thick silver-blond threads upon their heads.

His offspring hesitated, drawing up to stare at him, an odd expression of bewilderment wrinkling their new tender living skin.

The female was already developing breasts and both had a nest of curling silver-blond hair at their sex. How could they grow so quickly when they were said to be less than a month old?

The female snarled, showing a hideous mouthful of spiny teeth that reminded him of a barracuda. She hissed and snapped while the male remained immobile. She tugged at him, trying to urge him forward, but he moved only to try to haul her in the opposite direction. They tumbled over each other, wrestling, kicking and biting like two vicious little animals. The female, clamped her teeth onto the male's ear, triggering her release. He growled at her and then retreated behind the closest tree trunk. Nagi billowed in displeasure at the cowardly display by his offspring. This was not how he had pictured their first meeting.

His offspring were not handsome as he had hoped and seemed wild as wolves. The female remained where she was, on her hind legs now, her arms before her and her hands relaxed, but showing the vicious-looking claws that would have made a grizzly bear tremble.

He moved forward, past the carcass and closer to his little girl, extending his appendages in greeting.

"I'm your father, little one. I've come to teach you your place in this world."

She showed her fangs in a hideous smile and then ran full speed in his direction. It was another moment before he recognized that she was not rushing into his arms in greeting but attacking him. He was so appalled, he made no effort to defend or evade, but stared in shock. Fortunately his body was so ethereal that she simply darted right through him, falling over the deer. There she turned, placing herself between the kill and him. She slashed at the air, growling and barking like a dog.

Nagi was horrified at this wild thing he had sired. It seemed to have no intelligence or understanding and acted as the merest brute. Hideous, he thought as he slid away. One was a vicious little killer and the other a sniveling little coward.

Nagi did not remain long with his dreadful progeny, but slunk away. What was he to do with them if they would not obey? He had not anticipated that they would be unable to comprehend him or fail to fall gratefully before him to absorb his teachings. It was a problem.

And it could become much worse if the other Spirits discovered what he had done. He recalled that Tob Tob was the first to sire Halflings and the first to receive his directive to take charge of them.

Nagi had anticipated the process of instructing his creations, but now that he had seen them, he wanted nothing to do with them. Thank the Great Spirit they were mortal and would eventually die.

He stilled. They would die and walk the Way of Souls and their souls would be judged by Hihankara. The old crone would know instantly what they were. Nagi turned back toward the twins, then stopped. If he killed them they would arrive sooner, rather than later. But if they lived, they might breed. His dozen or so twins could multiply like the little animals they were.

He was about to abandon them when he sensed another powerful entity approaching. No, not approaching, hunting. A Niyanoka came this way. Nagi read his thoughts. He was tracking the blood trail of the deer, hoping to find Nagi's children.

A moment earlier Nagi had been ready to cut and run, but this Halfling threatened his brood and so he turned on instinct to defend his young.

Cesar found the deer, its neck stretched half over the walking path. Blood congealed beneath the body and clung to the fur. He paused at the edge of the trail. The thick carpet of ferns covered the rest of the body. Where were the flies?

Cesar glanced about. Something felt very wrong. Gone was the usual birdsong and the air grew still and fetid as the inside of a predator's den. His instincts kicked in and he began to back away. The last time he had faced Nagi's children he felt no sense of foreboding.

Then he saw movement. A head popped from the ferns to stare directly at him. The male, he realized, the one who had watched him before, but he was much larger already. He stared with his strange, glassy, unblinking bulbous yellow eyes. His ashy skin had grown more opalescent, almost the color of a morning fog and his hair grew thick and silver-blond in a shaggy mass that nearly reached his eyes. But his ears and wicked teeth still made him hideous in Cesar's opinion. Where was his sister?

As if summoned, he saw her just a few feet from her kill, her head down, her fangs bared. She did not seem to be watching him, but stared in the other direction. The hairs on Cesar's neck rose as he turned.

Before him, hovering several feet above the forest floor, billowed a gray mass that was roughly shaped like a man. Its eyes glowed yellow and round as the caution lights used by road crews at night and it focused on Cesar.

He did not need to ask who this was. He knew. This was no Skinwalker, not even a Supernatural. No, this was a true Spirit, the very first he had seen. Nagi. The collector of evil ghosts and the ruler of the Circle.

"Soul Whisperer."

The voice was a hissing, rasping sound that reminded him of a pneumonia patient gasping his last breath.

"You cannot even see souls, yet they call you this."

"Because my work helps find the evil ones who still live and sends them for justice."

"The justice of the living. But none escape *my*

justice. And you are not here to read a corpse but to create one." Nagi's voice held scorn.

"I'm trying to discover what they are."

"You already know. They are my children."

Cesar began backing up. Bess had been right.

Nagi's form began to shimmer, as if his body were a cloud blocking some unseen sun.

"You will not harm them, Soul Whisperer. Not you, not the raven."

Cesar raised his hands in surrender. No mortal could win a fight with a true Spirit.

"Death is coming. Do you sense them? My ghosts are hunting you both."

Cesar cocked his head, listening as he caught the sound of feet pounding along the ground. But you could not hear ghosts.

Ghosts were soundless, which meant that the things that were coming for him were alive. Human, but…possessed by Nagi's evil ghosts. Once possessed, the living creatures were slaves and would remained puppets until the ghosts chose to leave them, their host died or they were exorcised by the Seer of Souls.

He did not wait, but ran in the opposite direction, back down the trail that led to his car, praying as he charged through the undergrowth. *Please don't*

make me have to shoot innocent humans who are
being used by ghosts.

Nagi's voice trailed him, as if the Spirit sped along beside him. "Run and hide, Whisperer. Still they will find you and the raven. But fear not. If you have walked the Red Road, you will not join my Circle."

Cesar glanced back and saw three hikers, holding their long redwood walking sticks like clubs as they charged after him. He vaulted over the guardrail and hit the release for his driver-side door, gaining a few seconds as his attackers climbed over the obstacle.

He slipped into his car and hit the lock as the three reached him, pounding the hood, roof and driver's window. He started the car. The windshield cracked. Another blow and the windshield exploded but remained in place, a huge circular ring of shatterproof glass now held by only the film coating. He had his pistol, but he did not want to take the lives of innocents, so he threw the car into Reverse and gunned the engine.

Two of his attackers tumbled to the ground behind him, but the third clung to the hood. Cesar cranked the wheel, sending his final attacker careening from the hood and rolling along the parking area as he threw the car into Drive and raced from the lot.

Where was Bess? They were after her as well and he knew they would not stop until they found her or died trying.

Chapter 17

Bess left the Montana horse ranch and flew home, her thoughts a wide churning ocean of uncertainty. Could Cesar really be her soul mate?

Below her the patchwork of farm fields began to give way to the spine of the Rocky Mountains. If she flew hard and rested little she should reach him in four days.

As she flew, her anxiety grew and it took some time to recognize the warning that prickled her neck was different than her instinctive survival sense. Could she be picking up some danger directed at Cesar?

Bess called out her fear to the sky, hoping she was close enough for Tuff or some other of her people to hear her rising panic and be waiting when she arrived.

Bess pushed her tired wings to greater speed. What was happening to Cesar?

Cesar escaped the ghosts, but he knew that they were still out there, following Nagi's orders, pursuing him.

The Spirit had sent them the instant he perceived a threat to his offspring. Bess was right all along. They were the children of Nagi. Were they also the threat she believed?

What powers would they have?

He wanted to make contact with Nagi's Halflings, but did not want to risk meeting their sire or protectors again.

In the meantime there were three humans who were now possessed, trapped by the ghosts who inhabited them. To his knowledge, only the Seer of Souls could free them, but according to Bess, she was in hiding from Nagi.

Was there another way to free them, other than death?

He needed to speak to his Council about the ghosts and Nagi's misuse of men. He called Holly Black Hawk and told her what had happened. She seemed remarkably unsurprised.

"Keep this quiet. We don't want a panic. Leave it to the Council to handle the possessed men."

Cesar had a bad feeling but he agreed to do as she asked.

Over the next two days, he tried Bess's place several times and even risked returning to the forest where he had first met her, but he found no sign of her.

This morning, as he made his coffee, his cell phone rang and he snatched it up, glanced at the number and then released the breath he held in a frustrated blast. It was not her, but the liaison at the Council who coordinated which cases merited his special talents.

There had been a disturbing death at Fisherman's Wharf, and it wasn't long before he reached the crime scene.

On his way past the press and the bystanders, a man called to him.

"Detective Garza."

Cesar scanned the crowd, finally identifying the one who had spoken, by his stillness and the twin braids poking out from beneath a white straw cowboy hat.

"Tuff?"

Cesar motioned to the young officer on crowd control to let Tuff pass.

Cesar thumped him on the shoulder of his dusty denim shirt in greeting, feeling hopeful for the first time in days.

"I'm glad to see you," he said, and then had a dreadful, stomach-dropping thought. "Is Bess okay?"

Tuff's easy smile never faltered.

"Don't know. She sent out a distress call, but I can't pin down her location, so she must be traveling. The signal is getting stronger so she's close."

Cesar looked toward the sky.

"Hoped maybe you'd know where to find her," said Tuff.

Cesar almost repeated Bess's words that she never wanted to see him again, but he held back. Instead he shook his head. "She left."

"Well, she's headed back."

Could it be true? Cesar wanted to believe, but he also did not want his hopes dashed again.

He returned his attention to Tuff. "How did you find me?"

"You were leaving as I pulled up to your building. I followed you. Man, you drive a little crazy."

Cesar had been too preoccupied to consider someone might have been trying to follow him. He gave an apologetic grin and extended his hand.

"Thanks for coming."

Tuff looked at his offered hand and made him wait a moment before taking it. When the Skinwalker drew his hand back, wrinkles furrowed his brow.

"Your heart is hurting you."

Cesar guided Tuff past the young officer, now staring quizzically at them. There was nothing wrong with his heart. He was healthy as an ox.

"I think you got a bad signal. My heart's fine."

"Maybe heart isn't right. Maybe I should say that your soul is hurting you."

Cesar's sure step faltered and he came to a halt beside the Skinwalker.

"What do you mean?"

"I can feel emotional pain as well as physical. You feel like a man who has just lost someone in death, as if you are grieving a great loss."

Cesar did not want to explain to Tuff about the fight he and Bess had or how much more he missed her than he had any right to. But somehow it made sense that Tuff read his pain as mourning. Cesar feared he'd miss Bess for the rest of his life, but he was damned if he knew how to make her forgive him for something that was unforgivable. If he couldn't give himself absolution, how could he expect anyone else to?

"Hey, can you hang back here a little until I get the body read? Then we can go someplace private."

"I think we better wait for Bess. Her signal is strong and she's not injured, but she's jacked about something. Don't know what." He let that hang as if to ask if Cesar did.

"I'll be back. Anybody bothers you, just mention my name. Okay?"

Tuff nodded and then parked his butt on a yellow fireplug, gazing at the activity a few feet farther on. Cesar strode away, feeling better with the distance. That buffalo rattled him. Something about his calm and his perceptiveness put Cesar on edge. It was like dealing with Mind Walkers. There was no way to mask the truth, when they could snatch it from you with a touch.

Cesar's heart sank as he recognized the familiar scene. The body lay stretched out on the pier, beneath the bank of windows of a popular seafood restaurant. She had rolled to her back and lay in death, with legs splayed in a vain attempt to birth her babies. A third mother. If it was twins again that meant there were six Halflings now.

Why hadn't she gone to a hospital? Was that part of the directions Nagi had left with these women? The others had found a secluded spot in the forest. But here, on a busy stretch, there must have been witnesses. Why were the police not called until after it was too late?

Surely her screaming must have brought a crowd.

He looked at the now-familiar rupture in her abdomen. Cesar glanced around. Where were the twins?

They had been born here in plain sight and they'd be hungry. Great Spirit protect us, they might kill anyone here just to feed their voracious appetites.

Cesar didn't need to read the body, but he did and experienced the woman's death, just as he had with the two other mothers. This one believed that she carried the immaculately conceived child. Somehow, her confusion, mental instability, religious fervor and Nagi's suggestions had led her to believe that she carried the Lord's son.

He stood and looked back to where he had left Tuff.

"You done screwing up my crime scene?" said an unfamiliar voice.

Cesar glanced up at a man in a suit who stood, hands on hips, glaring. Had to be the lead on the case.

"Yeah, thanks."

"There are more of these?" asked the detective, pointing at the body.

Cesar nodded.

"Shit. We gotta find this guy."

Cesar stood. "Doing all we can."

The detective scowled. "Next time wear some gloves."

Cesar extended his hand. "We haven't met. I'm Garza."

He didn't take it.

"I know who you are. You're one of the SOBs with the Bureau. You guys took everything we got on these killings. Well, how about some reciprocity?"

He couldn't if he wanted to. Even the F.B.I. couldn't know what had actually happened here.

"You'll get my report."

This crime, like the other two, would go unsolved. How many more women had Nagi impregnated? And where were the newest twins?

Chapter 18

Bess saw the flashing lights of the police cars as she swept over the bay and into the city. The sheer number of units on the scene made her veer toward the pier on the chance that Cesar might be there. She could not explain the dread that held her heart, except that her instincts were good and they whispered to her of peril.

Instead of Cesar, she found Tuff, inside the police barricade, sitting on a fireplug as if he were waiting for a bus. She landed before him and he grinned.

"You are such a beauty, Bess. I hope you know how lovely your feathers are today. Each one shimmers like a rainbow of green and magenta. I heard your call from a long way away. My heart is glad to see you well."

She looked about. Officers came and went, photographers, various men in suits. There were far too many of them to give her the privacy she needed to speak or change to her human form without them seeing her.

"Cesar?" She chortled.

Tuff thumbed toward the end of the pier. "Over at the crime scene. He asked me to wait."

There seemed no emergency. Bess suddenly felt foolish.

"You could change in my truck, but I'm not sure we could get back inside here."

Bess was in the air an instant later, and soon spotted Cesar, who was stopped at the end of an alley and was staring at something she could not yet see. Had they killed someone? Had they finally crossed the invisible line that humans and Niyanoka drew between killing and murder?

She landed close behind him and glanced about, seeing only the deserted space between two large green Dumpsters to the right and a similar set of Dumpsters and refuge on the left. Bess quickly transformed, stilled for a moment by the zip of current that radiated through her body as she changed to her human form. An instant later she turned her feather cape into a black denim jacket, knit sheath top and trousers hemmed at her ankle since she elected flats instead of her usually elaborate footwear.

Cesar turned toward her, most likely drawn by the flash of bright light that accompanied her transformation.

"Bess!" His handsome smile lasted an instant to be replaced by a dipping of his brow as his gaze returned to the sound that had held him.

She now heard it, as well. Something was inside the Dumpster. Bess felt certain she knew what it was.

"The twins?" she asked.

He nodded. "I'm afraid so."

They turned in unison toward the thumping, tearing and scratching sounds. The black plastic lid flew up, revealing one small ash-gray creature swallowing the remains of a fish head. The yellow eyes scanned the ground before it and stopped on Cesar and Bess.

Tuff trotted out of the alley and skidded to a halt.

"Bess? What's…what in the wild world?" he said. "Is that what attacked you?"

"Not that one, but yes."

The creature gave a yowling cry and its twin popped up from the garbage, holding the red claw of a large lobster. Both the newborns remained where they were, still and watchful. Simultaneously, they began a low growl.

"Back up," said Cesar.

They all did. The growling ceased. Both of Nagi's newborns tumbled from the Dumpster and rolled onto their feet as nimble as acrobats. One stepped forward, the other back. It was the female again who approached in an aggressive mock charge, followed by an immediate retreat.

"They don't want us here," said Bess.

"Well, we can't leave them for the humans to find," said Cesar.

Tuff nodded. "Someone will see them."

The female sniffed the air, then huffed and began a series of rapid jaw snaps.

"She's hungry," said Bess.

"And afraid," said Cesar.

Bess grabbed Cesar's arm. "We've got them cornered. We need to give them a way to escape."

The female made another charge, trying to get past Cesar to Tuff. Cesar spread his arms like a basketball player and stepped between her and Tuff. The little female could not be more than two feet tall, yet it was trying to attack a full-grown human. But as Cesar moved, the female retreated again.

"Why didn't it attack me?" asked Cesar. "Why, Tuff?"

Bess and Tuff exchanged a knowing look, but it was Tuff who spoke.

"Maybe she smells buffalo."

Cesar took his eyes off the two little newborns, now huddled beside the open Dumpster yowling to each other like cats, recalling that the other twins had also attacked Bess and refrained from attacking him even when they had the opportunity.

"You think they recognize what you are?"

"Maybe," said Tuff. "Or maybe she just recognizes I'm not like you, because she only stopped when you stepped between us."

"Could they think I'm like them?" Cesar asked.

"They're not human," Bess reminded him. "And neither are you."

"Maybe they can see auras or scent the difference between us and humans."

He'd said "us" she realized, making no distinction between Niyanoka and Inanoka. Bess felt her heart squeeze in gratitude.

"You might be right," Bess said, nodding. "But I think they can tell the difference between our races."

Cesar flashed her a worried look. "I need you

both out of here. I might be able to communicate with them," he said.

"And they might kill you."

Tuff was already turning to go.

"Wait," said Cesar.

The two infants now huddled together, facing them, their big yellow eyes shining like twin moons, as they gave off little yips and chortles. Bess noticed that one of them had wet cheeks. Was it crying?

Cesar pulled out his cell phone and punched the buttons. "This is Special Agent Garza. I'm sending out a man. His name is Tuff. He's to bring my car to the alley between—" Cesar glanced up at the buildings and the restaurant names, printed on each rear door "—DiMondos and Gradies." He paused to listen. "Yeah, right away."

Cesar snapped the phone shut and dropped it in his front pocket. Then he turned to Tuff.

"Maybe we can get them out of here without the humans seeing them."

"Worth a try, I suppose," he said.

"Bess," said Cesar, "Go with him."

She kept her eyes on the dangerous things, feeling an odd mixture of empathy and envy at their tears. They were quite obviously frightened. Still she kept her head.

"The fear makes them more dangerous," she whispered.

"Then step out of sight, into the alley. You can still see me, but they can't see you."

She nodded her acceptance of this. Bess had only just found him and was not ready to lose him again.

"Remember they can fly," she said as she backed into the alley, worried she would be just a few steps too far away to defend him.

Tuff continued on, returning to the pier and then disappearing from her view.

Cesar dropped into a squat in the dirty alley and began to speak in low, soothing tones, extending his open hand to the little Halflings.

There was a howl as one of the twins charged Cesar. Bess rushed forward as Cesar staggered back. The black billowing cloud swept past him as the creature took flight.

She reached Cesar too late, but the twin did not strike. Instead it flapped around the space, enclosed on three sides, and then shot up and over the roof. The little male remained on the ground, hopping from one leg to another, reaching for the sky and howling.

Finally the arms dropped, the narrow shoulders sagged and its head sank forward so the pointed chin touched the smooth gray skin of its chest.

Cesar took a tentative step in the male's direction. It turned its head just enough to watch him approach, the wide unblinking eyes pinned on Cesar.

Cesar opened his arms, closing the distance to three feet. Bess held her breath, readying herself to launch at the thing with all she had if it so much as pointed a claw at him.

Instead it bent its knees and leaped like a tree frog, latching long, spindly legs about his waist and clasping skeletal hands behind his neck.

Bess stepped forward to drag it off, but it did not bare teeth to bite Cesar's exposed neck. Instead, it simply pressed against him, burying his face in beneath its own bony arm and Cesar's muscular chest.

She stopped her advance and stared, dumbstruck at the sight. This enemy was holding on to Cesar like any child in a parent's arms.

Behind her headlights flashed as the gray sedan pulled into the alley. Bess stepped aside to let Tuff pass.

"He wants to go to the forest," said Cesar.

"How do you know that?" she asked.

"I don't know. I just do."

"But you're not a Mind Walker."

"Perhaps it is not my gift but his."

Bess stared in wonder as she realized she knew nothing of these beings, their mission or powers.

Cesar walked toward the car as Tuff exited. "Hope the buffalo scent doesn't stir him up."

"He's hungry. You smell like food. He says you look like his mother, but you are not like her."

The male grasped Cesar's chin and turned his face to meet his stare.

"He says I'm not like her, either."

Bess took a step forward. The thing bared his teeth.

"He doesn't like you. Your scent is of the air, but also of the dead, like his mother."

"Is he talking about the Spirit World?" She turned to Tuff. "Do you smell death on me?"

Tuff shook his head.

"Maybe," said Cesar, "you should both follow me in Tuff's truck."

She didn't want to, for her instincts still hummed a warning. There was danger here, but the boy-child did not seem to be the cause. What then was making her instincts jangle like a ring of keys?

"We'll follow. But don't lose us."

Cesar sat in the car, holding the child of Nagi. After a few minutes of murmured conversation he managed to get the infant to release him, but the newborn then sank into the space between the passenger seat and the glove box, huddling and shivering as if he were freezing to death. Bess peered in.

"He's afraid," said Cesar.

"Can he understand your thoughts?" she asked.

"Not sure."

Bess straightened. "We'll follow you. Maybe you should cover him up until you get on the road."

"Yeah, good idea." He reached behind the seat and pulled out his trench coat, then draped it over the boy.

One little hand reached from beneath the shroud, his wicked claws puncturing the upholstery.

Cesar patted the tiny gray hand and then put the car into Reverse.

"I'm not sure about this," said Bess.

Tuff motioned at Cesar. "He is."

She and Tuff hurried back to his battered pickup and climbed in. Cesar passed them. Tuff followed.

"Are you getting any kind of a warning sign?" Bess asked.

"Besides yours?" He glanced at her then returned his attention to the street. "Nope."

The early-morning traffic was largely moving into the city so their ride from downtown to the bridge was relatively painless. Bess kept her attention on the empty space beside Cesar, half expecting his passenger to emerge.

He didn't. But Cesar did throw his coat over the seat when they had cleared the Golden Gate.

Bess stared at the rear end of Cesar's car.

"Wait a minute. That's not his car, is it?" She squinted. "I never noticed his plates, but the color is different. Isn't it?"

"I never saw *his* car before."

"I think it was navy. But that one is gray. Where's his car?"

"Maybe that's a cop car?" offered Tuff.

It was a long forty minutes to the state park and not the first time she wished she could carry a cell phone with her.

"You have a phone?" she asked.

Tuff shook his head.

They continued down the hill into the coastal valley where the giant redwoods grew amid the warm Pacific mist. Cesar returned to the same parking area where they had met, the trailhead for several nice hikes and one dead body.

Bess just wanted Cesar's passenger out of his car.

Cesar's brake lights had barely flicked off before Bess was out flinging open the rusty door and hopping from the truck.

Cesar stepped out of the car and held open his passenger-side door.

"Any trouble?" she asked.

"None."

"Why here?" she asked.

"He chose it." Cesar looked around.

She knew as well as he did that it was their responsibility to see that no humans discovered the existence of the Halfling races. But who was responsible for telling the little creature now huddled on the floor mat?

The tension in Cesar's jaw and the way his eyes darted from one spot to the next definitely put Bess on edge.

"What's wrong?"

"I had some trouble here yesterday."

Bess moved closer. "What kind of trouble?"

"I saw Nagi and two more Halflings."

"Nagi!" Bess now searched the shadows for anything that moved. "He knows that I know the Seer. This may be a trap to flush her out."

"It may be. So let's get him out of the car so we can go, before those ghosts come after me again."

Bess sucked in a breath. "What ghosts?"

Chapter 19

Something swooped in from the edge of Bess's peripheral vision and she ducked, thinking it was a ghost. She was already straightening when she remembered that ghosts could not be seen except by the Seer of Souls and the owl Skinwalkers.

The black billowing cloud landed on the roof of Cesar's new sedan, transforming into the female twin. She began to howl like a coyote and stamp her feet on the metal roof, her sharp claws causing such a racket that Bess clamped her hands over her ears.

Cesar still held open the passenger door, but now motioned them all to step back. After several minutes of howling and scratching the female dropped to the ground, placing the car between herself and them. She spotted her twin and began the yipping call they had used back in the city. The male at last crept from his hiding place beneath the dashboard.

The infants darted like deer beneath the guardrail and then stopped to stare at the three of them.

"What do you think they make of us?" asked Tuff.

"The female looks hungry," whispered Bess.

"And the male still seems frightened," added Cesar.

Bess shifted nervously. "I wish they'd go."

"Do you think they'll be all right?" Cesar asked.

She didn't know and she worried for them, but also worried that Nagi might appear. It seemed clear he was gathering his children.

Tuff opened the dented door of his pickup. "Want me to follow you or take off?"

"Take off," said Cesar at the same time Bess said, "Follow."

Tuff grinned until Bess said, "I still have that bad feeling."

The female was now tugging her twin by the arm, trying to get him to come with her, but he held on to the crossbeam of the wooden guardrail, whimpering. His eyes were on Cesar.

"What does he want?" asked Bess.

"Not sure. Help maybe."

"Or a parent," said Tuff.

Bess's jaw dropped as she stared from Tuff to Cesar. Was he right?

"They can hunt. They'll be fine," she said, more to herself than to the men.

"Babies need more than food," said Tuff.

"But unfortunately, *we're* the food," said Bess.

Tuff gave her a grim look, but didn't contradict her, which made her more worried.

Bess had no idea how to gather the little Half-lings or communicate with them even if she wanted to.

Cesar gave a sigh and then rubbed his hand over his mouth. "We better go, I guess. We're scaring the female."

That was obvious by the way she clacked her jaw, making her teeth gnash together as she gave a warning growl that would have made a German shepherd turn tail and run.

Help. Help. Danger now.

Bess heard the words as if they were spoken in her ear.

"What was that?" asked Bess.

The female had the male around the waist now and tugged as he clung to the rail with both hands.

"What was what?" asked Tuff.

Bess's neck prickled and she glanced around,

searching for the source of the voice, still trying to decide if it came from outside or inside her head. She spotted three hikers hurrying from the trailhead. "Great. Humans," she said.

She turned toward the three approaching men, noticing at first glance that something was not right with them. Their clothing was rumpled and bits of grass and moss clung to their disheveled hair. They looked as if they had spent the night sleeping in the woods without benefit of a tent or bedroll. They carried no gear except long walking sticks that appeared to be only redwood branches. They did not hold them as one would for walking but up before their chests as if they were clubs. They approached at a loping trot that was just short of a run.

Cesar stepped before her. "Get in the car."

"Why? What's wrong?" But even as she said the words she knew, because they were close enough for her to see their faces now. Their eyes were a ghostly yellow and their blank expressions looked as if they had been carved from wax. She had seen such men before, in Montana, at the fight between her friends and Nagi's ghosts.

Tuff must have noticed as well for he spoke under his breath. "Ghosts."

The twins now both began a chortling, crackling

sound that acted on Bess's ears like the collapse of sheet metal in a car wreck.

"Get to the car," Cesar ordered.

But none of them did. If it was to be a fight, Bess would stand beside Cesar and Tuff would stand with her.

The ghosts rushed at them with raised sticks. Bess dodged a blow that would surely have split her head open.

Cesar drew his service pistol and then sheathed it again. Of course he did not want to kill humans when it was his mission to protect them, even if they were trying to kill him.

When Bess had faced a similar fight the ghosts had been stopped only by the Seer of Souls.

This time they were on their own. So should they kill the humans or only disable them? It was certain by the swinging clubs that the ghosts did not face any such moral quandary.

Tuff nimbly dropped to the ground and used one foot to sweep the legs out from beneath his attacker.

"Try not to kill them," said Cesar.

The humans had done nothing to deserve death. They were merely the vessels the ghosts had taken.

Her attacker swung again and again she dodged, this time stepping behind him and kicking him in the ass with all she was worth. The blow sent him

sprawling. Tuff sat on his attacker, who flailed uselessly beneath him. Bess knew the guy would never
be able to dislodge a buffalo. Cesar had cuffed his
attacker's hands behind the man's back and the possessed man writhed uselessly on the ground. Cesar
grasped the ankle of the human who swung his
club at Bess, holding him as Bess relieved him of
his weapon.

"Now what?" asked Tuff.

The man beneath Tuff was trying to bite Tuff's
ankle, forcing him to lift one foot and then the next.

"Bess, could you get the rope from my trunk?"
Cesar spoke in a calm voice that seemed at odds
with his position, for he now had her attacker in a
headlock. The guy writhed and reached, trying un-
successfully to get a hold of Cesar.

She went to retrieve the rope, stepping over the
third man, who rolled about on the ground in a vain
attempt to remove his handcuffs.

Bess reached in the open window on the driver's
side and popped the trunk and then headed around
the back.

"We can't let them go," said Cesar. "Not like this
anyway."

Bess glanced toward the woods. The twins stood
on their stubby legs, leaning into each other. They
seemed so bereft it made her pause.

Alone, alone, alone. Afraid, afraid. Hungry.

Those were not her thoughts. Theirs? She cocked her head. Were they telepaths then, sending their thoughts to her or to everyone? It was the female. She knew it but did not know how she did.

"The Seer could send these ghosts to the Spirit Road. That would free the humans," said Tuff.

Bess slammed the trunk. "No. There might be more, watching us right now. They could find her."

"She can see them. She can send them for judgment just as she did the others at the ranch in Montana," said Tuff.

He had been there, fought beside her with the others and witnessed the Seer's powers.

"She has children to defend now. And Nagi is here," said Bess. "He *can* follow me and he'll kill her."

She brought Cesar the rope and he quickly used it on the man he held.

"First, we get out of this forest," said Cesar. "Then we'll figure out what to do."

"Ready?" asked Tuff, preparing to remove his weight from the final attacker.

Cesar tied the man's legs and then nodded.

Tuff drew aside, keeping hold of the hiker's right arm. His left was still pinned beneath him. Cesar trussed him like a captured boar.

Tuff dusted off the seat of his pants. "Why did they attack us?" asked Tuff.

Bess pointed toward the new Halflings. "Defending them."

"How do you know?"

"I can hear them. Or I hear the female. She called for help."

Both men stared at her.

"Didn't you hear her?"

They shook their heads.

"But I can understand the male when he's touching me," said Cesar.

Bess felt the prickling anxiety grow stronger, but now began to question whether the feeling came from her warning system working or the panic of the newborns sending out telepathic messages.

"Gun!" yelled Cesar.

Bess turned to see a fourth man, a park officer, emerge from behind a huge redwood trunk at the same instant Cesar tackled her. As she sailed through the air she saw the raised revolver and heard the pop of a single gunshot.

They hit the ground so hard it rattled her vision. Cesar reached for his weapon, lifting off her to return fire. His pistol report made her ears ring.

Three more shots came in rapid succession and Cesar crumpled to the ground.

Bess screamed as she rose to her knees beside Cesar.

The shooter was down and Tuff ran to him, retrieved the weapon and threw it. It sailed through the air and landed in his truck bed.

"I never saw him," said Tuff, stooping to check the ranger. "Dead."

Bess had Cesar in her arms now. She held his slack body against hers. Blood soaked his shirt and his head lolled back in a way that filled Bess with terror.

"No, no, no," she whispered as if it were a prayer. "He was trying to protect me."

Tuff left the shooter and returned to Bess, dropping to his knees in the dirt beside her.

Bess lifted her gaze from Cesar's unnaturally pale face to look into Tuff's eyes and found no reassurance there.

"Do something. Tuff, you have to heal him."

Tuff's eyes reflected the horror she felt. Cesar was so still. Was he even breathing?

"Hurry! Why don't you help him?"

Tuff sat fixed in stillness, his face a mask of dread.

She shifted Cesar, to lay him down before Tuff. He was a buffalo. He could survive these injuries and regenerate. It was his gift and his burden, the gift of sacrifice. She had never before seen Tuff withhold his powers to any living thing that needed him.

"Tuff!" she screamed at him. The terror burned her throat, making her voice shrill.

He reached out, not to Cesar, but to her, clasping her by the shoulders and turning her to face him.

"Bess, it's too late. He's already gone."

Chapter 20

"It can't be," said Bess. If she could only convince Tuff to try. If he would only listen.

"Bess. Look at him."

She did. Tuff flipped back the lapel of Cesar's suit to show her the bullet holes, still oozing dark red blood—two piercing his heart and another tearing through his lung on the right side. All three bullets had hit Cesar in the torso. He wasn't wearing a vest.

Bess pressed her hands over her face, trying to breathe past the weight of misery that suddenly fell down upon her. Her exhalation was ragged, choking. How could she still draw breath when he could not?

She shuddered and trembled as the world spun out of control. This wasn't right. It couldn't be happening. She had only just found him and never even told him that she loved him.

"He can't be gone."

Her mother, father. Now Cesar. Stolen, taken, it was the same. This was why she had not told Cesar that she loved him. The fear had stopped her. The fear of exactly this. And now her worst fear had happened.

She scrubbed her hands across her dry face, yearning for the release of tears and looked Tuff in the eye.

"No. Not this time. I won't let him go."

"But he *has* gone." Tuff's voice was quiet and full of concern.

He didn't understand.

"You can still heal his body."

Tuff's brows furrowed. "Why? I can't bring him back."

"I can. If I reach him before he crosses into the Spirit World."

"But Bess, do you have the right to stop him?"

"I love him."

She had not realized she had shouted until she saw the hurt and confusion on Tuff's dear face.

Bess tried to rein in her terror with her tone of

voice. "I will not let another person I love leave me behind. This time I'll fight. I'll bring him back or I'll follow him."

"No!" Tuff reached for her, his eyes wide with what looked like terror and she realized she had never seen him afraid before. A moment later he dropped his hands to his knees and nodded his acceptance. "All right, Bess. Bring him back and I'll see he is made whole."

Cesar was flying, up through the treetops and into the blue sky. The clouds swallowed him up and next he saw the stars glittering about him, spilling across the heavens in a sparkling highway.

Recognition arrived a moment later. He knew what this was, knew it even without ever having seen it before.

This was the Way of Souls, the road that all mortals must one day pass after their earthly journey was finished. It summoned him, humming softly, with a beautiful music that touched his soul and carried him forward. How did anyone resist such a call? It was sweeter than a lark's song, purer than water tumbling down a hillside. He wanted to bathe in the sound, roll in the carpet of stars and dance along the road that stretched out before him.

But wasn't there something wrong? He looked

back at the way he had come and could see nothing but more stars winking. Still he was unsettled by the feeling he had left something important behind. He paused, hovering, neither continuing forward nor retreating.

Why was he so torn? As if he were tied to two horses galloping in opposite directions.

He began again, sweeping forward. This was right, flying through the sky as easily as… He slowed his momentum, drifting in space. He was thinking that he flew as easily as Bess. His raven. His love.

Where was she now? More importantly where was he?

Cesar grew uneasy at the realization that he had no body. He seemed to be only a silver shimmering energy. How had he come here? He could not remember.

Something moved farther up the road of stars, something slow and ancient. He felt the age of this creature measured in eons instead of years, as if he stared at a cliff face instead of a living entity: a female, as old as the stars themselves and as much a part of this place as the sky.

She moved closer, not walking, but descending as if she rode some escalator that he could not see. One moment she was high above him and the next she was there before him, pinning him with eyes black as the holes in space. He had a feeling of irrational dread.

And then he knew who she was. So this was Hihankara, the elder who measured souls to judge if they were worthy to continue or be cast off the road.

He gazed down below his feet, looking through the gaps between the stars. Why hadn't he seen it before? The spinning vortex yawned like a great sprawling hurricane beneath him. But that was no storm. He was looking into the Circle of Ghosts. Each tiny wisp of each immortal soul combined with the others to give the cloud its shape and eternal spin. They trod from now until forever in that dismal mass.

Had he walked the Red Road? he wondered. Had his deeds been virtuous enough to overcome his mistakes? Or would he suffer the Circle? He thought of the Skinwalker he had shot on the word of his partner and thought he deserved to fall.

Cesar recalled his life now, watching the details flow by as Hihankara stared down at him. She was enormous, the size of an elephant by comparison, and strong and able enough to easily cast any soul from her path. How long would he fall before he hit the Circle?

He now saw that what he first assumed were wrinkles were actually an elaborate series of swirling blue-black tattoos covering her forehead and cheeks. They ran in twin arrows down her nose, curling over each nostril and continued around her mouth to coil on her chin like a resting rattlesnake.

"You seek to pass?" said Hihankara.

He did not know. He wanted to go back to Bess, but then he remembered she did not want him.

The Spirit leaned down so that her long flat nose nearly touched his.

"Show me your tattoos."

Cesar held out his arms and was shocked to see that they were as transparent as water except for the swirling silver spiral on his right arm and the symbol of a human hand upon the left.

"Hmm, a Soul Whisperer. That is odd, as there is yet no other of your kind upon the earth. Bad. The Balance will suffer."

"May I pass?" he asked.

She stepped aside, but he did not continue on his way. Nor did he feel the exhalation or relief he had expected. He had led a good life, despite his mistakes.

"What of Bess?"

"The raven? Nuisance, that one, always flapping and cawing her questions to those who have earned their peace."

"If I cross, can she come and speak to me?"

"Not until she crosses."

"But she told me she speaks to departed souls, that she calls into the Spirit World and they answer."

"True. But she cannot call the ones she loves."

"The ones she…but she doesn't love me. She told me so herself."

Hihankara laughed and the road beneath him shook as if rocked by an earthquake. "Did she now? Well, then it must be true. Ravens are not the sort of birds to deceive anyone, or play tricks or outwit men. No, wait, they *are* that sort."

"She loves me?"

Hihankara exhaled so forcefully that the stars brightened and one streaked away from the road, falling in a shower of sparks.

"Now look what you made me do. The Road has another hole in it. Harder to replace than cobblestone, I can tell you. If you are going…" She motioned, making a shooing gesture with both long, angular hands.

She said *if*. Did Cesar have a choice?

Bess flew faster than she ever had and still it was not fast enough. How long did it take a soul to cross the Ghost Road? All she knew was that Cesar was ahead of her and she had to catch up.

How would she know him from the others? They

all looked the same here, white energy, pulsing with power. She began to cry out his name, over and over until her voice grew hoarse and crackled like dry oak leaves skittering across the frozen ground. And still she cried his name again and again.

"Stop that racket," growled Hihankara, creeping down the road to wave her arms.

Bess veered and rolled, sweeping past her.

"He has the proper tattoos. Let him pass, Raven," Hihankara cried.

Let him pass. That meant he had not crossed the threshold yet. Bess flew faster. Ahead of her was the shimmering veil that blocked her view of the world beyond the Way of Souls. If he crossed that barrier, she would never see him again.

"Cesar!"

One of the souls stopped at the threshold.

Bess swept down to him, seeing now the familiar aura of the man she had loved, staring at his naked soul.

"Cesar, don't go. Don't leave me behind."

He hovered there, his aura pulsing more brightly. If he moved even another few inches he would be lost to her.

"Come back, Cesar. Tuff has healed your body. It is whole and waiting for you. Please, Cesar. Don't leave me."

She could not hear him, but she knew his thoughts, felt them as she always did when communicating with a soul. What she felt most strongly was his indecision. He wanted to end his lonely existence, trapped in a body on the earthly plane. He didn't believe himself worthy of love, but hoped to find peace in the Spirit World. He moved a little closer to the veil, drawn, it seemed, by some power she could not recognize.

How could she compete with all he would find there?

Bess flapped her wings before him, blocking his way.

Hihankara crept up behind them.

"Are you here to do what is best for him or what is best for you, little Raven?"

Bess felt her stomach drop. She didn't know. All she knew was that she needed Cesar and she would fight anything and anyone who tried to take him.

"You can't have him," she called as she beat her tired wings.

Cesar's thoughts came to her again. *Is it my choice or yours?*

Bess did not know if he spoke to her or to Hihankara, but it was the old wise Spirit who answered.

"There have been those who came this far and then turned back, some to their body and some to wait as ghosts for the one they cannot leave. But you have the proper tattoos, so you may cross."

And see my brother.

Cesar moved toward the veil and Bess beat him back with her wings again, desperate now to stop him.

"Your brother is not here," said Hihankara, and pointed below them, to the yawning vortex of misery. "But there."

Cesar's soul vibrated and Bess felt the agony sawing through him.

But it was an accident, a fall. Surely he deserves to enter the Spirit World.

Hihankara shook her massive head. "I pushed him off the Way of Souls myself. I don't make mistakes."

"But why?" asked Bess.

"Because he intentionally took a life."

Bess heard Cesar's thoughts as a shout in her mind.

What life?

Hihankara narrowed her billiard-ball-size eyes at him. "His own."

Cesar's anguish reviberted within her. *He was only a child.*

"No," said Bess, but she knew it could be true. Suicide was the murder of oneself, regardless of how old Carlos had been. As far as Hihankara was concerned any soul who intentionally took an innocent life must serve time in the Circle.

"He did not fall," said the ancient. "He jumped and in that instant his duty became your burden, Soul Whisperer. Did you not wonder why you have three gifts? Or why you discovered the last two so late? You are a Truth Seeker by birth. But the Whispering and the Memory Walking came because of him."

It's not possible, thought Cesar.

Bess did not know how much longer she could fly. Soon she would fall from the sky and into the circle where no living thing had ever gone.

Hihankara spoke. "When his brother learned what he was, he understood the path he must walk and rejected his duty."

"How could he keep this a secret from his parents?" asked Bess. "I thought the Niyanoka knew the gifts of their children and helped them learn to use them."

"Unless you use your Memory Walking gift to erase the memories of your parents each time they learned of it. That one could not keep up the ruse any longer. There were too many memories to erase and the guilt was too much to bear. So he jumped."

Cesar's denial turned to astonished silence. Bess

absorbed the black grief that poured from him, sharing the burden. Her wings grew heavy as if coated with tar. She needed to land, but there was no place here to rest.

My prayers? asked Cesar.

"Were not enough. You have lifted him to the highest level. In a few more mortal years he would have been free and moved to the Spirit World."

But my parents pray for him.

"Not often. They believe he crossed. But you cannot help him now for you are bound for the Spirit World."

I want to see him.

Her smile held no mercy. "Perhaps, someday, when he serves his time. But there is no seeing in the Circle of Ghosts. Each soul is blind, alone, while crushed against all the rest. They walk unseeing, ever searching for what they have not earned."

"What?" he asked.

"Peace."

Bess's tired muscles began to cramp. The vortex yawned beneath her.

Hihankara beckoned. "Cross over now. Your grandparents await."

Bess spoke in desperation. "He is here only because one of Nagi's ghosts took possession of a human and shot him to protect his Halflings."

Hihankara's expression blackened and a red aura of fury surrounded her. "Nagi? That one again? I spoke to him about his uncollected ghosts after the last attacks. He assured me it was an oversight."

"Do Spirits have oversights?" asked Bess.

"No," said the guardian. "They do not. And what is this about Halflings?"

"Nagi has children, fast growing, voracious."

Hihankara rubbed her long chin. "This changes The Balance."

"Do they threaten The Balance?" Bess prayed they did not for somehow she had become fond of the frightened little male and the small ferocious female. They both need...parents, she realized. And, although Inanoka protected The Balance, she would not judge them by their sire. Cesar had taught her that.

"They are dangerous," said Hihankara, "but if they are alive, their place is in the living world."

Bess wished she could keep silent, but she could not. "The Balance?"

"Like all creatures, they must find their place in the living world for they are now part of The Balance. And Nagi's responsibility is to teach them."

Bess could only imagine what horrors their sire would impart. "He's trying to take over the world. He'll only use them toward that purpose."

Hihankara turned to Cesar. "If he will not teach them, then it will fall to someone else."

Why did the Spirit look at him when she said that? Now Hihankara pinned her steel-colored eyes on Bess.

"We all remember the Skinwalkers' reaction when they thought The Balance jeopardized. I trust your kind have learned that war is not a solution."

Bess chortled at Hihankara's admonishment. She had lost her father to the aftermath of that war. If anyone knew the terrible cost of such conflicts it was Bess and, though she trusted Cesar, she did not trust his kind. But perhaps this connection between them was a start.

"Yes, wise one. I will do all I can to prevent another war between our kinds."

The Spirit turned to Cesar. "You were killed by a ghost?"

"I was killed by a man possessed by a ghost."

"It is an unnatural death and explains why you are here early. If your body is whole, you must return to it."

Bess felt a sagging relief until she saw Cesar's aura vibrate a dull gray. He was bereft at Hirhankara's decision. Cesar would return to her, but only because he had to.

"What about the tattoos?" he asked.

"All Soul Whisperers are born with the proper tattoos. Your life is of service and sacrifice. Until your brother, none of your kind had ever failed to cross my road. Go back now, Whisperer, and finish your work. There are innocents who need your protection. And do not cross again until the next Whisperer is born."

Cesar turned and began his descent. Bess called to him but he did not answer her. Had she saved him or condemned him?

Hihankara watched the two descend until they were gone from her sight. It would be many years before she would see the Whisperer again, but that nuisance of a raven would be back often.

Then she did something she had never done. She left her place on the Way of Souls and crossed into the World of Spirits to summon the three involved parties.

Niyan arrived first, the Spirit of Man, golden brown and irresistibly handsome. It was no wonder he had so many descendants, for no mortal woman could resist him. Soon afterward she spotted the great bear, Tob Tob, lumbering toward her. He was the guardian of all living creatures not under Niyan's stewardship.

Hihankara glanced about. Where was the other one? Her mood darkened.

Niyan opened his arms in greeting. He looked as she remembered, dressed in white buckskin adorned with hair from the tail of a white buffalo and rows of elks' teeth. His face held the perfect beauty that no mortal man could ever match and a glowing aura that shimmered with power.

"Guardian," he said, and bowed his head. "It has been long since we have seen you."

Why do you call us? asked Tob Tob, sending his thoughts to her without speaking. The bear was nothing if not direct.

"I also called Nagi."

They both looked about.

"He has sired living offspring."

Niyan laughed. "I hope they resemble their mothers."

Hihankara fumed. "I do not know, for I do not visit the living world."

I have been there recently, but I did not see them, said Tob Tob.

"He must instruct his offspring, just as each of you have done," she said.

They both nodded their agreement.

"And I must return to the Road."

"We will deliver your message, guardian," Niyan assured. "And see it done."

Hihankara returned to the Way of Souls, staring down in search of Nagi. He would not wiggle out of this. He'd been meddling in the living world again and this time she meant to see he did his duty. He was a father now and he had responsibilities.

Chapter 21

The air came back to Cesar's lungs in a gasp, as if he were surfacing from a deep dive. He opened his eyes to stare up at the golden columns of light pouring down through the high branches of the redwood trees. Tuff held him in his arms, supporting his head, which, for some reason, Cesar could not lift on his own.

Beads of sweat covered Tuff's face and he was nearly as gray as the Halfling infants.

"Welcome back, brother," Tuff whispered. His words conveyed his fatigue. Why was he shivering on such a warm day? "You've been gone a long time."

Cesar blinked and tried to move, but his arms did not respond to his command.

"Patience. You've been out of your body for nearly an hour."

"But that's not possible." The scratchy whisper of his voice frightened him and his mind scrambled for answers. How did he get here?

"Bess?"

"On her way back now, I suppose. I was afraid I'd lose her, too."

Back from where? He couldn't recall what had happened or why he was lying on the forest floor. Had he fallen? Bits and pieces of the day flashed through his mind, like fragments of a shattered whole. The pier, driving over the bridge, the twins howling. The ghosts. The gunshot. The pain ripping through his chest. He lifted a hand, pressing his palm over the cold, wet blood soaking his shirt, his muscles trembling as they responded slowly to his mind's command. Why did he feel no pain?

Then he realized what must have happened. "You healed me."

Tuff smiled. "Your body only."

Cesar did not understand this cryptic comment.

Tuff's trembling grew worse as they slowly switched positions, Cesar rising as Tuff fell into his arms. The Skinwalker looked as if he had just risen from his deathbed and Cesar was seriously worried about him.

"Are you going to be all right?" Cesar asked.

Even smiling seemed to take more effort than Tuff had. "In time. I've only done that once, but I had to stop. I wasn't as strong then." Tuff's smile faded and he squeezed his eyes shut.

Cesar touched Tuff and his Truth Seeker gift told him instantly that Tuff was downplaying the seriousness of his condition. The effort of saving Cesar had nearly killed him. No, that wasn't right. Might still kill him. Now Tuff's heart beat ineffectively and would until he finished regenerating.

"The bullet went through my heart?" said Cesar.

Tuff nodded. "And both lungs."

"You nearly died helping me. Why did you do that?"

Tuff shrugged, but the answer came to Cesar through his touch gift. Tuff had done it because Bess asked him to, because he would do anything Bess asked, even if it killed him. Why hadn't he guessed that Tuff loved Bess?

"I'm sorry," Cesar said.

Tuff cocked his head, not understanding. It wasn't fair to read his thoughts without his knowledge.

"I'm a Truth Seeker," he said.

Tuff's eyes widened. "Oh, then you know. She doesn't. Never told her."

The Skinwalker was such a gentleman; Cesar never even knew that Tuff was a rival for Bess. And the buffalo-man was willing to abide by Bess's decision. In similar circumstances, Cesar knew he would not be so selfless.

"Why haven't you told her?"

"She never showed any real interest in me. But I can't seem to get it through my thick skull. I thought one day she would see me. Shortsighted of me, I know. You won't tell her will you?"

"Not if you don't want me to."

"No. It would make her sad."

Cesar wondered if he might soon be in the same position, loving a woman who did not love him. Bess had told him she never wanted to see him again. Then why had she come back?

Then he recalled something, and the memory winked on like a firefly and off again before he could fully recall it. Someone laughing. Saying something about ravens and lies. It was important, he knew that much, but he could not summon the recollection from the darkness.

"Where's Bess?" he asked again.

"Coming. Any minute now."

Cesar struggled to drag Tuff clear of the wet

ground and up against the roots of the redwood where he sat back, exhausted, Tuff lying with his head on Cesar's thigh. For a time they rested in silence.

When Cesar opened his eyes, he noticed the dark red stain on the ground. His blood, he realized, and shivered. He glanced about the clearing.

"Where are the ghosts?"

Tuff lifted one finger. The effort seemed to take everything he had. "Tied over there."

"Alive?"

Tuff nodded. "But not really alive."

"We can't free them," said Cesar.

"Unless I can find an owl," Tuff whispered.

Cesar looked down at Tuff. "That's true? An owl can chase away ghosts?"

"Not just any owl, but a Skinwalker can."

Cesar was impressed. It was a great power, but nearly as terrible a burden as his.

"I thought owls could only tell when you will die," said Cesar.

"Any owl can do that." Tuff closed his eyes again and his breathing grew shallow.

"Where are the twins?" he asked.

Tuff thumbed over his shoulder without opening his eyes. "One flew off, and the male is hiding over there. I hear him and I smell him."

"You sure?"

"Buffalo usually know when they are being hunted."

"You think he'll try to hurt you."

"Not with you here. Wouldn't want to meet him on the plains. He's a formidable hunter for one so young. He seems confused that I walk as a man and smell like a bison."

Cesar tried to find the male but could see nothing of him.

Another recollection struck Cesar. "I killed a human."

Tuff's eyes fluttered closed. "No, you protected Bess. Nagi killed him with his ghosts. He was also possessed."

Cesar felt ill. Killing a human, one he was charged to protect, was a terrible offense.

"I have to call it in."

"No, you don't. I'll call from a payphone on my way out of town."

Cesar felt a wave of gratitude. "You don't have to."

"You saved Bess. I owe you for that."

Why did the way he said that upset him? Something about Tuff...he recalled his feeling of possession for Bess the first time he'd set eyes on Tuff.

Had he been right to feel Tuff threatened his right to her?

"Do you remember much of your journey?" asked Tuff.

"What journey?"

"My friend, you left your body and walked the Spirit Road."

Bess cried out before she entered the clearing. Dusk robbed the colors from her surroundings, but she could still see well enough to fly and she spotted Tuff, propped against a tree, his head cocked to watch her approach. Cesar sat beside him, long legs sprawled out before him as he shaded his eyes.

Cesar was alive!

All the weariness in her body and the aching of her tired wings evaporated like the morning mist. Power surged through her and she dove, performing a barrel roll. Just before hitting the forest floor, she swooped upward, transforming into her human form. She dropped to the gentle loam, landing on the thick layer of pine needles. She did not even take the instant required to change her feather cloak into some more traditional garment, but instead rushed to Cesar, hardly noticing Tuff at all.

Bess dropped to her knees beside him and trapped his jaw between her hands, staring at him in joy. Then she kissed him, drawing back when she recognized how very weak he was. She closed her eyes and let the breath slip from her as she gave thanks.

"You're alive," she whispered.

"Thanks to Tuff," said Cesar.

Bess glanced at her friend, only just noticing how drawn and ill he looked.

Had she asked too much?

"Are you all right?"

He nodded and closed his eyes for a moment, but then didn't open them. He tilted sideways in slow motion.

Bess released Cesar and caught Tuff as he fell.

"Tuff!" She lowered him to the ground and pressed an ear to his chest, hearing the strange, irregular beating of his heart, very fast, then nothing, then a slow increasing beat that raced too fast again. "There's something wrong with him. His heartbeat is all crazy."

Cesar lifted his bloody shirt from his chest, slipping a finger into one hole and out the other. "I had two bullets in my chest. Doesn't that mean he now has two in his?"

"But he will heal." Her voice trembled with doubt.

Cesar crawled over to Tuff and supported his

head. "I don't think he is supposed to bring back the dead."

Bess stared at him for a moment. "I never... I didn't think. Why didn't he tell me?"

She pressed her forehead to Tuff's chest. "No. This isn't right."

Cesar gave Tuff's shoulder a little shake. "Come on, buddy. Don't die on us."

Bess listened to his heart and gasped. "It's stopped. Cesar, do something!"

He laid Tuff on the hard ground and ripped open his shirt. The bullet holes that had been on Cesar's chest, now gurgled grotesquely, the only flaws in Tuff's tanned cinnamon skin. The sight stopped him for an instant. As he stared, the wounds began to close.

"Look." Cesar pointed with one hand, as his other went to Tuff's chest. "He couldn't heal if he was dead."

"He's still alive," whispered Bess.

But for how long?

Cesar felt weak and dizzy, but he lifted up to position himself with straight arms, his hands upon Tuff's breastbone. Bess pressed her fingers to Tuff's carotid artery.

"Wait. He's not dead," she whispered.

Bess tugged at Cesar's arms and he sat back on

his heels as Bess moved to press an ear to Tuff's chest again. "It's beating!"

"But he's not breathing."

Tuff gasped for air.

A moment later he began to tremble as if freezing cold.

Cesar stared at Bess. "How did you know?"

She flushed. "When we die, we change. He was still human so…"

Tuff's eye's fluttered open and he stared up at Bess and smiled.

"There you are, little bird."

"Tuff, why didn't you tell me it was too much?" Her words were hard, but she was crying or she sounded like she was crying, but her eyes remained dry. Did she love Tuff? "Don't you ever do something so foolish again."

He glanced at Cesar. "I fixed him, though."

The weakness in his voice troubled Cesar greatly. He feared the danger had not passed.

"Supposed to kill me. That's what I was told anyway." He stared at Bess again, as if drinking her in. "Maybe I didn't die because you brought back his soul."

What did he mean? Tuff was the one who had healed him. Cesar stilled as possibilities widened his eyes. He dropped to his seat and looked at them both. Tuff had healed his body, his already dead body, while Bess had…

He could almost see it, the glittering path strewn with diamonds instead of stars. He'd walked the Way of Souls and he had wanted to cross, but Bess stopped him, blocking him with her body and her beating wings.

Chapter 22

After drinking all the water Tuff carried in the cooler in his pickup, he was strong enough to stand, though Tuff still hunched toward the side where Cesar had been shot.

"Only take a day or two and I'll be right as summer rain," he said.

Bess kissed him and Cesar offered his hand, not wanting to hug a man in so much pain.

"You shouldn't drive," he said.

Tuff gave Cesar a look. "Got to."

"Then let me drive you. It's the least I can do."

Tuff glanced at the path leading into the forest. "Nope. You still have business here with the twins and I have to call in the ranger's death, plus get rid of those three ghosts."

Bess looked into the bed of his pickup where a blue rain tarp covered three wriggling captives. "You are sure you can find the owl?"

Tuff shrugged and then winced. "Have to. Those people are prisoners until I do."

"It's *my* job to care for them," said Cesar, who was the Spirit Child and protector of mankind.

Bess looked from one to the other. They both looked pale and weak and she had never felt this exhausted from a journey.

Cesar moved in an odd, stiff way, as if his limbs would not quite respond to him yet. She worried that the effects of being dead so long might do him permanent harm, but Tuff had assured her that he had taken all Cesar's injuries, including those caused by the organs shutting down. How could she ever repay him for what he had done?

"I'll find an owl Skinwalker. You two see to that little critter lurking upwind," said Tuff, pointing to their left. "Waiting for me to clear out."

"What about the ranger?" Bess asked Cesar.

His expression was grim. "Tuff will call it in and then later I'll use my memory gift to close the case. I'll have to notify District Council that I've killed a human. They'll call an inquest."

Bess cast him a worried look. Cesar would tell the truth to his council and he would be banished. She was certain.

Tuff reached for the door handle and winced.

"Where's the ranger's gun?" asked Cesar.

In answer, Tuff lifted his shirt, revealing the handle of the pistol pressed by the waistband of his jeans to his flat stomach.

Cesar nodded and held the door for Tuff, waiting until he climbed slowly behind the wheel before slamming it shut for him.

"Thanks," he whispered, then gave Cesar an odd look.

"What?"

Tuff's voice was barely a whisper. "Is it true you can walk in memories?"

Cesar nodded.

Tuff glanced at Bess, who stood back a few steps, hands clasped before her. She looked tall and elegant in a black sheath dress that flattered her curves.

"Can you, is it possible to make me forget her?"

Cesar shook his head. "Love is not a memory. I am sorry, my friend, after all you have done for me, I can do nothing for you."

Tuff gave a heavy sigh, nodded and then thumped his hand on the outside of the driver's side door. "Okay then."

Cesar stepped back. Tuff clasped the steering wheel and gave Bess one more long look. She smiled and waved.

"Thank you for my life, brother," said Cesar. "I won't forget it. If you ever need me, I am there for you."

Tuff slipped the clutch into gear. "Take care of her."

The pickup was barely out of sight when a familiar growling came from the bunch of ferns to their left. Cesar pushed her behind him, placing himself between her and danger.

She thought to shift and escape but she could not leave him. There was a yapping bark and then one of the two twins tumbled out.

Cesar waited, hand on his service revolver as the male twin emerged first from the foliage. He dragged the female behind him. She snarled and snapped but she walked behind him as he advanced purposefully.

"What do they want?" Bess asked.

Cesar glanced her way and then returned his focus to the twins. "Parents, I think."

"What?" She could think of nothing else to say, but she looked more carefully and noted the submissive approach of the male, shoulders hunched, his eyes darting to Cesar's and then away.

"I'm the first one they ever saw."

The two ashy creatures stood before them, staring up with huge owlish yellow eyes and fangs that they could not quite contain inside their mouths.

In the silence that stretched between them came a low rumbling growl from their empty bellies.

"They're hungry," said Cesar.

"The other ones ate an entire moose," Bess said warily. She wanted to help them, but hungry animals were dangerous animals and these two were voracious as bears emerging from their dens.

"Yet they didn't attack the dead ranger," said Cesar. "We have to feed them."

Bess wondered where he'd get enough meat and suddenly thought Tuff's departure was very well timed.

If Cesar wanted to feed these infants, she would help him and she knew exactly where they could go.

"My lodge is close. I have a freezer full. Just bought a half a cow from a farmer."

"Which half?"

Bess flapped her arms. "They don't just slice the cow in half and leave it hanging in your garage. I have packages of hamburger and several packs of long ribs and eight flank steaks and a bunch of porterhouse cuts, roasts, the works. It's three hundred pounds in total."

"That will do to start. How far?"

"Twenty minutes in a car. Five as the crow flies."

He gave her a smile at her joke.

"Do you think I can get them both into the car?"

"I don't know."

He released his pistol and extended his hand. The female tried to back away, but the male held on to her. He hunched, shifting uncertain eyes. Cesar motioned with his fingers. The male made a sudden hopping advance. Bess held her breath.

It grasped Cesar's hand.

"It's hot," he said, and placed his thumb over the male's small fingers. Then he turned and slowly led them to his car, holding open the passenger side. The little ashy infants tumbled into the footwell on the passenger side of his car. Bess looked through the open window at them.

"Do you want me to follow you or would you like to ride along?" he asked.

"I'm not leaving you alone with them." Her uncertainty roiled within her. They needed help, but they still frightened her.

"Get in." He held the rear door and she slipped behind the driver's seat.

The male hissed at her and he narrowed his eyes. But the female twisted his ear until he yowled.

The female's thoughts came to her clearly. *Mother. Mother. Mother.*

"Cesar? She thinks I'm her mother."

"She could do worse."

Bess didn't know what shocked her more, the infant's thoughts or Cesar's confidence in her. She knew nothing about these twins or how to raise them.

"It's all right, little ghostling," she cooed, feeling awkward.

The female closed its gaping mouth and stared up at her with wide eyes as if fascinated.

Cesar started the engine. "After we get them fed, maybe we should head away from people. I have a ranch in the Cascades. I think that might be a good place for them. It's secluded and there is lots of game."

He pulled out. The female began to whimper and the male held her. The two babies reminded Bess of orphaned monkeys, clinging to each other for protection.

"What about the other newborns?"

"We'll start with these two and later try to gather them. Perhaps these can help us find them."

Bess directed him toward her place.

The two passengers were jabbering together now, side by side on the floor mat.

"The way they are going, they'll be full grown in a week."

Cesar drew a breath and then exhaled his troubles. "But we don't know how big they'll grow or what they will turn into as adults."

Bess thought of her own change, which had come at puberty, and wondered what the future would be for these two. If they stayed like this, they could never be seen by men. One look would reveal them for what they were. What kind of life could they lead as outcasts?

She glanced to Cesar and understood suddenly why he felt a need to care for them. They faced what he had. Only he had managed to blend with humans.

Bess wanted to touch him so she could feel his emotions, but she didn't want to disturb him with hers. She was confused about the twins and about her role in bringing Cesar back without his consent. And she still needed to tell him that she was all wrong about him.

"Bess?"

She met his gaze in the rearview mirror.

"We'll have time to talk soon. I know you're upset. I can sense it without touching you. But hang on a little longer."

He was comforting her? Bess couldn't keep the anguish from choking her. She pressed her eyes closed against her shame and held on. She didn't touch Cesar, but she rested a hand on his seat, just beyond his shoulder.

The female made a sound that seemed an exclamation and hopped up beside Cesar, staring at her from between the bucket seats. Could the little Halfling read the chaos of her emotions?

The ghostling laid her hand on Bess's and gave her a pat, looking up into Bess's eyes with her wide, unnatural ones. Then she leaped back down to the floor mats to hold her brother.

"Burning up," she whispered. "Her skin is so hot. A fever or is that normal?"

Cesar glanced at the two. "They don't look ill."

An inappropriate laugh erupted from her. "He doesn't? He's gray, with burning skin and eyes as yellow as egg yolks."

"Good point."

"Turn here."

They ascended the private driveway and Bess punched in the code for the fence. In another moment she was entering in the code to open the garage. She swept inside and opened the chest freezer, transferring packets to a large cooler. Cesar waited outside as she wheeled the offering to the driveway.

The female charged her, knocking the cooler from her hands and diving into the neatly wrapped plastic. The male hesitated, gave her a look she could swear was apologetic and then joined his sister.

Cesar stood beside her watching the two swallowing chunks of frozen meat, bone and wrapping together.

"We're going to need the other half," he said.

"That plastic will make them sick," she whispered.

"I don't think so."

Cesar and Bess spent the rest of the evening obtaining a butchered cow and two slaughtered pigs. The truck delivered them to the barn and somehow Cesar kept the twins in the garage until the truck pulled out.

Bess opened the barn door and she and Cesar stood back as the twins gorged themselves, then curled into the hay and fell asleep.

"That is going to give me nightmares," said Bess.

Cesar laughed. "I wouldn't blame you."

"Doesn't bother you?"

He gave her a sad look. "I've seen worse."

Of course he had. He'd seen the very worst things one human could do to another. Perhaps that was why he needed to help them. He was impervious to their appetites, dauntless about their care and unaffected by their appearance.

She felt humbled, wanting to help him, join him in doing whatever he thought best. She longed to touch him, to know his thoughts.

Instead she used conventional methods.

"What now?" she asked.

He used his knuckles to scratch the stubble of his jaw as he considered the sleeping twins. "We've discovered what they are and that they are not killers. We have done what we set out to do. They will affect The Balance but I do not believe they will destroy it."

Hihankara had said much the same.

"I was wrong about them," she admitted. "Very wrong."

He looked surprised. "Well, they attacked you."

"Still, I'll not be so quick to judge again. I've learned my lesson."

"Lessons can be costly."

His smile of approval was a balm to her tired soul.

"I'm thinking I will try to bring the others together."

Bess knew that felt right, but had to raise the obvious concern. "Nagi may come for them."

"They are his children. He has the right."

"Even if he plans to make them into a private army?"

Cesar's jaw tightened. "That I would not allow."

She did not ask how he would stop a Spirit from doing exactly what it chose to do.

Bess nodded, taking up Cesar's cause as her own. "We'll face him when the time comes, then."

"You'll help me?"

They stared at the twins, nearly buried in the loose hay and snoring softly, clinging to each other as they slept. She had been mentored by a great swan after her change came, so she understood a family that was not of blood. She could think of none better than the two of them to help these creatures find their way.

"Of course."

His shoulders dropped a little, as if he had been bracing for her refusal. He didn't know yet that she'd do anything he asked.

"What will they grow into, I wonder?" she asked.

"I only know some part of them will be like their father. I pray they will also serve the living."

"Should we leave them to sleep or watch over them?" she asked.

"They can kill anything that is stupid enough to threaten them. I say we leave them to sleep and go in the house."

"What if they wake up and can't find us?"

"They can track and kill game, they'll be able to find us in the house," he assured.

She took her eyes off the twins and met Cesar's worried gaze. Instantly she felt a dread. The look in his eyes was so troubled, she braced for what he would say.

"Bess? We need to talk."

"The porch then, it's private, but we can still see the barn."

She led the way across the yard, leaving the circle of light cast by the single electric light in the barn. Cesar followed a few steps behind as the silence between them stretched to eternity. Bess gazed up at the stars winking and, just beyond, the Way of Souls. She recalled Hihankara asking her if she was saving Cesar because it was best for him or for her. She told herself she had brought him back out of love, but was that true? He had not wanted to come back to her. What would happen when he remembered that?

Bess could not bear the thought of the harsh electric lights, so she led him to the wide front porch that more resembled something from Charleston or Savannah than California. The long sectional couch formed a U, capturing the coffee table with the center. She motioned and he sat. She perched beside him, staring out over the porch rail at the single light blazing from the barn as she thought of the two souls sleeping in the hay.

"What happened on the Way of Souls?" he asked.

Cesar waited for an answer.

She had clasped and clung, fighting and clawing to keep Cesar. She'd even beat him back with her wings to keep him from crossing.

Now, he asked for the truth. In giving it, she would lose all her dignity, for she knew she would throw herself at him and beg him not to send her away. Once he knew what she had done, would she lose him forever?

Cesar sat beside her in the darkness, close to her side but distant as well, the tone of his voice, the uncertainty cut at her. He deserved the truth. Bess gathered her flagging courage and faced him, seeing his strange black and white aura now spiked with the bright green of emotional anguish.

"It's all fractured, like looking through ice on a pond." He knitted his brow. "I remember asking the guardian about…" His eyes went wide. "Oh, sweet mercy, Carlos!"

Cesar trembled with the force of memories suddenly unleashed upon him, to sweep away his peace under a tidal wave of grief. It all came back to him like water bursting over a ruptured damn.

He covered his mouth with one broad hand, failing to block out the memories battering him. Bess moved closer, trying to cradle him, her fingers brushing his bare neck. At the touch, her fear assaulting him, merging with his pain.

He pushed her aside. "No. Wait."

Cesar squeezed his eyes shut.

"Carlos is in the Circle of Ghosts."

"Yes," she whispered.

He opened his eyes and stared up at her, seeing her brown aura now shimmering golden, making her sympathy a visible entity about her.

"Why?" But he knew, knew exactly, understood the terrible truth. "He killed himself because *he* was the Soul Whisperer."

"It was his duty to perform. Not yours. When he died, his powers became yours."

He lifted his open hands toward her as if pleading for answers. "How is that possible?"

She shook her head. "I do not know."

Bess wrapped her arms about him. Her sorrow and her grief over his pain swept through him like a spring rain, tender, soft and nourishing. Bess understood his grief for she had lived many years with questions that had no answers.

"He needs our prayers," she said.

Yes. That was right. His brother must walk the

circle until his soul was clean, but Cesar could help speed the process with his prayers. A few mortal years Hihankara had said.

Bess released him, leaving him with his own thoughts again.

"I can't believe it."

"He couldn't live the lie any longer. He couldn't go on hurting your parents and you by erasing your memories. I don't think he knew that his ability would pass to you."

Cesar thought of the life he might have had as a Truth Seeker—he might have been a minister or a member of the District Council. But Carlos had taken that chance when he had taken his life.

Cesar rubbed his hands over his eyes, trying to remember the face he had not seen in a century. Whatever he had done, Carlos had more than paid for his mistakes. Cesar wanted nothing more than to free him from the Circle.

He stepped out onto the lawn, into the cool darkness and fell to his knees in the wet grass. Raising his arms to the night sky, he began to pray for his brother's lost soul. A moment later he heard her voice join his.

When they had finished, he guided Bess to her feet and she led him back to the seclusion of the porch and they sat side by side on the wide, comfortable couch. She released his hand then, leaving him with his own thoughts. Or was she shielding her thoughts from him?

"I'll pray for him each day," he vowed.

"And I'll call to him each time I fly the Spirit Road. One day, he will answer."

Cesar stared up at the crystal-clear night sky shimmering with stars.

"I remember the sparkling light of the Way and the pull to move forward. I recall wanting to…" He stopped, swayed, and righted himself. Bess remained where she was, hands folded, a shadow waiting in the darkness beside him.

Bess knew what he had been about to say. He recalled wanting to leave her, wanting to go to the Spirit World.

"It wasn't your time."

"Is that why you faced Hihankara?"

"You *do* remember."

He inclined his head. "Pieces. Like a dream."

"It's my fault, Cesar. I asked Tuff to heal your body and I nearly killed him. I followed you and told the guardian Spirit about the ghosts. I never even considered that you wouldn't want to come back to your body, to the world or to me." Bess rubbed her nose, refusing to let herself cry. He'd once assured her that he would not fall in love with her.

His words now seemed some horrible prophecy. It took a moment for the burn in her throat to dissipate enough for her to speak. "I only thought about what was best for me. What I wanted. It was selfish and I'm sorry."

He gave her an odd look, studying her face for a long moment before speaking.

"What do you mean, Bess?"

He was going to make her say it, make her humiliation complete.

She drew a long breath in preparation. If he wanted this, it was small payment for stealing his chance for perfect peace. She'd never heard of a person born with the proper tattoos to gain entrance to the Spirit World, as Cesar was. She knew she would have to earn hers by the deeds of her life.

"I—I… Cesar, I came after you because I thought I could convince you to forget that I'm a Skinwalker and forbidden to you. Jessie told me everything. About your partner and I'm so stupid. I should have let you explain, instead of flying off and… Well, she has a soul-mate connection with a Skinwalker wolf named Nicholas. But she had to give up everything to have him. I don't want to have to ask that of you. Not when you have lost so much already. I don't want you banished, but…" Her misery overcame her and her words trailed off.

He moved closer, sitting beside her in the cool air, the soft glow of his aura outlining his form against the silver-blue darkness.

"I have read of this connection. It is said to be only legend."

"She said it's real and that's what we feel when we touch, that it's the soul-mate connection. That you are my perfect mate."

His eyes widened. "Soul mates?"

"That's what she said. And Cesar, I'm in love with you."

She knew that look, the one filled with resentment and hurt.

"Is that why you say you love me, because you think we share this connection?"

Bess shook her head, feeling no hesitation now. She'd say what was in her heart and leave him to make his choice.

"I love your sacrifice for the dead and how you protect men by finding dangerous killers. I'm humbled by how you would not take my word or the word of anyone else about Nagi's children. You kept true to your beliefs and kept me from making a terrible mistake."

"The mistake that I once made."

"But you learned from it and you changed. You don't just protect the living victims. You protect the accused, as well. I want to be like that. I want to help you. We both have connections with the dead. You can talk to the victims, read the bodies and I can speak to souls who have crossed. And I can help you with the newborns. I can help them fly and find food. I can teach them of The Balance and you can teach them to protect mankind."

She realized she was making this arrangement sound like some kind of business partnership.

When he spoke, his tone held a note of humor. "And I thought you loved the way I kiss."

Bess stared down at the rounded toes of her black boots. "Don't tease me now. I can't stand it. I love you, Cesar. I can't fight how I feel any longer."

"You fight well. You fought death itself to have me."

Her chin sank to her chest. "I'm so sorry." She motioned toward the sleeping twins. "You had to come back because of me."

He lifted her chin until he met her gaze. The familiar buzz of heat and power pulsed at the touch. "Perhaps *you* are why I had to come back."

She stared into his dark grey eyes.

"I've never had anyone care so much about me. It's true I felt the pull to cross over. But I didn't know then that you loved me. I didn't know you would risk so much to have me back. I'm glad you succeeded, because it gives me the chance to tell you that I love you, too, Bess. I was prepared to cross only because I believed that I had lost you forever."

"I was so stupid."

"No, you were right. I made a terrible mistake."

"He tricked you."

His smile was wise and sad and dear. "The Dream Walker told you this?"

She nodded.

"What she did not tell you is that I was naive enough to allow myself to be tricked. Since then I've grown cynical. I didn't even trust the woman I love enough to tell her the truth." He stroked her cheek and she closed her eyes as she sensed his tenderness for her. "If I had known you wanted me, that you loved me, I would not have walked the Way of Souls. I would have stayed, even as a ghost, just to be near you."

"Oh, Cesar." She threw herself into his arms, feeling his love through the connection and now something else. She drew back to look at him, keeping her arms clasped about his neck. She could read his thoughts.

First the joy mingling with the love. Then the astonishment that she wanted him. And finally the realization that, for the first time in his adult life, he was not alone.

He grinned at her.

"Anywhere?" he asked.

She flushed. Obviously he could read her thoughts as well. She'd been thinking of loving him, needing to seal their connection with a physical joining. "Well, yes."

He slipped his hands beneath her jacket, sliding them down her torso and over her hips, taking possession of her at last. Bess pressed against Cesar and kissed him, letting him feel the rush of heat he aroused with his touch. She needed this, needed to show him with her body just how much she loved him.

She grasped the lapels of his sports jacket and pushed, taking him down to his back on the soft wide cushions of the couch. He went willingly, accepting her kiss, his tongue dancing over hers as she felt the rush of his excitement fuel her own. Bess broke away, to straddle his thighs, pulling back to struggle with the small buttons of his shirt. Cesar lifted up on an elbow his shoulders shrugging as he battled to remove his jacket and shoulder holster. She pushed, he pulled and together they tore the clothing away from his upper body. When he was naked from the waist up, Bess hummed her satisfaction, admiring each luscious contour and enticing inch of male flesh. She kneaded the warm, taunt skin and hard muscle beneath, drowning in his scent.

His aura changed as she touched him, the golden glow now pulsing with waves of salmon showing the strong sexual energy of arousal. Her aura flared as well, the soft chocolate brown replaced with iridescent pink, the swirling hot glow of desire.

She fell forward and before she landed on the wide open plains of his chest, her clothing had vanished. She pressed her full breasts against him, rubbing and grasping, straddling his hips, offering herself to this man who she could no longer live without. The glow about them brightened as their lips met again.

Bess kissed his mouth, his neck, the long center of his chest, over his taunt stomach that twitched with each swirling stroke of her tongue. His thoughts were now a mad jumble of images of her, them, locked together in passion. She licked the hollow of his navel as she worked his belt away, opened his trousers, releasing him. She took him in her hands, stroking the long velvet length of him, first with her fingertips and then with her mouth. Cesar arched back and groaned as his thoughts broke apart, replaced only by wild emotions. He wanted her, wanted to feel her wet and hot as she rode him. Yes, she thought, she would do that. But before she could move, Cesar took hold of her shoulders and brought her body against his. His lips pressed to the erogenous zone just behind her ear.

"Not so fast, little black bird. First I want you to come for me."

Bess trembled at the images flying through his mind and next at his touch as he stroked her back and then clasped her bottom, lifting her and bringing her down beside him. He left her to peel away his trousers, toss aside his boots and return to her naked and ready. She reached with greedy fingers, pulling him down on top of her. She felt the blood beating in her veins, the rising desire that prickled each raw nerve and offered her mouth to him again. His lips were warm satin, sizzling hot and needy. She grew breathless, their auras glittering with desire.

She released him as he headed south, his teeth scoring the sensitive skin of her neck, each nip a tiny, tingling knife of pleasure. His tongue delved into her ear, curling her toes. Bess arched back against the cushions as his fingers caressed the curves of her heavy, aching breasts, toying with her aroused nipples, turning them into hard knots of sensation. He pinched her and she shivered with need, arching to offer herself to him.

He took one nipple between his lips and sucked. Bess moaned, at the aching pleasure that corkscrewed through her. His hand slipped between her legs, gliding over the soft folds, spiraling over the needy nub of flesh and driving her to madness. He kissed his way down her body, leaving a wet trail that cooled in the evening air. She shivered, cool on top, and hot where his mouth now worked between her legs.

Bess arched back, delving her fingers into his hair, holding him against her. He kissed her, his tongue licking the sensitive nub of flesh that became the epicenter of all her need. She drew her legs up, curling her toes into the cushions as the first starburst of pleasure rocketed through her quaking body. She cried out her release in one long sigh of ecstasy. But even as her orgasm rocketed through her, she wished they had come together.

"Yes," he whispered. "Me, too."

He rubbed the slickness of his mouth against her warm thigh and then climbed upward, pausing to kiss her breasts again. She resisted, tired now and wanting to rest, but he did not stop and the resistance gave way, replaced by another curling wisp of wanting that billowed and built inside her like a summer storm. Soon she was clasping his head, holding him tight against her breast, relishing the sharp shards of pleasure that pierced deep into her belly and groin.

She wanted him again, still, always. But this was more than just filling her need. She recognized the difference. She no longer merely took what she wanted. She gave Cesar access to her body, to her emotions, to every part of her in a way that felt both foreign and right. She trusted him completely and held nothing back as he rolled, taking her with him, bringing her on top.

Her legs straddled his thighs and she felt his erection pressing, hard and ready between their bodies. She lifted and he sprang into position, the tip of him poised, willing. She lifted her hips, the soft, wet folds of her cleft encircling him, her needy, pliant flesh taking all of him.

She lowered herself, moving down, down, settling her body over his, taking him deep inside, relishing the sensation of his hard shaft penetrating her. He gripped her rump between two strong hands and lifted her up, setting her in motion, thrusting smoothly against her as she fell. Bess threw her head back to savor each wild stroke as she felt his need rising with her own. This time they would come together.

She perceived his jumbled thoughts and the wild, scorching hot images of them locked in violent sensual motion. Fuel to the fire. She sensed that he was close to his release, wanting her, waiting for her. The tenderness he felt for her began to burn to ash against the jagged instinctive need to take her, to come inside her, deeper, deeper.

Her release burst upon her at the same instant Cesar's orgasm fired within him like a booster rocket. The hot surge of sensation hit her like a shock wave, throwing her into a second orgasm and then a third. Their pleasures merged together, overwhelming her until she did not know if she experienced her pleasure or his. She arched like a bow, surrendering to the power of their coupling and as the waves gradually receded. Bess fell forward as if struck by a blow, sprawling over his warm, muscular body as the delicious waves of ecstasy ebbed slowly away. She snuggled against his neck, feeling the blood surging in the great vessel there. He lifted a clumsy hand and thumped it against her back, patting her twice before his hand fell away.

His voice was a low, rumbling rasp. "You nearly killed me."

"Multiple orgasms," she muttered, the effort of speech nearly more than she could manage.

He groaned.

She rolled onto her back beside him on the wide couch, tossing the pillows of the backrest away to make room for them both on the cushioned bed. A moment later she tucked tight beneath his arm, curling against him. She threw one long leg stretched across his legs so she could press against him from chest to thigh, her thatch of hair now nestled intimately against his hip. She gave a contented sigh as she realized the restlessness that had driven her through the century was gone. For the first time in her life she felt certain that she was now, suddenly, exactly where she was meant to be.

She blinked her eyes open, turning her head to see her aura was no longer chocolate brown, but now a pale soft tawny color, like the back of a newborn fawn, made lighter and brighter by the soft pink now glowing all about her. He turned his head to stare at her, looking up at her aura.

"I know that color—pale pink." He stopped speaking, but his thoughts rolled through her. No longer the madness that overcame him during the loving, they were now perfectly sensible, back in order and clear as her own. *Pale pink, the aura of a soul in love. It was true then, the words she had spoken, true that she loves me, can love me.*

She inclined her head to touch his. "Yes, it's true."

He drew a long breath and then released it.

His thoughts came to her again. *I didn't believe it possible—to be loved.*

But he did believe it now, she realized and the wonder filling him made her chest ache. He had been alone so long. Had really believed he was untouchable. Bess vowed to spend every day of their lives proving how wrong he had been.

Gratitude reached her next, his gratitude.

I've never loved a woman. But I love her, love the perfect blended balance of animal and human and the honesty that is absent from the Niyanoka. I am as much animal as Bess. How could I not have seen that before? She is just like me, better than me. That's why the loving was so intense, so powerful, so freaking perfect, because we are just the same and because I belonged to her.

Bess lifted a hand to caress his cheek, already rough with stubble.

"I belong to you, too," she whispered.

He cradled her head, bending to kiss her and she read something that had not been there before, his optimism. Gone were the dour, dark thoughts and his perpetual air of solitude. Now he held hope. She could feel it as clearly as she felt his steady heartbeat. He thought of their future together with anticipation. He was thinking of her as…as his wife.

She broke away.

"Wife?"

He grinned and gave his head a slow shake of reluctant acceptance. "I wanted to ask you properly, with a ring."

Bess swept her right hand over her left. When she drew it back, she wore a perfect faceted round diamond set in platinum and encircled with smaller diamonds.

Cesar gasped.

"Skinwalkers don't wear jewelry very often because we lose it when we shift." She extended the engagement ring for him to admire. "Did you want to pick it out? I can make it look any way you like."

He shook his head in bewilderment. "Makes me realize how much I still don't know about you."

"But think of the fun it will be finding out."

He slid from the couch and knelt on the porch before her. She rolled to sit beside him, the cold wooden planks now solid beneath her bare feet. She thought to dress but as he was on his knees, naked before her, she did not. He took hold of her left hand. His love for her zinged up her arm and filled her with a warm flush.

"Will you marry me, Bess?" he asked.

It was a question she had never expected to hear and one she had never wished to hear until today.

Because of this man she had lost her loneliness, shed it as surely as she could shed her feather cape.

Bess squeezed his hand.

"You honor me, Cesar. And I will spend the rest of my life honoring you."

"Just love me, Bess. Now and always."

"Here, now and into eternity," she promised, and then rose up to kiss him again.

*   *   *   *   *

Terminology

DREAM WALKER*

A NIYANOKA with the ability to visit another person's dreams and work mental and/or physical healing during the visitation. The human visited has no memory of the visit.

CIRCLE OF GHOSTS

The final home of all ghosts who once led evil lives and are punished when HIRHANKARA pushes them from the SPIRIT ROAD into the circle, where they drift for eternity in endless circles. This ghostly prison is presided over by NAGI. Some ghosts have been released from this prison by the prayers of those who live a pure life.

CLAIRVOYANTS*

A NIYANOKA or INAOKA with the ability to foretell future events of a person by touching that person or something that belongs to that person. They have an unfortunate blind spot in that they cannot foretell their own futures or that of anyone they love. This is to prevent them the agony of trying and failing to change what cannot be changed.

GHOST

The remains of humans after they have left their earthly vessels.

GHOST TRAIL

See **SPIRIT ROAD**

HALFLING*

Any creature with one SPIRIT and one HUMAN parent.

HANWI

The moon is a reflective female SPIRIT who warms MAKA when the WI is absent.

HEYOKA

SPIRIT of chaos who is a double-faced SPIRIT with a split personality and emotions. He represents joy and sorrow, war and peace and all other opposites. Humans who see WAKINYAN (THUNDERBEINGS) become living HEYYOKAS and do the opposite of what is expected.

HIHANKARA

The crone who guards the SPIRIT ROAD. If the soul has walked the RED ROAD and leads a righteous life they bear the proper tattoos and are allowed to pass.

If they have led a wicked life, she pushes them from the road and allows them to fall into the CIRCLE of GHOSTS.

HUMANS

Mortal creatures without firsthand knowledge of the SPIRIT WORLD or SPIRITS.

INANOKA*

MORTAL beings born of a human female and the SPIRIT TOB TOB. They are SKINWALKERS who shape-shift into the animal of their mother's tribe at will and maintain all attributes of that animal while in human form. They are called HALFLINGS and live an average of 400 years. They are despised by NIYANOKA for being beasts and possibly because they live longer. They protect animals from capricious SUPERNATURALS. Each animal is gifted with a different power.

BEAR: Has the ability to heal all injuries and wounds.

BUFFALO: Is a creature of sacrifice that can absorb injuries, illness or grief into its body and then heal at a rapid rate. They are not healers and must feel all the pain they take from the one they relieve. It is said they can raise the dead, but only at the expense of their own life.

HAWK: Receives messages from the SPIRITS and sees into the future. But they are helplessly blind to their own future or the future of those they love.

MOUNTAIN LION: *Has the power of clairvoyance and can see things far beyond the realm of normal sight. This gift gives cats the appearance of telling the future, but they really see things as they occur in other locations. They are especially good at seeing what is happening to those they know well.*

OWL: *Said to have the ability to exorcise disembodied souls (GHOSTS) from their unwilling hosts and send them for judgment on the WAY OF SOULS. They also can predict a human's death. It is for this reason that seeing an owl is considered a warning of death.*

RAVEN: *Is the only creature that can travel the SPIRIT ROAD and speak to the souls in the SPIRIT WORLD.*

WOLF: *Can track anyone on earth by their scent trail.*

KANKA

Old woman sorceress. She travels in dreams and helps people purify themselves. She can see the past, present and future and is a SUPERNATURAL.

MAKA

Mother Earth, holds the female power of birth and is a sacred SPIRIT.

MEMORY WALKER*

A Niyanoka with the power to make another forget a person or event. They cannot erase another's memory, but only make slight alterations. This gift is helpful to reduce grief after a loss and to allow a person to go unnoticed by erasing the memory of an encounter.

MITAKUYE OYASIN

A closing for a blessing. It literally means "All my relations included" or "We are all related" and reminds us that humans are connected to everything of the earth.

NAGI

This shadow creature is the ghostly guardian of the CIRCLE OF GHOSTS *and is a* SPIRIT.

NIYAN

A SPIRIT BEING *that teaches man to understand the cycle of life and death and the return of the body to* MAKA (the earth) *as the spirit returns to the* SPIRIT WORLD. NIYAN *is a* SPIRIT.

NIYANOKA*

MORTAL *beings born of a union between* NIYAN *and a human. They are called* SPIRIT CHILD *and are charged with protecting humans from the interference of* SUPERNATURALS *and* SKINWALKERS. *In addition they consider themselves shepherds of mankind, working for their benefit, helping them walk the* RED ROAD *and preparing them for the* SPIRIT WORLD. *They have a live span of 300 to 400 years.*

PEACEMAKER*

A NIYANOKA *with the power to influence the moods*

and emotions of those nearby. They are highly persuasive and sought after for their ability to assist in all forms of negotiation. Since their suggestions are difficult to defy and their proposals hold such influence, their ethics must be above reproach.

RED ROAD

The RED ROAD *is a metaphor for the correct way to live. One who walks the* RED ROAD *exists in balance with all things of the earth, behaving in a manner that is both proper and blessed. Walking the* RED ROAD *allows for entrance into the* SPIRIT WORLD, *while ignoring the proper way might lead to being cast from the* WAY OF SOULS *and into the* CIRCLE OF GHOSTS.

SEER OF SOULS*

A NIYANOKA *member of the Ghost Clan, thought to be extinct. Such a* HALFLING *has the ability to see not only* SPIRITS *but earthbound souls in the form of disembodied* GHOSTS. *They a have the power to speak to* GHOSTS *and to send them to the* SPIRIT ROAD *for judgment. See* HIHANKARA.

SOUL WHISPERER*

A NIKANOKA *of the* SPIRIT CLAN *with the power to bear witness to a death by touching the corpse. The* WHISPERER *sees exactly what the departed saw in the moments prior to his death and also experiences his thoughts. This makes* WHISPERERS *essential* for solving crimes such as murder, but also makes them unclean in the minds of their kind, making them outcasts. None will touch them for they are believed to be unclean.

SKINWALKERS

Another word for INANOKA, *the* HALFLING *children of* TOB TOB *the* SPIRIT BEAR. *Legend says these are animals who remove their skin to masquerade as humans, but their ineptitude often reveals them.*

SPIRITS

All of these creatures are immortal.

SPIRIT CHILD

Another name for NIYANOKA, *a* HALFLING *child of* NIYAN *and a human parent.*

SPIRIT ROAD

(SKY-ROAD, SPIRIT TRAIL) *The Milky Way that is the path leading to the Spirit World. Those without the proper tattoos are pushed off the trail and wander endlessly in the* CIRCLE OF GHOSTS. *Souls without the proper markings have led an evil life on earth and do not merit entrance to the* SPIRIT WORLD.

SPIRIT WORLD

The home of all ghosts that have successfully crossed the SPIRIT ROAD.

SUPERNATURALS

There are eight SUPERNATURALS including KANKA. They are immortal but less powerful than SPIRITS. They live on earth.

THE BALANCE*

This refers to the balance of nature, the fragile connection which the LANOKA protect from careless or malevolent damage by SUPERNATURAL creatures, NIYANOKA and HUMANS, who all tend to feel a certain entitlement to the earth.

TOB TOB

Translates as "Four by Four," meaning a creature that goes on four legs. This great SPIRIT BEAR has wisdom and healing powers. TOB TOB is a SPIRIT.

TRUTH SEEKER*

A NIYANOKA who can divine the truth to any spoken question, merely by touching the one he questions. TRUTH SEEKERS are hard to deceive and make excellent judges in the NIYANOKA community.

WANAGI

The soul of a dead person, a GHOST.

WAKAN TANKA

The Great Spirit, The Great Mystery, Creator of all. A holy immortal entity who is more than SPIRIT.

WAKINYAN THUNDERBEINGS

(THUNDERBIRD, THUNDERHORSE). *The power of electric energy on earth. Thunder comes from the opening of the* THUNDERBIRD'S *eye and thunder from the drumming of the* THUNDERHORSES' *hooves.* WAKINYA *are* SPIRITS. *They also cause clouds, hurricanes, tornadoes and storms. They are known to strike dead any human foolish enough to lie while holding a sacred pipe.*

WAY OF SOULS
See **SPIRIT ROAD**

WI

The Sun. WI *represents power and sustains life. He is a great teacher and a* SPIRIT.

WONIYA

The soul of a living person.

*These terms/beings are fictional and do not exist in Lakota legend.

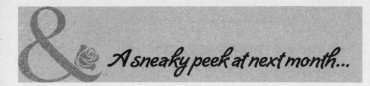

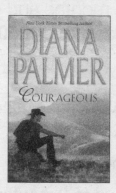

Mills & Boon® Online

Discover more romance at
www.millsandboon.co.uk

- 🌹 **FREE** online reads
- 🌹 **Books** up to one month before shops
- 🌹 **Browse our books** before you buy

...and much more!

For exclusive competitions and instant updates:

 Like us on **facebook.com/romancehq**

 Follow us on **twitter.com/millsandboonuk**

 Join us on **community.millsandboon.co.uk**

Visit us Online — Sign up for our FREE eNewsletter at **www.millsandboon.co.uk**

WEB/M&B/RTL4